VEINS OF EVIL

KRISTI DOWNARD

Black Rose Writing | Texas

ISBN: 978-1-68513-545-4
PUBLISHED BY BLACK ROSE WRITING
www.blackrosewriting.com

Printed in the United States of America
Suggested Retail Price (SRP) $23.95

Veins of Evil is printed in Garamond Premier Pro

*As a planet-friendly publisher, Black Rose Writing does its best to eliminate unnecessary waste to reduce paper usage and energy costs, while never compromising the reading experience. As a result, the final word count vs. page count may not meet common expectations.

PRAISE FOR
VEINS OF EVIL

"*Veins of Evil* is a nonstop thriller from Kristi Downard. Hold on tight when you dive into this one. Just when you think you have a handle on the characters and the messes they have created, the plot takes a sharp turn into new territory. Over and over again, I was halfway through the book thinking what more could happen, only to discover much more! This book is like riding a speeding rollercoaster forcing the reader to lean into every bump and twist."
–Dale Ward, author of *Killing the Butterfly*

"Floored by twists. I fell in love with Libby and Patrick immediately and was blown away by the circumstances that befell them! Kristi Downard had multiple twists I didn't see coming and had me enthralled from the beginning. A great addition to the thriller genre."
–Yvonne DeSousa, author of *Shelter of the Monument*

"Downard leads readers through a dark narrative with twists, turns, and a shocking ending."
–Cam Torrens, award-winning author of *Stable* and *False Summit*.

ACKNOWLEDGMENTS

I started writing around nine years ago and it was this book about Libby. Five years ago, I stopped this book and brought to life "Out of the Wormhole." Then I came back to "Veins of Evil" with part two. It has been a challenge to make myself sit and write, but it is the story I love to develop and tell. I want to thank Black Rose Writing for seeing something special in this book and for their support.

I would like to thank these people for their support from the beginning: Mary Ann Sewell, Janna Vigue, Sara Mora Burcham, Tim and Lori Byers, and especially my husband, Jimmy, for loving the fun and scary sides of me. I want to thank my editor, MEB. Authors Dale Ward, Yvonne DeSousa, and Cam Torrens for helping me shape my characters. I want to thank some late readers for their kind words and encouragement: Lacey Cooper, Angi Sollie, and Matthew Suber.

A few folks I interviewed for their expertise were Darrin Flick, Tony Terry, Joseph Mannella, and Lori Byers.

I want to thank you, the readers. If I didn't ever hear how crazy my books are, I wouldn't do this.

VEINS
OF
EVIL

LIBBY

I love a walk in the woods to clear my head. What better way to feel more connected to life or just feel better in general. We live on eighty-eight acres of hilly, sandy land in Alliance, Ohio. As I walk around the outskirts of our property, I find myself talking out loud. You don't lie to yourself when conversing to the path ahead or with the trees. The truth comes out, your inner feelings or desires. Sometimes life can be going great, but you still feel like something's wrong. That's how I feel today. A subtle wariness looms in my bones. Cold but not shivering. Guarded yet unaware. I feel a presence in my soul. Does God know something, and He's trying to tell me? Honestly, I don't know if I believe in God. Maybe this pull is just nature's way of telling me to get ready for adulthood or maturity. I walk by the biggest tree we own. What must run through its veins? The rain it has absorbed from the sky? From laden clouds transversing the continent? It has particles from India and Greenland inside of it. This tree doesn't have to travel the world to know pollution, smell fire, and soak up nutrients. The thought amazes me.

I just started my senior year at Alliance High School, and it's still the same old problems. The girls are all about clothes, hair, and boys while the boys are full of acne and only talk about sex and sports. It seems kids my age don't see the big picture. This tree, right here, with its twisted roots and smooth bark has more awareness than most high school kids. "Please give me peace to calm my restless spirit," I plead. My name is Elizabeth Jane Simon, Libby for short. My mom died of lung cancer when I was 11, and it's just been Dad and me ever since. The company of the woods is sometimes more stimulating than Dad.

"Who are you talking to now? The tree or a squirrel? Perhaps it's the sky this time? No, I know it isn't the sky, you're in a mood today." I turn around to see my boyfriend, Patrick, walking towards me. I hate it when he catches me openly talking. We've been together for almost two years. We found each other because we both love the outdoors, and we're both a little bit broken. He had asked my dad for permission to hunt on our property. That's how we got to know each other. I've known him most of my life, but we didn't know we were so compatible. Patrick and I are rather reclusive. We have friends, but we like solitude. I feel that Patrick has really blossomed since having me in his life. He smiles and is friendlier than when we were younger. I'm surprised he wasn't bullied more because he was always alone and his clothes looked too small. I think the other kids found out very quickly that Patrick could take them down if provoked. He has purposeful movements, but he can also become a statue with a stare that disturbs. That's why he is such a good hunter.

Patrick wastes no energy fluttering about or talking nonsense. I enjoy our afternoons engaging in conversations about life and our futures-when I can get him to open up.

"You know what? I saw that same buck again. He's mocking me. I don't even want to kill him now. It's more fun to play the game with him. He walks around slowly as he looks at me from afar. Deer don't normally do that. This buck is provoking me. I feel one day he'll draw a gun on me." Patrick talks about this deer like he's human or smart. I laugh as he smiles. We both feel a strong pull to the natural world.

"Hey, Libby, let's practice your throw again." I agree because I know he'll insist. Patrick thinks I need to be able to protect myself and always be prepared. He says if I'm going to be out walking around alone, I better be skilled at fending off creeps. "I brought two kinds of knives today, and that looks like a good tree." He points to the one I was just talking to.

"No, that's the best tree here." I point to one that doesn't have near as much distinction and looks almost dead already. The heaviness of the knife will decide the distance from the tree. I miss the target with both of them. I hurry to find the knives for another try. Finding them is sometimes difficult, but Patrick waits patiently and positions himself to watch. Standing without saying a word, he knows I think this is foolish, but he worries and feels this is an unsafe town. Things are happening in this small town: the typical drug problem, industry is shutting down, and of course, the missing people. Sometimes drownings in the river occur. At least rapes are not an issue. I point that out to him, but he doesn't care. He just waits for me to throw again. I miss most of my throws.

"Libby, step a little closer." I try that and get both stuck dead on. Throwing knives is fun, but I don't think it will be practical in a bad situation. I don't even carry a knife with me, while he always has one on him. He insists on throwing more. "Next, we'll work on punching and kicking." I nod in agreement. I catch him gazing at me. "You're much cuter than you think you are in those baggy clothes." He smiles. "I'm not the only one who notices. I see guys watching you walk away."

I am about 5' 4", and I have long blonde hair that is mostly kept in a ponytail. My eyes are brown. I don't wear much makeup because I'm usually just at school or hanging out outside. Not much need to be made up for that. For me, school is not a popularity contest. It's a chore to get through.

"I carry mace on me when I go exploring," I say with a smile. Patrick and Dad both hate it when I go hiking without them. Our land does not have nice trails, so I like to venture out sometimes. When we're done with drills, we walk back to the house and grab something to eat. I have leftover fried chicken and macaroni salad. We both love my macaroni salad. I realize we seem about 62 years old right now, which fits with the rest of our personalities. Simple needs make life less complicated. This beautiful earth is calling, but so much of the population ignores the call of the wild. We both have smart phones, but we hardly look at them. Our future goals are similar too. I want to work for the national parks or something like that. Patrick just talks about hunting and wants to get away from this town. He doesn't desire material things, so he isn't worried about his future job. I do most of the talking about careers.

Patrick didn't have the best home life growing up. His parents are divorced, and he hasn't seen his father since he was 13. Not a subject he ever wants to talk about. His mother works two jobs. She works as a receptionist at a dental office and at a diner some weekends, so she isn't home much. All I know about his father is that Patrick is glad he left. Like me, he's an only child. Patrick takes care of himself and fixes anything that breaks around the house. He's very utilitarian. I feel he has had to become the man of the house at a young age, and he seems much older than he is. The quiet type.

As for me, I'm used to being alone. We have a very small family. My mom's sister, Janna, lives in Canton, Ohio, along with my two cousins. That's only a half hour away from us. We see them occasionally and during the holidays. My aunt is great, and we have a close relationship. She has helped me through the years with girl stuff and taking me shopping. That isn't Dad's expertise. He seems depressed sometimes, which started back when Mom died, so Aunt Janna helps me out from time to time. Maybe my feelings about something being wrong are because of Dad. He does have a girlfriend now, but he seems so distant most of the time.

"Do you want to go kayaking this weekend?" Patrick asks.

I shrug. "I'll think about it." This year will fly by, and I realize I should be visiting colleges and talking to advisors instead of the trees.

"We need to plan for our future, remember? And no, sitting with you in a deer blind is not part of my future," I say. I have to draw the limits somewhere. I'm not into killing and cutting animals open. Patrick feels like it's a skill I should know, but I'd rather starve. He likes to think about getting a little cabin deep in the woods and living off the land, but I'm not quite as prehistoric as he is. He doesn't even plan on going to college at all. I like to tease him about his reclusiveness, but I know he has come a long way. Before we met, he had never gone on a picnic, or bowled, or even played a board game. He only knew how to play go fish and hide and seek.

"Perhaps you should join the Amish society. They aren't far away, and we can easily commute to visit each other, me in a car and you with your buggy." He looks at me with those deep brown eyes. No comment from him. Neither of us will have big careers as doctors or lawyers. We just don't have that type of discipline or desire. Books are for enjoyment or learning a quick skill. We couldn't tolerate all the classes involved for a big career life. Life and existence are what makes us happy. That's something we totally agree on. Will Patrick and I get married and have kids? I have no idea. Patrick doesn't want kids for a long time. He says he needs to be at peace for long as possible. We both agree that when we see people with small children, they don't seem very happy. They look stressed and tired. Patrick can't actually have kids. He had a hunting accident years ago that ended that possibility. Sometimes I wonder if that is why he doesn't have many friends, perhaps he feels inadequate. I fell for him before knowing about his injury, which didn't change my feelings in any way. As for now, we just need to get through our senior year, and then the future is ours. I feel lucky to have Patrick in my life.

We finish eating and Patrick needs to help his mom out at the restaurant tonight.

"See ya tomorrow." I sneak a quick kiss walking him out. He leaves. After waving goodbye, I walk back towards the house and notice the garage is open. It's piled with camping gear on one side. Dad and I both enjoy camping and primitive trips. Now he goes on trips with his girlfriend. Right now, Dad is dating Becka, one of the waitresses at Bob Evans. I think she looks sleazy, but I don't say anything. If he's happy, that's what matters. We both just do our own thing. Life is pretty simple. I walk into the house and hear Dad.

"Hey Libby," he says.

Hi Dad, I'm going to do some homework." Homework doesn't take long most nights. My grades are good with minimal effort.

He smiles. He's covered in dirt like always. "I have to put a new fuel pump in the backhoe, and Ivan is stopping by later." He grabs a 100 Grand bar and heads outside. He loves them. He keeps several boxes of them in the freezer. They're getting harder to find, so he likes to stock up. The thought of Ivan stopping by puts me in a foul mood. He's my dad's buddy, and they have a few beers together every now and then. I've never warmed up to him, but he seems to have warmed up to me. I'll have to make myself scarce when he gets here. He looks at me too long, or could it be my imagination? Seems like Ivan comes by more and more.

Maybe he's noticed Dad being depressed and wants to be a good friend. I hope that's why. But their friendship seems strange. I don't think they have much in common or do anything else together but sit around here and drink beer. He just feels creepy.

I head to my room and crash on my bed. I feel safe here. My bedroom doesn't have any posters or flashy items. The walls are tan, and the carpet is a mixture of more tan. It is very plain, but I like it that way. I have a queen bed in the corner with a blue comforter. My dresser is full of baggy sweats, my favorite attire. I have a lot of books, mostly mysteries or about animal species. Since I was little, I've learned many useless facts about animals. Mom and I used to go to the library a lot when I was young. We would get stacks of books and read together. I miss her. Or do I just miss the idea of having a mom? Because most of her memories are fading. I struggle, wanting to hang on to them but finding almost greater comfort in letting them go. Shaking off that thought, I run downstairs quickly to grab something to drink and run right back up to avoid any contact, with Ivan.

Later on Dad knocks on my door.

"Hey, Libby, Ivan wants to say hi to you before he goes." I don't want to disappoint Dad with his friend, so I go downstairs.

"Hey there, sprout, you're too young for sleeping during daylight hours. "I guess that's what high school kids do these days," Ivan says with a grin.

"No, I'm just doing some homework."

"Still got that same boyfriend, I hear. Must be getting serious."

"Yep, same boyfriend." I turn and go back upstairs. Ivan Sipos is some sort of teacher somewhere that I don't remember, so he must be a smart guy. I don't want to know anything else about Ivan. Just wish dad had a better friend. One that he had more in common with and wasn't so unnerving. Somehow, he looks too fancy for my Dad. I'd like to ask Dad why he spends time with him, but again, if it makes him happy, fine, I guess.

"Hey there, Libby, before you go!" I hear Ivan plead. I turn back around trying to look interested. "Did you hear about the missing kid from your school?" I shake my head, now interested. "Well, it sounds like another one has turned up missing. Stay on the right side of town. You don't want to get hurt." Ivan looks at me with a hint of a grin. Creeeeeepy.

"Good to know," I say and retreat. Not again. Who is missing now? Strange disappearances have been happening in the last couple of years. In the northern Ohio area, teen boys and young men have vanished. The odd thing is, the disappearances have been people known to sell or transport drugs, and so in consequence, not much has been done about finding out what happened to them. Families aren't in the picture to push for answers, if the victims even had families. Some people in town even talk like it's okay. I wonder if this is happening in other states as well. If a person is playing a dangerous game, hazards will happen. Is this latest disappearance someone I actually know? I know that brothers Billy and Thomas Ruff are hardly at school, and

I've heard rumors about them. They deal or use or steal drugs of some kind. Kids at school tease them about becoming the next victim. Dealers from the Cleveland area come around here looking for high school kids to deal for them. Ray Squires is another kid at school who has been mixed up with illegal activities. He has a changed look about him-drawn face, skinny, and dirty. A few months ago, Steven Foster came up missing. My cousins in Canton knew him from their school, and they said he was in the drug world. Never heard anything else about him though-like he didn't even exist. Someone sure has it out for drug pushers.

Tired, I climb into bed, eager to find out tomorrow at school if anything did happen. But sleep is elusive. Sometimes I have nightmares. Usually, I'm drowning and wake up choking. Same dream. Glad it isn't often. Patrick thinks I should see a therapist, but it just doesn't seem bad enough for that. I lie down thinking about Dad and wondering if he'll be okay when I'm out of school and leave him.

2

I wake up on Monday morning wondering about what Ivan said. Is he right? I turn on the news while eating cereal to see if anything is said. I only catch the weather and commercials. I decide to get going early and find out. At school, obvious whispering and chatter is in the hallways. I can tell by the way everyone is acting something did happen. I find my best friends, Hope and Rashin. They know about the missing kid. Turns out it was Thomas Ruff. His brother Billy reported him missing yesterday. The last place he was seen was close to Rockhill Park. Thomas was driving his car, and it was found yesterday morning in the park. Thomas is nowhere. They're getting a search team together to look around the park today. How is school not cancelled so we can help search for him? This time it has happened close to home. Ivan was right.

Apprehension creeps over me, like on my walk yesterday. Do the police assume he'll not be found due to the fact that no other missing boys are ever found? My stomach feels sick. The teachers are trying to conduct their classes, but police are going by the rooms and pulling out students for interviews. It is mayhem. The only thing taking place is the realization that the plague has infiltrated our school now. Looks and stares are permeating. I know most people don't care about Thomas Ruff, but he's still our classmate. It has marked us as a whole. The unsettling sickness close to home. I knew something was going to happen.

I have lunch with Hope and Rashin. Patrick is nowhere in sight. He doesn't have my lunch period, but the school has lost all order today, so I figured I might see him. My close friends and I huddle together. We have been close for many years, mostly because we all think beyond today.

Hope is a total girl jock. She plays basketball and is fabulous. She stays very busy with that. Her parents want her to get a scholarship to attend Ohio State University. We have known each other since kindergarten. When she was 12, she doubled in size. She's 5' 11" now. Her father is a realtor and owns several properties. Her mother runs a greenhouse, and over the years, my dad has provided her with dirt or sand from our property. Dad is an excavator by trade and has all the big boy toys. Hope's family has given us vegetables and plants in exchange. We don't get much anymore since mom is gone; she was the gardener. When Hope and I were young, we would go back on our property and become little explorers. That's why I have all the animal books. We would read about them and study them with binoculars. Dad would get me straw all the time. I played the park ranger and had to make homes for the wildlife, and Hope would help me. We would put little snacks on the beds like hotels, and I could just picture all the animals safe and warm at night.

Rashin is from Pakistan. Her family moved to the area when she was in 7th grade. Hope and I liked her right away because she came to school with army boots on. She helps her parents run the convenience store and gas station, Jafri's. Since she always has to work, we don't do much together beyond school. Rashin gets the good gossip before anyone else does though. She hears all the talk of the town while stocking shelves at the store. Both of my friends are busy with family and work, and don't have time for being drama queens. I love that about them.

I'm not as busy as they are unless you count the time I spend in the woods. I've helped my dad out on some weekends while he's excavating. He's taught me to run the bulldozer, excavator, loader, skid steer and mini hoe. Moving dirt from one pile to another pile, it's a living. One time, I got to move dirt at a small airport. I had to watch for planes before driving up and down the runway while moving topsoil. That was one of my favorite days with Dad. Most girls I know would think that's stupid, but I love to help him out. He works all the time and says he just wants to provide for me as much as he can. I tell him I'm not going to some big expensive college, but he just says, "You never know."

Dad's kind of funny. He hardly uses his bank. We have a big safe in our basement where he keeps most of his cash along with important paperwork and guns. Perhaps he's more paranoid than depressed. My friends think Dad is cool.

But today, our talk isn't about our families. It's about the Ruff's. Thomas Ruff has been going to our school for years. He and his brother have always been in trouble. It's not a surprise that they got themselves mixed up with the wrong people. Their father is a drunk, and their mother left them years ago. They were all too much for her to handle, I bet. When we were younger, I felt sorry for them. They always had on torn clothes and seemed hungry. But now in high school, they just exist for their next score. Billy will be lost and alone without Thomas. I wonder if it will be enough for Billy to change his ways, but I doubt it. This will probably make him worse. The whole world will be to blame.

"No one will be going to that park anymore," Hope says. "It will forever be known for this. They should just close it down."

"I heard Billy say he was with Thomas at the park but went home with some other guys because Thomas wanted to stay longer. I'm sure he was selling. Why else do you hang out at the park after dark?" Rashin whispers.

Rashin is always cautious. She knows which streets in town to avoid after dark. She and Patrick get along well. They have a mutual respect because they're both into guns and self-defense. Rashin and her family have a lot of security at the gas station. They occasionally come out and practice shooting on our land. They seem prepared for war. No coincidence that they have never been robbed.

"Maybe he didn't want to go home because of his drunken father," I say, trying to give him a positive perspective, which I know is pointless. Their father doesn't have control over them anymore. Billy and Thomas are a product of their upbringing, and I'm sure they have to take care of themselves. Selling drugs gives them enough money to get by.

Before lunch is over, I get a text from Dad wanting me to have dinner with him tonight. This means going to Bob Evans. We have standing seats at the bar. No one else is ever sitting in those seats when we go in. I think people just know the seats are ours. I tell him sounds good.

Heading back to class, I think of Ivan stopping by last night and shiver. I'm glad it will just be Dad and me tonight. I suppose Becka will be our waitress. My chemistry teacher is talking, but all I can think about is how Dad could do so much better. Becka isn't even that pretty, and she sure likes to talk about herself. Sighing, I realize he probably doesn't have a chance to meet many women stuck in a machine all day.

As I'm about to leave school, Patrick walks across the parking lot towards me. He's very handsome. Thick dark hair all scruffy around his ears and neck. He is 6'2" and built of solid muscle. I bet most girls are jealous thinking about this hot guy pounding away on me. If they only knew how our lives really work. He's just a simple guy, and I like that. His brown eyes can take your breath away. Sometimes I wonder what he sees in me. Hope he doesn't just like me for the hunting privileges.

"Dad and I are going out tonight. What are you going to get into?"

"Mom wants me to fix the shower door, and I am going to clean some guns. Since I won't have you distracting me, I might even work on my tractor." That boosts my ego.

"Don't blame your laziness on me." I smile at him because I have no choice. Sometimes the way he looks at me makes my stomach do flip flops. I don't tell him those details though. I get into my car, and he shuts the door for me. I drive a little blue Toyota Camry. He drives a Ford F-150. I don't know the year, but I know it's old. Easy to fix he says. Mine is easy to fix since it never breaks, I argue.

When I arrive home, I can ever so faintly hear Dad running some equipment in the yard. He's home early. I walk out to see him, and he waves. I have to make sure he sees me before I get too close to him. Don't want the boom taking my head off.

"I have to go dig out a culvert a couple miles away and drop a pipe, and I will be right back."

"Okay. I'll just take a walk." I need to enjoy the warmer days while they're still here.

The ground is mostly sand with lots of piles of scrap laying around like old railroad ties here and different sizes of pipe there. There are mounds of different sized stone: fifty-sevens, eights, and berm. Big heaps of broken up concrete sit waiting to be used. It's like an earthy cemetery waiting to be woken up and brought out of the dead. Everything just waits in anticipation for a purpose. Sometimes I find feral kittens hiding away. As always, there are a few 100 Grand wrappers lying around blowing in the wind. No surprise there.

Once Dad is done working, he gets cleaned up and we head out for dinner. We walk in and our seats are waiting for us, along with Becka and her big smile as she sees Dad arrive. No greeting for me. Nice. As we sit at the bar, Becka takes our order. She chews her gum while she runs her fingers along her necklace with a little grin. Did Dad give that to her? Make me puke. Not sure I can eat now. She talks about her son, Johnny, in Columbus, and how he's going to mechanic school and how hard it is for him. Then she talks about driving up to Niagara with Dad soon before it gets too cold. He likes that idea. Still no greeting for me. She then talks about her sore feet and her shoes wearing out. Does she not have other people to wait on? Completely bored, I go to the bathroom to get away from her. It gets worse every time. How does he not get sick of that? I mean, she only talks about herself. Perhaps she's uncomfortable with me sitting with him, and she feels the need to make conversation. I would love to tell her we're here for Dad and I to talk to each other, but I'll just try be nice.

We somehow make it through dinner. Dad pays with cash. We never did have a chance to talk. In the car, he looks at me with those sad eyes.

"I know you aren't fond of Becka, but we have a good time together."

"She sure can talk. As long as you like her, that's all that matters. I just want to see you happy, Dad."

"Thanks, sweetie." I look out the window as we drive home. "Did you hear any more details about the missing kid from school today?"

"I did. It was Thomas Ruff. Remember his messed up family? School was crazy today. I wonder how much effort the police will put into the investigation." I shivered. "I wonder if their father even cares that his son is now one of the missing."

"I don't like you being out by yourself. Patrick or someone needs to be with you when you go wandering. I don't want to have to worry about you."

I smile and try to comfort him. "I understand. Don't worry. I'll take precautions. Patrick has been teaching me some self-defense moves. His little lessons never seem to end." I don't know if Dad would like to hear about the knife throwing, so I leave that out. "I also always carry the pepper spray you gave me."

"That's good. I do remember Thomas Ruff's family. His father asked me one time if I needed any help while he was stumbling around. Some people just need to go away." Dad gets angry talking about unresponsible adults, so I try and change the subject.

"I love the rock you put around the pond last week. I should put a coat of paint on the bench before winter comes. Do we have any paint left?"

"I think so. I'll look when we get home," he says. He looks straight ahead like he's in a daze. I watch him and wonder what he's thinking. Could it be Mom, or Thomas missing, or about work tomorrow? Will he even see the red light coming up?

"Stop!" I yell, and the car jerks to a stop. Dad shakes his head and checks if I am okay.

"I'm fine. Are you okay? Where were you just then?" He doesn't answer. Do I see tears in his eyes? I bet he was thinking about Mom. It's so weird how she died of lung cancer. She didn't smoke and rarely drank. Life is shitty sometimes. Soon after that, I became very independent, and Dad and I both just started doing our own thing. That might be why I'm not quite like the other girls. They had someone to fuss over them and listen to their little sorrows. Mothers comfort and take care of the household. After she died, Dad and I just folded up into our little shells. We don't speak much about her, and that is sad. Wish we would because I can't remember much anymore. She was sick for a while before she died, so what I remember is her being in bed a lot. Dad and Aunt Janna were there for me, but no matter how much they tried, they couldn't replace her. I try to think how life would be if we still had her. I would definitely be a different person. I would probably be like the other girls at school. We would be shopping for cute girl clothes and checking out colleges. I would learn about cooking and maybe wear makeup. Patrick and I would not be together though, because I would not have been hanging around in the woods. That's how we found each other. Would I change the life I have now to have my mother back? Of course I would, but most days, I'm happy.

It's a nice evening when we get home. We go down to the basement to check out the back wall that has a long shelf with all the paint supplies along with the old Christmas stuff, suitcases and canned goods. Standing tall next to the shelf, close to the corner, is the safe. Only he and I know the combination. I don't get into the safe hardly ever though. We quickly find the paint for the bench, and then I see Dad take a long glance at the Christmas boxes before heading up the stairs. Not another word is said.

It's dark outside now, and I decide to take a walk down to the pond by myself. It's not far from the front of the house. I think Dad knows I need to be there alone because when I sit down on the bench, a presence comes over me. There's a marked feeling I get when I come to the pond. It's a good feeling, but I can't explain it. My eyes close, and everything is calm and quiet. I can feel my heartbeat in my chest because it's so tranquil and still. I can hear the bluegill splash in the water. Sometimes mallard ducks alight here and occasionally a blue heron. I've read all about these birds. Male mallards have a soft sound while female ones have a loud quack. Ducks also sleep with one eye open, and only half of their brains sleep. Fascinating. A heron will not only eat fish but reptiles and even other birds. Again, I'm full of useless animal facts.

I gaze towards the water. This windless night has left the surface a plate of glass. I wonder if my special fish is there looking at me in the dark? I don't know fish like I know birds and mammals, since they don't interest me. But there is this one bass that comes to the edge of the surface and stares at me whenever I sit on the bench. It intrigues me. He's rather strange looking. His eyes look like they're bugging out of his head, like someone squeezed him too hard, so I call him Boggles. As I scan the water's edge looking for him, I notice the new rocks around the side are lighter in color. They give the water a subtle glow as the moonlight bounces off their smooth surface.

For a few minutes, it was nice to think about ducks and fish, but then I remember the real world. Someone is missing from the school that I grew up in. It's not an accident or illness that took him. He was snatched; it was a crime. I know he's not coming back, none of them have made it back. How many have disappeared and haven't been reported? A chill runs up my back. How can this crime not be solved yet? I would think that dealers are going to start working differently now. The job has become not only illegal but life threatening. Perhaps they need to find another living. Maybe we should move away from this area. However, it seems that if you're not in the drug world, you're safe. Someone wants vengeance.

I want to stay by the pond longer, but the air is starting to blow and I'm getting cold even with my coat on. Winter is coming. I return to the house to find Dad watching TV. He has been looking older lately. Perhaps it's from the sun. I don't know how long he'll continue to work at his job. He gets plenty of work without any advertising. He charges a fair rate and works fast. Sometimes he brings a guy named Wayne in to help him out on big jobs. Dad pays him in cash, of course. Wayne used to be an equipment operator before he got into a car accident and became a paraplegic. But he's still able to run the skid steer and the John Dear 120 excavator since they don't have foot pedals. It gets tricky getting him into some of the machines, but they work it out. Wayne keeps his arms strong and his weight down. Now he gets disability and has a van he can drive. He's a very cool guy. Nowadays, he helps out other kids with disabilities. I wish he was Dad's close friend. They seem to have more in common.

"Can I get you anything?" I ask.

"No, I'm fine."

"Dad, why don't you do more with Wayne instead of Ivan?" I have to ask.

"I don't know. Wayne doesn't drink, and he likes to go to bed early. He gets tired. Ivan and I like to talk about people in town. We joke about them, have some laughs. I think he feels like he needs a friend after coming to the area. He knows I won't judge him about his past."

"What past?"

"He used to be a doctor until he lost his license, so now he teaches."

"Why did he lose his license?"

"Something about writing too many prescriptions. I don't ask. He seems lonely."

"Jeeze, Dad." He goes back to watching TV. Not much for long conversations. I head up to my room, holding my head. He has the worst taste in friends and girlfriends. Dad and I used to do more things together. We would play cards, make cookies, and go to the mall and people watch. We don't do much together anymore. I still enjoy spending time with him though. Does he think I'm too old for that stuff? I need to make more of an effort. Good chance I'll be gone in a year starting my new life, and I want Dad to have great memories of us together. I don't want to think of him with just Ivan and Becka in his life, yuck.

3
MIDGET FINSTER

Oh my God, oh my God. It happened again. Where's is my bag? Frantic, I gather my personal effects while I categorize my possessions in my head. What do I need? I survey the apartment I share with my brother and another coworker named Sparky. It's a crappy apartment in the town of Parma, south of Cleveland. Crime in this town has escalated over the past few years. Part of that could be my fault, but now is not the time to debate. I've got to hit the road and fast. My brother, Cola Mass, needs to realize this is getting serious. House mother I am not, but savior of your ass I am, and right now, I need to save my own- and his, if he'll let me. Cola Mass doesn't get that. He was born taller, hotter, and gets all the pussy he wants. Most of the time, he doesn't listen to me.

"Mass, where's my bag!" I yell. No reply. I storm into his room, and there he is asleep with some big ass, small tits, bleach blonde piece, snoring in sync. Damn! It stinks like tacos and lavender in here. I spy my suitcase in the corner, unzip it, and dump the contents on the floor. Closing his door behind me with a bang, I try to wake him. At least my suitcase is somewhat clean. I open it on my bed and double check all the compartments. I don't want any surprises later. My three tailor-made polyester suits go in first. They're my signature outfits. When I have these on, I'm working. I become king boss of my block. At 4'7", I need a motif. These suits give me plenty of pockets and ample hiding for my piece. This moss green one is my favorite. Oh yea, careful with my fedora. My door opens and Cola Mass comes in scratching himself.

"What is yo problem? Whey yo goin?" Cola Mass has potato chips stuck to his chest hair, yet he still looks handsome. My brother's real name is Collin Stevens. My real name is Marvin. To be a drug lord, you have to have a good name. Marvin Stevens was not it. My parents still live in Milwaukee and they think I'm in Ohio working at the Anchor factory. Not hardly. Midget Finster is my street name, and the streets are becoming too dangerous for me. I try to explain the situation to my brother.

"Spark didn't come home for the second day. He's gone, man. Ya hear what I'm sayien'? It happened on our street. I'm out."

"You don't know nuttin," Mass says.

"Have you ever known Spark not to play Xbox for longer than three hours, and I stopped by Leo's. They haven't seen him for two days. Has he ever missed his coffee and Krispy Kremes?" Mass looks at his fingers-is he counting?

"Did you call 'im?"

"Yes. Look, Mass, dis area is tainted, an' I'm gone. Spark went off an' pushed al' alone; his dumb choice and look what happened." I look into his eyes, pleading for clarity.

"Dey violatin our rights!" Mass yells. I can't carry on further conversation with him. I kick him out the door before I lose it.

"Like I said, I'm gone. You're welcome to come wi' me." We sell drugs locally and word has it dealers are turning up missing in the greater Cleveland area. Some vigilante is taking us out. Nobody knows who; there's no snitching in the drug game. Sure, people get shanked every day. But this is different. No gang fights or drive-bys, this is people just gone. People like me, like Sparky. I shudder thinking about him. He was a nice guy. Not greedy. Gave some of his coin away. That's not my style.

I open my safe in the back of my closet behind a false wall. Already have a bag for my Paper and gold bars. My financial advisor hooked me up with this little set up. Ready to go on the flash. I also keep my Pandora box in my safe. It's just an old puzzle box with a landscape picture. In it I have some pictures my brother drew and cards from my grandparents who tried to raise me right. I call it Pandora because it's all I have of my childhood memories, a box of my past. I don't keep many pictures, too hard to look at. I grab my teeth clip too, but I think I'm done with the gold grills. It's just not me. I'm more retro, and they just don't bring the outfit together. You don't want to stand out too much. I close the safe and put the wall back up. What else do I want to take? I find my bacon skillet and my Tupperware set. I finish packing the suitcase with my day-off clothes and underwear. That's all my necessities. The rest can stay. I leave the stuffed bass fish plaque on the wall. I load my case on wheels, money bag, and piece into my Range Rover.

Cola stands in the doorway, and I wave goodbye. I hope he understands the danger and joins me. We're good together and have made some serious cash. I'm heading west.

4
LIBBY

When November reaches an end, it's feeling like winter. Hiking is fun in the cold months because most of the vegetation has died down and the ground is bare. I can see further through the woods, and the landscape is hypnotizing. Each tree has a shape all its own. Some trees are alone and some all run together. If they were alive, each one would have its own personality. Just like us. Around this time of year, I don't talk so much as listen. The forest beckons contemplation, answers to life's puzzles. It's calmer at school, too. And as predicted, nothing on Thomas Ruff ever surfaced. His brother Billy is like a lost soul. He's not as obnoxious which makes it sadder in a way. I heard their father is still a drunk, as always.

We'll be going to Aunt Janna's house for Thanksgiving dinner today. That's our tradition. Janna is divorced, so it's just her and my two cousins, Regina and Cory. They go to GlenOak High School in Canton. Regina is a sophomore, and she plays volleyball. Cory is a senior and he's a book worm. He plans on going to college to become an engineer.

He plays a lot of video games and comes out only to eat, and then he disappears again.

Regina and I get along really well and always catch up on our lives. She asks where Patrick is, and I tell her bagging and tagging a deer somewhere. Regina doesn't know what she wants to be when she grows up. Unlike me, she's not interested in the outdoors. She wears nail polish and looks at her phone every other minute, and she wears too much makeup. I made myself a bit fancier today with some makeup, jeans, and a sweater. I chose to wear my hair down. I miss my comfy clothes, but it's fun to dress up sometimes. Regina talks about getting her driver's license soon, but they can't afford a car for her. She might get a job, but I don't see that happening. If Janna didn't buy her so many clothes and shoes, they could afford to get her a car. I just keep my mouth shut. I don't have a job either.

"Everything is ready, come and eat!" Janna yells. We all stand around the table. I sit down before everyone else because I'm the only one who drinks milk, and my milk glass stands out amid the tea for everyone else. I always just bring the green bean casserole. We all eat too much and then eat pie. There goes Cory to the basement. We sit around and talk about graduation plans, though I don't seem to have any. Then the subject of the missing people come up. Some disappeared from the Canton area earlier this year, like Steven Foster. Regina says her school has a memorial sign up for him. I wonder what it says-don't do drugs? I am guessing someone lost a loved one to drugs, and they are wreaking some serious vengeance.

"Libby, can I help you with a graduation party?" Aunt Janna always wants to help. She's the next best thing to Mom. She misses her sister, I know. They were close. Nobody really talks about her anymore. Dad doesn't say much of anything around Janna. She looks and sounds similar to Mom, so he might find that hard. He acts like he's looking at magazines, but I know he is just trying to look comfortable and contented. Aunt Janna tries to talk to him alone sometimes, but it always ends with him walking away. I never ask what they talk about, but I assume it's about me looking or acting like a tomboy or something like that.

"I'll let you know." I tell her. I don't plan on having a party, but Janna doesn't need to know that yet.

It's getting late, and we say our goodbyes. Driving the half hour home is overly quiet. It always ends this way when he goes to her house. I'm surprised he still goes at all. Dad must feel like it's an obligation. I decide this is a great time to make an effort to do something together.

"Are you doing anything this weekend?" I ask.

"Becka wants to go up to Niagara Falls. Would you be okay with that? Do you and Patrick have any plans?"

"Sure, Dad, go ahead, I'll be fine. We don't have any plans, but he will be around," I assure him. Maybe if he is with her that long, he'll get sick of her talking and complaining. Patrick turns into a barbarian this time of year, hunting season galore. He is sometimes gone for a couple days, so I'll have to amuse myself. Maybe some movies would be fun. I could watch the next season of Animal Kingdom or read the next Stephanie Plum novel. I promised both Dad and Patrick that I will not go hiking off the property alone. Perhaps I can get Hope or Rashin to do something. On the other hand, I might enjoy time to myself. Maybe I could teach myself some new survival skill and impress Patrick. What could that be?

Two days later, Dad is gone. He doesn't work as much this time of year. As a nice surprise, Patrick is done hunting and comes over to see me. Snuggling close to him on the couch, I love being next to him; there is so much mystery to him. I don't let him know how much he affects me though. He has this strong, silent charisma that is very appealing. His body is perfect except for the one Major thing. That's okay though, other ways exist to be close. I'm just wondering when we'll do some of them. We kiss for a while, but then he stops. Damn.

"Why does your Dad trust you to be alone with me?" He asks with a grin.

"I've come to the understanding that males are not the smartest species. That's what it says in all my books." He grabs me and throws me over his knees and acts like he's spanking me, and I scream in delight. He can move fast when he wants to. I know why Dad trusts me with Patrick. I told him last year that Patrick is very old fashioned, and we do not have sex. Dad can always tell if I lie. We never have to keep secrets from each other. He also knows I'm almost 18 and he can't stop whatever might happen anyway. Dad likes Patrick for that reason and that he never gets into any trouble. Like I said, simple life.

We make some popcorn and get out the milk duds and settle in for a movie. We love the Denzel movies. I try not to fall asleep on the couch. He doesn't spend the night; says it's not proper. I try to kiss him more before he leaves to convince him to stay longer.

"Don't go yet," I whisper in his ear while holding his strong arms.

"I better go now." He can see my frustration. "The chicken made it across." Now he smiles, and I smile too. That's what he always says to calm a situation down, along with a little hand scoot motion. He makes sure I lock all the doors and I have my mace in my room ready to go. Then he goes home after a kiss goodnight. We really are like 60-year-olds. Perhaps I do need to get out of these frumpy clothes. That's what I can work on. I need to be more girlish. I can think of many things we could be doing that could be very stimulating without having sex. I need to be more seductive. New survival plan.

5

I ask Dad for a little money to buy some clothes, supporting my new survival plan, and he gives me way too much. Dad is very generous, and since Christmas will be here soon, I accept. Dad and I don't get each other many gifts. This time of year is hard for us. When he is home, he sits in his chair and stares at the TV. Mom loved this time of year, and she died this time of year. She would bake every day, and the house smelled so good. We all would take holiday goodies to friends around town. Dad would grumble each year about having to do it, but then he always had a good time. Mom had plenty of dessert recipes. She must have had a sweet tooth, although I am not sure about that. I'll have to ask Janna. Christmas memories are special, but she died just before Christmas. After losing her, we would try to get out decorations, but each year, we put up fewer and fewer. One year, we put up a real tree, but no one ever got the decorations out, so it was just a pine tree in the living room. After that, we didn't decorate during the holidays. We just head to Canton for the big dinner and take the white elephant gifts. That seems like enough to me.

Once Mom was diagnosed, she lived for about two more years from what I understand. Aunt Janna came to live with us during the last couple weeks. Her husband stayed home with Regina and Cory. They were still married back then. I don't really know why they broke up. Maybe Janna and Dad both changed after Mom died. Dad's parents were killed together in a car accident, so I never met them. And Mom's parents live in Arizona. I have seen them four times that I can remember. They have no interest in our lives, too busy golfing at the country club. I don't think Dad really gets along with them anyway; they never talk. I wonder if Mom's parents think Dad should have taken better care of her, or blame him for something, or maybe he wasn't good enough for her.

Mom grew up in the Cleveland area. She and Dad met at a Journey concert, but he never talks about those times. I just look forward to the New Year and hope Dad perks up after the holidays. Patrick will be a nice Christmas distraction for me.

With Dad's mood, I hate to trouble him, but I had another nightmare last night. The water was so cold, and I couldn't swim with my heavy clothes on. I had a knife in my hand, and I was trying to keep from fully falling into the water by stabbing the top of the ice, but it didn't work. Dad had to come and wake me. It worries him more than me. It's always the same drowning struggle. I just tell him I'm okay, and it was just a dream. I'm good at pushing painful feelings away. I just go into my shell, and I'm fine. It's not a lie. Dad's face is distressing, so I put on a smile.

"Dad, I'm fine now," I calmly say, while I'm shaking inside. He doesn't know what to say. Patrick is the same way. Men have a hard time expressing feelings. I stay strong for the both of them.

Safety is imperative to Patrick. Tonight, we're taking the evening off from defense practice. I've mastered the knives, so we can now have some down time. My thoughts are more towards the let's-get-physical route, but I'll take what I can get. I bought some tight-fitting jeans and a lower cut sweater to wear around him. This is all in my plan. I can tell he notices the new clothes, but he doesn't say anything about them. Look at me! I'm curvy! He is very backward about that subject. We will kiss and hold each other, but then the romance stops. I don't talk about it; I know he'll feel bad. Snuggling in this cold weather will have to do right now. Plan not working. He decides it's time to go home. He kisses me goodbye and is off in his truck. It is hard to get warm again after he's gone. Hot cocoa in bed is not quite the same.

It seems that life is back to normal. The kids at school hardly talk about Thomas. The talk is all about Christmas gifts and Christmas break vacations. Hope is going to a basketball camp, of course. Rashin and her family will be working like always. I'll plan some hikes, and Patrick says he'll take me to Wayne National Forest during break. Perhaps we could rent a cabin. Wonder what Dad will say to that?

The next evening, I'm waiting for Patrick in more new tight-fitting clothes. He said he would try to make it over, but he had some things to do for his mom. Dad is out with

Becka. The doorbell rings. I can hear Ivan yelling, and he's looking at me through the window. Wish I had on my frump clothes. I open the door. He rubs his hands together and steps into the house.

"Getting cold out there. Is George home?" he asks. He knows Dad isn't home or his truck would be outside. "I was close by and thought I would stop. Where is Patrick tonight? You didn't have to get all fancy for me." He moves his hands in a curving pattern up and down. Think Libby.

"He's coming over; I expect him here anytime now," I say as I head back to the couch to cover up as much as possible with a blanket. "I can tell Dad that you stopped by." I can hear some noises outside and hope that Dad is back. Ivan slides down onto the couch and starts to watch TV. Two Broke Girls is on. What the hell is he doing? I want to scream at him to leave, but I bite my tongue. This man makes my stomach turn.

"I like the brunette one," he stammers while clearing his throat. "I need some water." He walks into the kitchen and helps himself then sits back down. So now, he's just going to sit here with me? Ivan watches more of the show and laughs to himself. Guess that wasn't Dad outside. I can tell he keeps looking over at me as I stare at the TV. I text Patrick to let him know I'm sitting here with Ivan. He knows how I feel about him. No reply. He must be busy with something. Patrick does not sit much. I text Dad to let him know Ivan is here waiting for him. He says he's on his way back. I can relax more now. I can't focus on the show, so I head into the kitchen for some chips. I look out the window and see Ivan's fancy car parked off to the side of the drive. It's a Tahoe, very shiny in the security light. I suppose I should be nicer to Dad's friend. He really hasn't done anything to make me dislike him. Dad said he was a teacher now since he's no longer a doctor. Looking at his car, he must be doing well. Ivan drives a nice car, has on expensive clothes, and has a good haircut. His face is more doglike, which is also how he acts.

"What do you need that big car for?" I ask from the kitchen. He mumbles something about moving equipment around for jobs he's doing. "What jobs are you doing?" Perfect time to ask and find out more about this fancy person who likes to hang out with my dad.

"I teach some medical classes at Ohio Northern University, and I haul around some display items. I teach anatomy mostly but also biology. I like to travel in comfort." His smile is wide, clearly bragging. I see Dad pulling up now. He comes in and sits down with Ivan. Dad seems happy. He and Becka must have had a nice time together. She must be different when they're alone.

I listen to them talk about some new city council agendas, so I decide to go check out the fancy Tahoe. I put on my boots and coat and quietly sneak out the back door. I wonder what else Ivan might have in his fancy car? I peek into the driver's side window and look around. Can't see much, so I test the door handle and it's unlocked. Bingo. After glancing back at the house to be sure no one is looking, I open the door. It's surprisingly clean. I look over the driver's seat into the backseat and don't see anything but a coat. Wouldn't there be some books and papers piled up? Where is all of this stuff he has to haul around? I gently close the front door and open the back door. Peering over the backset, I see something in the very back. I glance back towards the house to make sure no one is looking out the window. What am I doing? My heart starts to race. I'm snooping for anything that makes Ivan look bad. Why does someone like him stop by to see my Dad, who is quite opposite? Then I get in and lean over the backseat. It's dark, but I spot a couple coolers in the back. I open one, and I see a Ziploc bag surrounded by ice. I lift the bag out of the ice. It's heavy. I can't tell in the darkness what it is. No lights come on in the back. I use the flashlight on my phone to make it brighter.

"What the hell is this?" I say to myself. It looks like a big piece of flesh. I pick up another bag and it's smaller. These look like organs or something very squishy, and they don't seem completely frozen. I put them back in and get out of the car and shut the door quietly. I look at the house again. My legs don't seem to be able to move right now. It's biology stuff because he teaches anatomy. That's all it is. He needs this for his classes. My legs finally register to move, and I run around to the back door again. I can't go in the house yet, my face must look sickened. I walk towards the back yard and sit down in a chair. Yes, he must pick this stuff up from some butcher, and those are cow or deer parts. I take some deep breaths and calm myself down. Can I go in and act normal? Almost there. I take some more breaths. I guess you have to be unusual to do what he does; most of those smart guys are odd. Ivan the Terrible comes to mind, but I don't remember what that's from. I can't think. I quietly enter the house and take off my boots. Dad comes around the corner, and he gives me a strange look.

"What were you doing outside?" he asks, looking at me.

"I thought I left a book in my car to finish my homework, but I must have left it at school," I say. Dad looks at me longer. Then he looks at my clothes. Crap, he knows when I'm lying, but he doesn't say anything. "I'm going to go to my room to do some reading." I kiss him on the cheek and say goodnight. "Bye, Ivan," I force myself to say and head upstairs.

"Good night, Libby." I hurriedly go upstairs and get under the blankets to think about what I just saw. I tell myself to forget about it, but I can't. Perhaps organs don't freeze very fast. They could have been from a horse. I just can't get the bags out of my mind. Were they warm too, or was that my imagination? I grab my book and decide to catch up on Lula and Stephanie and put that out of my mind. Patrick finally texts me back. He says he was outside fixing his mom's brakes and he was covered in grease, so he couldn't answer his phone. I decide not to mention what was in the bags. I don't want to sound like a lunatic. It's not a big deal. Ivan uses that for his job.

The next day at school, it happened again. Another boy is reported missing, Ray Squires. Ray also went to my school. This time, they decide to cancel the rest of classes and send us all home; it has become a bigger deal now. He is also a known drug user and possible dealer. I know Ray. He used to be on the football team through his sophomore year. Last year, he wasn't even on the team. Somehow his life changed. He got mixed up with the wrong crowd and quickly changed into a stranger. When I would see him in the halls, he might make eye contact, but he wasn't there just a hollow emptiness. I remember having a crush on him when we were younger. Of course, he only dated the cheerleaders when he was on the football team. I can't believe this happened again here.

I feel bad for his parents, Earl and Nancy Squires, They used to be good friends with Mom and Dad. I can remember them coming by when Mom was sick. Nancy would make us casseroles, and she would do some cleaning around the house. Earl would take Dad out somewhere. I suppose to get a drink or something. They tried to keep in touch with Dad after Mom was gone, but Dad holed up into his shell. I know they love their son, and this will be hard on them even though they knew he was into the drug scene. Ray was their only child, but they had already lost him.

Later at home, I hear from Rashin that Ray was close to Berlin Lake with his buddies. That's about eight miles north. They had a bonfire going, and Ray never went home. His car was found still parked at the same place. That's close to where I like to go hiking. Yikes. Maybe he just fell into the lake. It would be easy to do if you're high. The cold water temperature would make it a quick but painful death. I shudder to think about it because it's like my nightmares. I think about Ray when we first entered high school. He always had a smile on his face, and he was nice to everyone. Such a waste. This has to be an accident. Ray still lived at home and carried on a somewhat normal life. He was not living on the streets, and he wasn't like Thomas, who didn't have someone who loves him. I know those things probably don't matter, but I'm getting scared.

Since his body was not found over the next three days, the search is called off. Just like the others-no body.

I tell Patrick I want to go hiking near where he was last seen; I really just want to think about how fragile life is. He rolls his eyes and agrees to go. We drive to Berlin Lake and find the area Rashin was talking about by the Berlin Lake trail head. Their bonfire area is loosely secured with yellow tape, and a few people are hanging around talking. We walk on by and head to the trail. What is going on around here? Overdoses are one thing, but people are just disappearing. Patrick has nothing to say about the issue. He is more of a listener. The cold air makes it all the more grim. Poor Earl and Nancy.

As we start walking away onto the trail, I look down and see two 100 Grand candy bar wrappers just off the trail. The bright red is hard to miss. Patrick sees them too. My heart skips a beat or two or three and pounds very hard in my chest. I think of Dad being here. Why would he be here? Then follow that with the coolers in Ivan's car. My stomach knots up, and I think about Ray. I will myself to move and breathe. Neither of us say anything. I pick up the wrappers and put them in my pocket. It's just an impulse thing to do.

"Why did you do that?" he asks. I still can't form words. My legs are going numb. Breathe, I tell myself. "Libby?"

"I don't know why. I just don't like litter on the ground is all." He looks at me and lets it drop. Why wouldn't I pick up trash? But he knows what I'm thinking. That Dad was here. So what if he was. Is he incapable of throwing those wrappers in a trash can? Again, why would Dad be here? He doesn't go hiking unless someone drags him. Quit thinking about Dad. Someone else might like those bars too. Why is this even worrying me?

"Let's head home now. I'm getting hungry and thirsty, and we didn't bring anything with us." We walk in silence for a stretch. I feel silly for picking up the wrappers. "Let's go to Jafri's and see if Rashin has heard anything else about Ray," I calmly say.

"Okay, whatever you feel like." We walk back by the fire and car area. Ray's car is not there anymore. I wonder how many police cars were here for Ray. Do any of the officers know that Ray used to be a great kid? That he could have gotten help and recovered. Do they care? I feel like I'm the only person who knew him. In reality, I hardly did. It's just so hard when this happens to people you know: schoolmates, friends, and dumb ass kids. Patrick opens the car door for me, and I get in. I know Patrick's wondering what I'm thinking about. I'm wondering why Dad and Ivan are friends.

"They probably found him by now. He might not even be dead." Patrick tries to make me feel better. Over the past two to three years, this must be close to the 20th missing boy or man in the greater northern Ohio area that has been reported on the news. Most of the news shows civilians talking about the fact that they are not that upset about the situation. Something is seriously going on here. Now it feels personal, like it is somehow happening to me, my town, my people, and my backyard. We arrive at the gas station, and I go in to see if Rashin is working. She's stocking shelves in the back. She hugs me and can tell I'm shaken up.

"What's wrong Lib? You look spooked." She holds my hands.

"I was just wondering if you heard any more about Ray," I ask her.

"Yes, well nothing about Ray, but a new detective stopped by who is new in town. I hear the police feel it could be a serial killer. I imagine that will bring the media front and center. It's all crazy around here with people talking about it. The disappearances are becoming more frequent, and none of them are ever found. It might be trafficking." Rashin talks very fast. She normally doesn't get excited about anything. I get us a drink when Patrick walks in. He filled up his tank while he was waiting outside.

"I can tell the town is in a heightened state of panic. Did they find him?" he asks.

"No," I answer, "but a new detective is here to investigate."

"Really," Patrick says slowly. He seems unimpressed.

"It makes sense, something needs to be done," I say. "Someone might get taken just because this freak feels like doing it, without being a dope head." Now I'm getting pumped. Then I suddenly think again about the wrappers in my pocket and the contents of the Tahoe. My mind is swirling with thoughts of Ray and his parents, and Dad and Ivan and the Tahoe.

"Libby," Patrick is holding me by my arms and giving me a little shake. "Libby!" I look up at him. Tears start to form, and I look down to wipe my eyes and get a hold of myself. Rashin tells me it will be okay and to go home. She'll call me if she hears anything else. That sounds good. I just want to go home and cocoon up. We say goodbye, and I tell her to come over and practice her shooting skills sometime. She gives me the thumbs up. Rashin's dad is working behind the counter. I can never remember his name, but he always gives me a wave. Her mom is probably in the back doing paperwork.

Patrick drops me off and tries to make me smile with his "the chicken made it across" saying, but it doesn't help my mood this time. I don't think everything will be okay. He probably thinks I'm too much to handle at this point. Dad is still working somewhere, so I go hide in my room. Thinking about the detective being here makes me feel a little better. Hopefully, this is being taken more seriously now. My stomach feels like a knot, and I just need to calm down.

The next day is Saturday, and Dad and I have breakfast together before he goes off to work. I offer to help him, but there's nothing I can do. Today is not a job for Tony or me. Spreading stone from a dump truck is something only Dad can do. It is very precise work, and he does not want to shovel the mistakes. I tell him I'll be staying close to home. He drinks his coffee while staring at the news. We talk about Earl and Nancy for a little while, but Dad doesn't have much to say. He seems distracted.

When I stand, he says, "Still have your pepper spray?"

"Sure, how about your AR-15, also? I can sling it over my back," I tease. He is not amused. "Can I do anything to help you here? It has been a while since you needed me."

"Just keep yourself safe, that's all I ask." I give him a hug and kiss goodbye. "Everything I do is for you, that's all that matters to me." Then he's gone, never much for conversations.

I put on my boots and coat, which already has the pepper spray in the pocket, and head out. I first walk by the equipment yard. New tracks are visible in the sand, yet the same piles of material. I walk for a while and find a tree down. I sit and find myself talking, talking out loud about anything but the missing classmates: my future, my boyfriend, my breathing, my stomach ache, my Dad, and Ivan Crap. Should I tell Patrick about my apprehensions?

"Let Ray be found. Please let him just have skipped out for a while and then come back. I don't want my town to become a circus. I'll need to get out of here. Seems like Alliance is becoming polluted or soured. Perhaps Hope and I could be dorm buddies together far away, and I can join a sorority. Then I can actually find out what it feels like to have sex and be daring. No more hometown dramas and aloneness. People all around me going to parties and drinking; that would put my mind in a completely different place. How funny I am trying to talk myself into those things. That life is not for me. I can't lie to you." Looking up at the tree, I say. "But I do need to get out of this town. It feels corrupt. I need a small college with my own place and my classroom could be at Yosemite National Park. That sounds about right."

A chill comes over me; like I'm being watched. I stand up and slowly look in all directions, while quiet and listening. I can hear several types of birds and the occasional scurry in the brush. I decide to walk towards the pond and tell myself I'm not cracking up and no one is after me. Partway, I stop fast and look behind me again. Still nothing. God, Libby, just calm down. I reach the pond and sit down on my bench.

Looking down at the water's edge I find my special fish, Boggles. "I see you buddy, why don't you swim away? Do you have something to tell me? You look like a mutant." I look around again. I can hear Dad's dump truck coming back now. I decide to stay here for a while longer. The sky is blue, and the sun is warm today. I stare back at my fish friend. Just push the feelings away, Libby, go into your shell. Everything will be fine.

Dad pulls up to the house in his truck, and he looks like he's in a good mood. That has to be a good sign. He yells to me that he's going to repair a driveway beside Earl Squire's house today. Earl is Ray's dad, and Ray has been gone six days ago now. I'm sure Dad will talk to Earl. They've known each other for a long time.

"Tell Earl I said hello," I mention as I walk back towards the house.

"I will if I see him. I won't lie; I hope I don't see him. What can I say?" I shrug my shoulders. There are no words for someone who has lost a child. He nods then drives off.

6

It's Monday morning and classes are back in session. School is not school anymore. The impact of the disappearing boys has turned it into bizarro world. Assignments are not assigned; tests are not given. It is a jumbled walk from room to room with stares and silence. Patrick and I see each other throughout the day, and we just go through the motions. Not only is the situation hard on the community, I feel like something has happened to me personally. Am I right to feel this way, or does everyone feel this way? Am I neglecting the signs in front of me? I'm good at shutting my feelings away, but maybe I should be worried about my suspicions. Can people look at my face and see my questionable thoughts? Why do I feel like I have to be secretive; I know no secrets.

Patrick has been quiet lately too. He doesn't have much to say about the missing classmates, which seems about right for him. He has come out of his shell during the time we've been together, but he has a long way to go in sharing his feelings. Another reason why we are so compatible is our need to be alone. We both have days we don't talk or pry. I know his life hasn't been easy. He hunts to escape into his other world. I get it.

Dad and I end up at Bob Evans that evening for dinner. Becka isn't working, so that's a relief. I can't help but wonder about the circumstances I've come across. I look at Dad, and he's like a stranger to me. Holiday memories and depression are evident on his face. How can I ask him anything? This time I almost wish Becka was here taking up the silence.

My world at school is like the Titanic. An iceberg has been hit, and it will sink-no saving or going back. My world at home is like being on the life raft; everything should be okay, but it could still go wrong. There is no safe place. The next time Ivan comes over, I will investigate again, and then I'll determine what to do or say. I consider again the wrappers on the ground. I'm sure I am overreacting-my life is great, right? It's better than most kids I know. I hear them talking about fights at home, no money, and they feel hopeless. I'm thankful for what I have. I have no unmet needs. I turn to Dad and make a conscious effort to start a conversation.

"How's Ray doing?"

"He's not doing well," he says. "He feels like the police department is inadequate. One new guy has talked to Nancy and Earl twice. No clues were found at the scene, and no witnesses have come forward. I can't give him any comfort." Dad looks concerned. "Are you done eating? Because we have to get going. I've got a meeting tonight with some of the townspeople to discuss new prevention protocols and safety measures," he says.

"Sure, let's go." It was hard just sitting with him anyway. We drive home. I'm glad Dad is taking an active part in the problem. That makes me feel better. The thought of Dad and Ivan being involved in anything sinister is ludicrous. Besides, Dad wouldn't do anything to hurt Earl and Nancy's son, right?

I finish some homework on the couch and go upstairs to get ready for bed. Dad's meeting must be long, or maybe he was meeting Becka later on. It's almost 10 p.m. He likes to be in bed by now when he has to get up for work. The house feels different tonight.

Then I hear the doorbell ring. I immediately think of Ivan and feel sick. If that's him again, I'm not opening the door. I peek out my bedroom window carefully and see a police car. This makes me feel even sicker. Grabbing my robe, I head downstairs and open the door.

Two officers are on the doorstop. They ask me my name and then if they can come in. I nod but my legs stop working again, and a cold sweat takes over. They help me to the couch. Breathe, Libby, breathe.

"I'm Officer Tim, and this is Officer Nick. Libby, we have to tell you something very difficult." Officer Tim holds my hand. I look at his name badge because I can't look him in the face. His name is Timothy Moore. He must be around 35 and has a soothing voice. I look down at my hands, and I'm unable to breath anymore. I lift my head to look up at the ceiling, forcing myself to breathe in and out. I know this policeman is going to tell me something bad.

"Did something happen to my Dad?" I ask, my voice barely a whisper. Tim nods his head. The room is silent for a minute. I freeze into the couch. He finally goes on.

"He was found outside his car shot in the chest. This happened out on Bonner Road near Berlin Lake."

"Berlin Lake? Where Ray went missing?"

"Yes, about two miles past that spot. Your father's body is en route to the medical examiner's. They want to retrieve the bullets for ballistics. I am so sorry to have to tell you this. The event was called in by a family driving by. Can we call anyone for you?"

I can't talk for what seems like a few minutes, trying to absorb what I'm hearing. I try to pull myself together. This cannot be real. I knew something bad was going to happen. I could feel it, but this is much worse than I could have ever imagined. My father was killed! My mind spins out of control. He said he was going to a town meeting. Was that a lie? Did Dad lie to me, or did someone lie to Dad? Why was he out on Bonner Road?

"Please call my Aunt Janna for me." I numbly hand him my phone with her number. She's my only close family." Officer Nick takes my phone and goes into the kitchen while Officer Tim stays sitting with me. I curl up into a ball on the couch crying. They text Patrick for me too, and he said he'll be right over. The officers are patient with me, but they need to ask a few questions.

"Where were you this evening?" I know this is routine but still very hard to take. I sit up straight.

"I have been here since we got home from Bob Evans earlier, around 6:30." Is this really happening? My dad is gone. He's not coming home-ever. I shiver despite the blanker around me. "Dad said he was going to a town meeting somewhere tonight to talk about new safety measures because of the disappearances." The officers look at each other.

"There was no town meeting. We would have heard about that. Do you know who told your dad that information?"

"No, I have no idea. He worked over by Earl and Nancy Squires today. That's all I know." My hands are shaking, and I can't stop crying. I now feel hysterical, while the officers look at me and remain calm. I try to figure out what happened, but it makes no sense. They ask if Dad had any enemies or any other details that could help. I can only shake my head.

"We need to get back to the crime scene. We'll have to take his truck for a while. We didn't find any cell phone, so it might have been taken. Here's my number if you think of anything," Officer Nick says, handing me his card. "Do you have any guns in the house?"

"We keep some in a safe," I say.

"Are they all registered?"

"I would assume so." I really have no idea about that. Then Patrick arrives, just as the officers get ready to leave.

"We'll be in contact tomorrow. A detective, Jason, will be in contact with you soon, and we are truly sorry about this. One more thing. Before we leave, we need to swab both of your hands."

"What's that for?"

"Standard procedure, it checks for gunshot residue," he answers. I nod. Officer Nick takes out two little bags from his car and opens each one and pats around my hands and lower arms with a small cotton ended tip. Then he does

Patrick's hands and arms as well. The swabs go back into the kit with our names on each. They apologize to me again and leave. Patrick just holds me while I cry. We sit on the couch in darkness. I tell him what happened to Dad between sobs and snot. I'm so lost inside. I don't remember ever having this much pain.

Janna arrives, and she takes me up to my room to put me to bed. I can't make my body work right. I look at her helping me into my pajamas. I miss not having a mom. She's crying too. I haven't seen her cry since Mom died, and it brings all those feeling crashing back. Now both of my parents are gone. My ship has sunk to the floor, and my life raft has a hole in it. Someday, I'll be gone too, my reasoning tells me. Death keeps taking from me. Finally, sleep takes over the numbness.

Janna stays with me for a couple days and takes care of the funeral arrangements. I eventually make it out of bed and eat a few bites. The fridge is stuffed with food from friends, but I make Patrick and Janna take most of it home with them. I have no interest in eating, and I'm not up to seeing anybody. My body is immobile; it takes effort to make myself move. I want my Dad back. What has happened to my simple life? I have no direction, and my mind is broken. I don't know if I should be worried for my own life or furious my father was murdered, but I'm distressed to the point of agony. What am I supposed to do now?

Janna goes home to Canton for a while and will come back for the funeral. She's right there to take care of everything for me. When Mom died, she stayed with me for a few weeks. We took several walks together to get me out of the house. That's when I decided hiking was my new favorite pastime. As we strolled, I taught her fun animal facts. For how bad I felt, she made the best of it. I don't know what I would do without being able to count on her. She tries to keep me from crawling too deep into my shell which is my favorite spot. I don't think she is succeeding.

Officer Tim calls me the next morning. He lets me know the bullets retrieved are from a 9mm handgun. He asks again if I have any idea what Dad was doing there or if he had any problems with anyone. I realize there was no meeting, but why Dad was out on some back road close to the latest abduction site troubles me deeply.

"I don't know of any problems he was having." I answer him. I'm glad right now to be on the phone, so no one can read my face. They might be able to tell I'm holding back bewildering thoughts. I don't mention anything about Ivan to them. What would I say? There's this friend of Dads who had some unusual parts in his car last week. I think it was the same night Ray disappeared. That's the part I don't want to tell myself. It was the same night.

"If you think of anything, or if we can help you in any way, please don't hesitate to call," he says.

Nausea takes over again. "Do you think this is related to the missing high school kids?" I ask.

"That is a consideration we are investigating. Anything you can think, please let us know. It could be of help. A detective will also stop by to ask you some questions today."

"Okay, thanks for calling." I don't know what else to say. This whole situation is like a never-ending fall.

Patrick skips school again and spends the day with me. He's very quiet. He knows there's nothing he can say to make this any better. We just hold each other, and he wipes my tears away. I will have to leave the house eventually, but the first place I'll end up going is to my father's funeral. Maybe I can put myself in another place. I'll try to picture a scene in a national park picture that I love. I see the Needles with all of the rock formations, but now that seems like a cemetery. I cry again and scare Patrick with my sudden eruption.

With his arms around me, Patrick tells me the police asked him where he was that night. He was working at the diner with his mother, then went home with her. I guess since he's dating the daughter, he's a suspect. The plague of this town has found me. It's personal, and it's devastating. The hurt is so much different than when Mom died. I'm older, and this was sudden. Dad and I were a team together. How am I going to go on without him? He was my rock. I don't know if it's possible to go deeper into my shell.

The funeral home is done up with Christmas decorations. Again, a December death. Aunt Janna talks to the director because I am still not quite functioning. I sit towards the back in the hallway. I can't go in to see the casket. I've been numb for days now, and my clothes are hanging on me. Janna got me this black dress I'm wearing. This used to be my size. My hair is down to hide most of my face. That works well. Patrick tries to get me to come into the gathering room, but I can't do it. I don't know how I feel about this whole situation or even how to feel anything. I need it to all go away. I don't want to think about it anymore. I can't bring my dad back, and his life has left me with mysteries, which might need to remain mysteries. I want to know who killed my father, but I also don't want to get involved. I don't want to ever hear from Ivan again. This town needs a break from whatever has invaded, or has it just begun?

Where will I live? I don't think I can live in my house by myself. I turn and look towards the exit. I could just walk out that door and leave it all behind. That sounds easy, but my mind is not functioning. I feel the door is telling me to get away? I can't look at people right now. Patrick embraces me, and I'm brought back to reality as he looks into my eyes.

"Let's go sit in the back row for the service. I'll be with you the whole time." I let him lead me in and we find a seat. I see folks turning around. My cousins, Regina and Cory, are up front with Janna. Most people I recognize, but I don't remember all their names. These are people Dad probably did jobs for or grew up with. I can't look at them. Then I see Wayne in his wheelchair off to the side. He's wiping his eyes. I feel a strong connection to Wayne. He has been around me many years, and shown true friendship to Dad. I will just focus on him and picture the good times we had working and laughing together. He was always in a good mood and upbeat. I'm sad he probably won't be around anymore. No, no, I will think happy thoughts. Just focus on Wayne. Patrick is holding my hand. I can get through this. Breathe in. Breathe out.

The sermon is about a hardworking man who has had loses in his life. Something about how a tragedy can strike and take a loved one too soon. Songs are played with intermittent silences. I didn't hear hardly any of it. I feel so alone and overwhelmed with what to do. The pain is overpowering. I try to remember the pain from my mom, but a person must slowly forget. If it could be a year from now already, I would gladly lose a year of my life to get rid of some of this sorrow.

The service ends, but I barely notice. Since Dad will be cremated, there will be no graveside service. Janna glances my way, but she that I won't be greeting anybody today. She does her best to thank people for coming. I feel bad leaving all of this to her, but I only want to talk to Wayne. Walking over to him, I hug him with all my soul. He feels like family to me.

"I am so sorry, kiddo," he says.

"Me too, Wayne, I don't know what's going on."

"George was the best guy I ever knew. This makes no sense to me either. Life is unfair sometimes, Libby. When life knocks you down, you'll have to make a choice about what you'll do about it." He smiles and hugs me again, then turns to leave. I'm about to follow him when life stops me again. Ivan is standing beside me. He apologizes for showing up late. He forcibly hugs me and keeps his hand on my back for too long. It's like he is trying to guide me somewhere.

"I'm here for you, Libby and if there is anything you need...," he whispers in my ear like it has to be a secret. "I have watched you grow up into a fine young lady, and now you'll have many responsibilities. Please allow me to help you out." He almost smiles.

Why are you smiling? Get the hell away from me, you freak, I'm yelling at him with my eyes. Ivan slithers away as fast as he slithered in. Patrick is waiting for me in the back. I'm sickened by Ivan. I don't plan on seeing him ever again. Janna eventually finds me in Patrick's truck, and she takes me back to my empty house. There's nothing to say. I just shut my eyes and she rubs my head while I lay on the couch. My cousins go home with their dad, but she stays with me.

"Do you think it would be okay if I come and live with you for a while?"

"Of course you can, Libby, whatever you want to do."

Patrick comes in to check on me. "Hope and Rashin were at the service and wanted me to tell you they were sorry. They'll call you soon," Patrick says.

I forgot about them. I didn't even see them. I was too focused on Wayne. I wonder who else I missed that I should have spoken to. I just want to go back to bed, so I tell them goodnight and take myself to bed. Janna will be sleeping in a little guest room we have. Patrick will go home. I stare at darkness again for hours before falling asleep. So many questions with no answers. In the morning, I use the bathroom and head back to bed. Food doesn't sound good. I can hear someone coming up the stairs.

Entering my room, Janna says, "I need to talk to you, Libby." My room suddenly becomes heavy to breathe in. She looks wrecked and sits on the side of my bed. "There's something I have wanted to tell you for a long time, but your father insisted I wasn't allowed to." I feel myself becoming sick again. She looks at the wall and takes a deep breath. I can't even imagine what she needs to tell me. I have never seen her this way; she is always a rock. "Libby, you had a sister. She was one and a half years older than you. Her name was Cassandra." She lets this sink in before she goes on. I am mute. What is she talking about?

"One day, you were outside by your pond on a blanket. You were just a baby. Cassandra, 'Casey,' was running around. Your mom was not home, and your dad was outside with you both." She hesitates before going on. "Your dad had a problem with drugs back then. He used Percocet and Vicodin after having a back injury and got hooked on them. When they didn't work anymore, he started to get into more serious drugs, and he took some that day. Well, he fell asleep beside you on your blanket, and Casey fell into the pond and drowned. He slept through the whole thing." I am in a tunnel. My mind is having a hard time concentrating on what she's telling me. Words cannot form. She goes on. "Your dad never forgave himself and couldn't bring himself to tell you. He never took any other drugs again after that day and has worked hard to provide for you and your mom ever since. I have always felt it was something you should know. Your mom couldn't handle telling you either. It was too painful for both of them. Through it, they bonded together instead of Casey's death driving them apart. I've always admired that. Yet, he was never the same. How could he be? I have some pictures at my house of Casey if you want to see her."

The room is quiet except for both of us sniffling. My pillow is wet with tears as I think back to my earliest memory. My life just feels like a blur now. I had a sister; I had a sister. She rubs my head and gets up to leave. My mind swirls with this information. "We can talk more about this later, but I felt you should know."

Alone in my room, I envision what that day would have been like. I run to the bathroom to dry heave into the toilet. When done, I sit on the floor and empty thoughts flood back. Thoughts that I have no answers for. The coolness feels good, so I just lie here. The house is silent. My heart is broken while my brain endlessly circles. My body can't handle anymore, and I sleep.

I get up later that afternoon. Wondering if anyone is even here, I creep down the steps. The muscles in my body feel weak and frail. I need to eat. Patrick is asleep on the couch, and it almost makes me smile. It's cloudy outside, and I look through the window for a while. Like when I was staring at that Tahoe. My mind starts to circle again. Not being able to help myself, I'm back to feeling that Dad was somehow involved in the disappearances of these people who sell drugs. Did he and Ivan work together? Like some form of retaliation to dealers that got him hooked. Vengeance for his dead daughter. Dad had been depressed about Mom and my sudden sister, Casey. Was he capable of this type of crime? I believe Ivan could be part of it, but Dad? Depression is powerful, but would he turn into a murderer? Do I tell the police any of this? Do I tell Patrick?

I don't want people to be talking about Dad and investigating his life, my life. I need this all to go away now. Either the disappearances will stop, or they won't. Then I'll have my answer. Ivan can just stay away from me, and my life will go on. I have no other choice. Telling anyone else will not change what happened, and I'm sorry for the families. But I can't bring them back. I have to live on. Ray and the others made their life choices, and so will I. I can't help them now. I look over towards the couch and stare at Patrick. What direction can my life go? When should I get out of this town?

7

Christmas break is coming up soon. I don't see myself going back to school before then. I bounce around between home and Janna's house. I open the safe to get out some of the paperwork the lawyer needs, and I see plenty of cash. Pulling everything out, I find the titles, deed, and insurance policies. The insurance policy is for $300,000 if Dad passes. I had no idea that much was in place. Suddenly realizing, Dad may have thought he was putting himself in a risky position. I leave the cash alone, but I plan on opening an account with the insurance money.

I look closer in all the envelopes and find one in the back that's not marked. There are pictures inside that I have never seen before. It's a baby and a little girl. She looks like me with darker hair. She's smiling and happy in all the pictures-Casey. Mom is also in some of them; she looks so young. This was my sister. I think about the pond outside and imagine that day. Understanding dawning, this is why Dad rarely went down to the pond with me. I imagine the feeling that comes over me at the pond. The water is calming, and it calls to me when I'm there. Is Casey connecting with me somehow? I then think about my drowning nightmares. Casey is affecting my dreams. This is stranger than I thought. The world can't always be explained, especially when the unexpected is at your door. Dad was living a secret life all along. Casey has been trying to connect with me, and I had no idea. I shriek loudly sitting on the floor with my dead sister's pictures clutched to my chest. I spend hours again on the floor, crying.

Finally, I decide it's time to put all that into my shell. I have to continue life. After shutting the safe with the pictures placed back in their envelope, I go back upstairs. I've actually been feeling hungry lately; I cannot lose any more weight. My body is still recovering from days of numbness and immobility, and so Patrick put most of Dad's equipment into the buildings for me. Patrick is hunting today. I needed alone time, and he likes to escape life too. I hope Patrick doesn't feel I'm pushing him away, but he can't help me with my dilemmas. I'm trying to protect him; he might need to stay away from me by the end of this. My life seems cursed, stained, and I'm just floating in the cold abyss clutching my raft.

My doorbell rings, shaking me from my thoughts. Looking out the window, I see a man standing and looking around. "Who is it?" I ask through the door,

"I'm Detective Jason Burkhart." He is holding out a shield.

He seemed young for a detective, but I open the door. It has been two weeks since Dad was killed. It's about time.

"Elizabeth Simon?" he asks as he steps in.

"Yes, just Libby."

"Glad I caught you today. I've been here two other times, but you weren't home."

"Sometimes I spend time at my aunt's house. Please sit down." He looks at me and the pit of my stomach falls. Like he can already tell I'm hiding something before he asks me anything. We both sit.

"Libby, I've been investigating your father's murder and some of the other incidences that have been happening."

"Okay." I can tell I'm acting nervous.

"I want you to know, we don't think of you as a suspect. You and your boyfriend's hands were clean, and your car was here and cold when the officers showed up. There's a security camera not far from the crime scene that would have shown you coming or going. It did show your dad driving by the area, but we can't tell much from the other cars that passed by. It was dark, and no license plates are visible. You were quickly ruled out. You also have no motive from what we can see. They could tell by your reaction, you were truly unaware. I'm just having a hard time finding any witnesses or clues as to who might have done this. Whoever it was may have been hiding out in the area for a long time. It was execution style with one shot." I cringe hearing that. "And it does seem strange that he was killed so close to the location where Ray Squires disappeared. Were you familiar with him?"

"I went to school with Billy and Thomas Ruff, and I knew Ray from way back when. We were close with his family."

"How so?"

"My parents knew his parents for as long as I can remember."

"I know you said your father was going to a town meeting and that was all you knew about that day," Jason says. He smiles and seems genuinely concerned. I'm very comfortable with him. I could almost tell him all my thoughts to unburden myself, but I just can't bring myself to do it.

"That's all he told me. I wish I had more information for you." I look at his chest. Then I make myself look into his eyes, make eye contact. Hopefully, my reactions don't make him more curious. Do I seem nervous or uneasy? He's so young. I'd like to ask him how old he is, but I don't want to offend him. He asks if Dad was dating anyone. I can answer that question.

"Yes, he was dating Becka something. I guess I don't know her last name. She works at Bob Evans. I haven't seen her since before he was killed, now that you mention it." Was she at the funeral home? I wonder. I have no idea. I missed most people there.

"We'll return his truck to you later today. I'll talk to this Becka next. I'm sorry to tell you, we don't have any leads on his killer at this time. Overall, we don't feel it's related to the disappearances given the circumstances. I understand you're alone here now. Your aunt lives in Canton, correct?"

"Yes, I go back and forth. Just trying to get straightened out," I say. He looks at me with probing eyes. Awkward silences.

"Libby, I'll continue to investigate," he says while he stands. "Were you here with anyone the evening your Dad was killed?"

"No, I was alone here."

"We've had patrol cars come out this way more than usual to keep an eye on your place. I don't feel you're in danger, but I wanted to watch the area for a while. I've got your number if I have any more questions, and now you have mine." He hands me his card, and he stands there. Is he leaving or not?

"Thank you." He shakes my hand and gets in his unmarked car to leave. I wonder what cars the camera did show. The detective seems nice and not threatening, thank goodness. As much as I want to find out what happened, I don't want to know any more. I decide to take a long bath and go to bed. Tomorrow is another day.

Hope and Rashin stop by to see me the next day. They don't know what to say. Rashin isn't saying much, and I wonder what she's hearing at the gas station that she's not telling me. I'm sure it's gossip about Dad. The circumstances are fishy. Rashin knows that I want to hear the news too. I ask her, and she says it is mostly about what a tragedy it is, and how this is different than people just going missing. People wonder if he was into the drug scene. I roll my eyes at that.

"I want to get past all of this and get back to school, but I just can't yet." Do I tell them about my sister? Do I seem like a recluse in this house by myself? At least I bathed recently. I feel if I'm around people too much, they'll read my thoughts somehow. Guilt by blood.

"Why don't you go up to our cabin in Michigan for a few days during break?" Hope suggests. "It's secluded and quiet. I know you like that." she smiles. "I know my parents won't mind; you're like a sister to me." That comment brings tears to my eyes. I forgot about that cabin. I used to go there with Hope and her family many years ago. Learned how to water ski and shave my legs. It was only about three or four hours away. That sounds like what I need. Escape this life for a while. Reboot and-make a plan.

"What was that town called?" I ask her.

"Kalamazoo."

"I'll keep that in mind, and thanks for offering. Go ahead and check with your parents to make sure it's okay with them."

After they say goodbye, I hit the couch again. I text Patrick to stop by after he's done doing whatever he's doing. He tells me he's working on his tractor today. I want to tell him about my sister. I need to share it with someone. We could go for a hike together. That sounds great. Not surprisingly, I haven't been able to go down to the pond yet. I can't look at that fish and then think of my sister. Maybe if I tell Patrick about Casey, we can go together and sit on that bench. He needs to help me cope. If Patrick is going to be in my life, he'll have to know about her eventually. I lie on the couch and wonder what it would have been like to have a sister. We could share clothes and tell each other our deepest secrets-talk about boys, sneak out, polish each other's nails. It would have been great. I close my eyes and picture us together.

I suddenly wake up to Becka yelling at me and waving a gun. Am I dreaming? No, this is really happening. I am wide awake now and sitting up. This woman is crazed.

"Listen, you little bitch! I know George kept all his cash in the basement. We're going to go downstairs, and you're going to open that big safe for me, or I'm going to start shooting!" She is frantic, looking out the window then back to me while pointing her gun at me with her hands shaking. I have no idea what kind of gun it is. Is this the gun and the person who killed my father? I try to stay calm. I believe what she's saying. Becka must have taken some kind of amphetamines or crack because she is amped. This is a desperate person and completely unreasonable. "Get up!" she yells. I slowly stand up, and she shoves me through the kitchen toward the basement stairs. My legs are failing me again. "I don't have all day, girl, and if you keep moving slow I'll start shooting your toes off first!" she screams. "I know he has lots of money from all his jobs." She says that smugly.

What's she talking about? Does she know something about Dad? Did she know what he was doing? Could she have been in on it? How many times can my boat sink into the water before I never resurface? Okay, girl, what would Patrick do now? What would he tell you to do? Think. Think faster. She is crazed. It's like fire ants are in her pants. Her head is shifting on her neck unnaturally. Arms are still shaking that gun all around.

"Okay, okay, just take it easy," I say with calmness that surprises me. I wonder what she's going to do after she gets the money. She'll have to kill me because I can identify her. She is desperate, and Dad isn't around to help her out anymore. Think of a plan, Libby. I start through the kitchen and see the knife still on the cutting board from earlier. I act like I tripped out of sheer terror and use the cabinets to help myself up. Glad she's too high to notice that I seized the perfectly sharp knife.

"You stupid girl, get up and move!" she yells while checking the driveway with that shaky gun pointed at me. I hold the knife carefully between my fingers and hug myself to look more scared. Now my adrenaline has kicked in, and I am ready to fight. I knew this woman was a good-for-nothing loser. When I reach the top of the steps, I descend fast in the dark to get some distance between us. I run and stand over by the far side of the safe and get into position. As soon as she reaches the bottom of the stairs, she feels for and flips on the light. Then I throw. The knife sinks all the way in under her collarbone on the right side. I then hide behind the side of the safe in case she starts shooting. I hear her gasp and gurgle for a few seconds. Then it's quiet. I peek around at her. She's looking down in disbelief at herself. She falls to her knees.

"You bitch! What did you do to me?" She coughs and blood comes out her mouth. She coughs again, and more blood spills. The gun drops from her hands as horror fills her eyes as she looks up at me. She pleads for help and reaches out. Then she falls all the way to the floor, and she gasps for breath. I turn back towards the wall. I can't look anymore. A couple minutes, I think, go by and there's no more sound. It's deadly quiet and smells of copper. I'm frozen. What have I done? I just killed her. Just then, Patrick comes down the steps and looks at the floor and up at me. We lock eyes, and tears are falling down my face. He doesn't even yell or get hysterical. He comes over to me and holds me.

"Oh my God, Libby, what happened?" He looks down at Becka. "Did she have a gun on you?"

"Yes," I cry. "She told me to open the safe or she'd kill me. Then I threw a knife into her chest." He holds me tight knowing I got it right on the first throw.

"I guess we better call the cops, Libby. Don't touch anything."

"Wait," I say crying through my words, "I think I need to tell you something first. I need to sit down somewhere." We sit down in another corner of the basement. "Remember when I found those candy wrappers close to Ray's car, and you know how Ivan comes by sometimes? I think Ivan and Dad were the reason for the disappearances. My dad lost my sister in our pond while he was using drugs of some kind, and he had it out for drug dealers. Maybe he was seeking some sort of revenge. I think he and Ivan were taking them and harvesting..."

"Libby, stop." He looks down. "I know all about the harvesting. And you had a sister?"

8

I look at Patrick with utter confusion.

"What are you talking about?" He looks down at his lap and over at Becka before he talks. Nothing in my world is what it seemed.

"I saw your dad when I was hunting one night. As I headed over to say hi, I saw something that made me stop. I started watching him from behind a pile of stone. He had a body of one of the boys, and he was cutting it open. He took the organs out, put them in bags, and threw them in a cooler. I froze in disbelief, afraid he would know I was there. Wish I never saw any of it in the first place. Then Ivan came to the house, and your dad put the coolers in the back of his Tahoe. They must sell the organs to some black-market underground. I figured the teens were causing turmoil to the town anyway, and that's why your dad was willing to do it. I just didn't want either of us to get involved. Why he ever started this with Ivan is a mystery to me. I didn't want to get him in trouble, because I love you." I'm not processing what Patrick is telling me. "Ivan probably has connections and convinced him, and the money is too hard to resist. Then I saw him take his excavator and dig a really deep hole in the sand and throw the body in. I mean a very deep a hole so that even a dog couldn't smell it. I just hope it will end now. I hoped you would never have to find out or become involved."

Patrick knew all along. I can't process any of this. Stay calm. He talks so easily about it. Now, I really want out of this town, house, and this world altogether.

"One night I snuck into Ivan's Tahoe and looked in. Ivan mentioned a while back that he was teaching anatomy, so I thought the parts were from some animal for his class. Well, I told myself that." I looked over at Becka. "I think she knew about it too. She talked about his jobs and all the money. I don't want the cops here again. If this all came out, my life would never recover from the shame. My dad would be notorious forever. This would never end. Patrick, what do I do? I killed her. What if she told her son, Johnny, what Dad was doing? She knew there was a lot of money!" Patrick looks at me and looks at Becka.

"Why do you think she knew?"

"She mentioned Dad's little jobs with a smug tone."

He thought about it for a while. "If she knew about it, then we should just get rid of her, and no one will know. I can bury her body like the others, and we can dump the car far away. Not many people are going to care that she's gone, and I'm sure she didn't tell anyone she was coming here with her gun in hand." Was Patrick really willing to do this for me? "People will just think she left town. If her son knows anything, we will deal with that later." My worst thoughts have come true, and now I'm involved.

"Are you serious? Would this work or are we being stupid? Maybe I'm not thinking clearly now." I hold my head in my hands. What has my life come to? I thought I had a normal life doing mundane daily activities, and now I have a dead woman in my basement and people buried on my land. Ivan must have convinced my father that the money will take care of me in the future. When Dad said everything he did was for me, I didn't think he meant murder. I can't ask Patrick to get involved in this.

"It's now or never, Libby, your call." Maybe I'm more like my dad than I want to acknowledge, but making this situation go away is all I want to do. Talking to cops right now would make this whole ordeal come out. I stand up.

"I know where there are large pieces of plastic used for concrete," I say in disbelief before ascending the stairs, heading out to the yard, and taking in the fresh air. Think, some deep breaths in and out, in and out, and I consider my options again. Dad, what were you thinking? Ivan is the reason all of this has happened. His failed career as a doctor led him into a dark world of pure greed. Dad did it for revenge. Did Ivan know about my sister? If so, was he using my Dad? My God, I look up into the sky and say, "Look at me, Dad. Was this in your plan?" Now I have to keep this hidden. Yes, Becka needs to disappear.

I find the plastic and take it back inside. Patrick takes out the knife, and we lay her on one end. We get her belongings from the car and wrap it all up along with the gun. What if this is the gun that Dad was shot with? Again, I can't get him back, and this needs to go away. I grab the keys for the John Deere. Patrick easily carries her up the stairs and out to the yard. I watch for cars to go by. It's a quiet night, and I hand the keys to Patrick.

Numb, I hear the excavator start up. I know that sand packs well, and the ground can easily look undisturbed. Perfect hiding spot. I head back to the basement with some sort of cleanser, a bucket and sponge. When I see the blood stain on the floor, I have to go to the bathroom and vomit. The smell is nauseating, and the task is sickening. I can't do it. I'm still in the bathroom when Patrick returns. My mind and body won't work together. I can hear him scrubbing the floor. How and why is he doing this? Then I smell the bleach. I walk out and see him finishing up like he's cleaning up a deer that he butchered himself.

My life has forever changed and not for the better. Who am I protecting: me or Dad? When Patrick is done, he goes into the bathroom. He didn't even get anything on him. I have vomit splashed into my hair and on my clothes. Patrick wipes it out of my hair, and my clothes go in the washer. My mind is a swirled mess, but Patrick has taken charge. I don't even care that he sees me in my underwear and bra. I'm unable to process all of this.

I follow Patrick outside as he walks to her car with a screwdriver and wipes. He throws the wipes in her car and starts to remove the VIN plate from the dashboard along with the front license plate. When he's done, he turns to me and holds my head in his hands. He looks me in the eyes. "You're going to follow me in your car, Libby. Just follow this car. Can you do that?" I nod yes. I will myself to help him; I have to. He's doing this for me. He gets into her car, and I get into mine, such a silent night. I stare ahead and try to only concentrate on driving not thinking. I don't even know what roads we're on because I can only stare at her car in front of me. The two-hour drive could have been fifteen minutes for all I know. I feel my life fading away, the life I knew. Like father, like daughter.

How can Patrick stay so calm? I start to notice signs for Columbus. We take a few exits then end up in a dark, scary neighborhood. I follow him down a back alley off Cleveland Avenue. We stop, and he gets out. He takes the plate off the back and wipes the car down and leaves it there with the single key in it.

"I don't see any cameras in this neighborhood," he comments as he takes over driving my car. I scoot over. Who is this person? He puts the plates on the floor under him. He even checked the car one more time for personal items.

"Have you done this before?" I ask. We look around, and the area is deserted and quiet. "What if someone is looking out the window?"

"The people who live here don't report anything they see. I probably look like a Mafia man, don't you think?" He's making a joke now. Smiling is not going to happen for the rest of my life. My life is done. I'll be living in a national park somewhere, but it will not be for a job. I'll be hiding out and eating squirrels roasted on a stick and turn myself into a half man half wild animal. Focus on the task, Libby. "People will come out when we leave, I suspect," he mentions.

Barely registering what he says, I think maybe this is where I should just stay and live. The life of the felonious. That's me now. Murderer. Realism sets back in. I think of the bodies on my property. What am I going to do about that? Do I just leave them there? I would assume this is all going to end now. I think of Earl and Nancy Squires. They're wanting their son back. At one time, Ray was a great kid. I cannot fathom that he has been dismembered and buried, but I'm forced to deal with this. It makes me very angry at my father. Look at me, Dad, thank you so much.

"Libby, are you with me?" I look over at him, and tears start to flow again. "Just recline your seat back and rest." I lie back and picture life in a cell compared to life on the run. Which one sounds better? All I know is my previous life is over.

Back at my house, Patrick wakes me. I'm slumped over in the passenger seat.

"Libby, are you still with me?" I sit up.

"What am I going to do?"

"Nothing, the chicken made it across. It's all over. I'm going home now so I can collect my thoughts and make sure we have everything covered. You just need to go to bed." I walk into my house, too guilty to care that I'm here and alone and frightened. I watch him get into his truck and leave. I wonder if I'll ever see him again after this night. He may get smart and never want anything to do with me. I would be happy for him. I go back down to the basement to look at the scene. Did we miss anything? The knife is clean and, in the kitchen, but it needs to go. We should have wrapped it up, too. I wonder what Patrick did with the license plates. Everything will be fine; just give it time he says.

Can I even stay in this house tonight? I think to myself. I'm too tired to decide anything else at this point. What does it matter? I better get used to being alone more than ever before. Facing exhaustion, yet my eyes won't close all night while staring out the window. I wish Dad had left me a note in the safe explaining why he started doing this. Why did he think we needed the money? He must have held so much pain inside. I remember seeing him one time walking out of a store. He didn't know I was there in the parking lot. He lit up a cigar and started smoking. I had never seen my dad smoke any other time. At the time, it did make me wonder what else he did that I wasn't aware of I just shrugged it off, but now that difference is grand. Why did he date Becka? He could do so much better than her. Perhaps he felt bad about himself. I would sometimes catch him staring off into space. Was he dealing with the guilt?

In the morning, Hope sends me a text. Her mother is fine with me staying at their cabin if being at home is too hard right now. She has no idea how great that sounds. Getting away from the killing zone, this town, and even Patrick sounds good. Patrick needs to get a break from my crazy life. I shower again and drive over to Hope's house to get a key to the cabin and the address. They have a beautiful home, complete with her mom and dad, a dog, and a white fence. Did I brush my hair or my teeth? I don't remember. I forgot a coat, and it's cold out. I'm hungry but also nauseated.

I visit them for a little while. What must they think of my appearance? I pull out my smile and thank them for the getaway. Walking back to my car, I hope they're not watching me. I feel thin and weak. Very sad girl, they're probably saying. Very bad girl, I'm feeling.

As I drive, tears once again form. Deciding to eat, I hit the Waffle House to see what it feels like to be around people. For sure, I can never go to Bob Evans again.

I'm a different person now. I stepped over the line that can't be redrawn. Looking around, can anyone tell? Is it apparent? Libby, Lib...look around you. You are not the only criminal. The world is full of immoral people; join the club. The wicked will rule...right? The weak will fall. Only the strong survive. No...I don't want to be cruel or corrupt. I want my simple life back. When have I gone hiking last? I have not talked to the trees for what...like weeks now. That's the problem. I should have consulted with them first. What have I done? How could I just hide Becka's body? I can't eat. What was I thinking? Need to vomit. I head to the bathroom and squat by the toilet. Oh boy, here it comes. Body is down, the weak will fall.

I don't know how long I stay in the bathroom, but when I emerge, the waitress looks at me and asks if I'm okay.

"Yes, thank you. I feel better now." I pay and leave. Going home to start a new life is my only option. What's done is definitely done. I head home to pack. Must get out of here.

9

I tell Janna where I'm going, and that I need to get away. I give her the address of where she can contact me in case of an emergency. I figure my cell won't work there. To help her not worry, I let her know I will come back to her house on Christmas Eve. Lastly, I let Patrick know where the cabin is, but I also tell him I need to be alone and not to come. I do invite him to Janna's on Christmas for dinner along with his mother. Until then, I need to evaluate my life and future. The insurance money will come after the investigation. Most things are taken care of by the lawyers. I now own way more than I know what to do with. My grief process has turned into more anger and confusion.

I drive towards Kalamazoo with my laptop and books. I need some time where nothing happens. I used to go to school and worry about too much mud on the hiking trail or what TV show to watch. I wish I could flip back to my old self. When did this madness start? Thinking back, Ivan started coming around three years ago. Did they know each other already? Dad had the land and the means and the tragic drug history. Ivan must have talked him into it because a person can't make that much money moving dirt around for a living. Ivan played him, and money changes people. Or was it all about my sister? Ivan must have shown Dad how to…I can't even think about it. If Becka knew, she must have told him it was okay and that he was doing the community a service. Did she kill Dad so she could clean out his safe and skip town? I'm glad she's dead. Her son might cause some problems, but I can't worry about that right now. I wonder where her car is.

I think Patrick should have told me what he knew, but I can see why he didn't. He wanted to protect me. I don't know what I would do without him. If it wasn't for him teaching me some self-defense, I would be dead. Patrick is unusual in his own way. We're perfect together, but he's better off without me. I hate to get him involved in this situation. It's good I'm getting out of town for a while to decide my life's future. Guess finishing high school will have to wait. The thought of school, hallways, crowds, and rules seem pointless now.

After driving over two hours, I see a sign for The Cascades. I pull off and decide to take a little hike. Hope's family stopped here twice with me many years ago, and I loved it. This is just what I need. Examining the parking lot, not much has changed. I see the touristy fountains are still here, and I decide I don't need to spend any time looking at them. They're pretty, but I'm not really in the mood for that, so I drive a little further toward the Swains Lake campground. I remember the wetlands area beside the biking trail over there. I loved to see all the creatures.

After parking, and with water and granola bar in hand, I start off on a trail. Other people walk along, smiling, laughing, and happy. It makes me weep inside; happiness feels lost. I discreetly jump off the trail to find a spot all to myself close to the edge of the golf course, secluded. My stamina needs improvement-not even a mile walk and I need a rest. My own new demons and depression have already ravaged part of my body.

Finding a tree that looks old and wise, I settle down beside it. It's a red maple. It must be over 120 feet tall and so elegant. I look up at the tree. Have I seen you before? Maybe years ago, you caught a glimpse of me running along with another girl. We might have been giggling and talking about boys. You might have thought we were sisters, but we were just good friends. I had a sister once. You won't recognize me now because that person you saw last time is gone. You saw me when my life was fun and I didn't have any cares.

"I am vile now," I say out loud. "Not worthy of being free to do what I want. I should be hiding in a dungeon, eating bugs off the floor and kept out of the light. I'm not worthy of your presence." This must be how I truly feel about myself. Yes, I hid a terrible incident. "I'm not a bad person, but grave events have crossed my path. Where do I go from here? Death is all around me now. Death has taken all my family. They've been snatched away from me. And now, I have also taken a life and can't go back. Is it in my DNA to do this? I picture Becka's lifeless body on the floor. It had to be done. I'm kneeling now.

"What am I supposed to do?" I yell, desperate and feeling broken. I just want to feel free again, but has that possibility expired. "I need you to hear me and help if you can." I look around to make sure no one has followed me, and I close my eyes to listen. Only the critters and birds are around. Think about something else, Libby. Remember you're here to focus on the future. This is not my fault. Only I can change my path-no one else can do it. I make myself smile and get back up. Keep your eyes closed; open your senses. I can smell fungus. Dead leaves cover the ground like a carpet. The air is crisp and cool and fresh. Glad for the warm jacket hugging me. Thankful for solitude and peace. My mind and body can be in a safe place. I am not in a dungeon or on a sinking ship. I open my eyes looking around again to check my surroundings. I see a male and female cardinal chasing each other. His bright red color stands out against the brown background. They're so in love and young. Usually only the male songbird can sing, but with cardinals, the female can also sing.

Will Patrick and I chase each other around anymore? Our relationship will drastically change now, I can assume. I should set him free. He didn't ask for this; he fell into it. It's not too late for him. He could find a nice girl and have the simple life he wanted. My life has turned complicated and flawed. The tree has not given me any signs or said anything back that I can tell. That's okay, some people don't deserve it. I stare straight ahead at the bark, full of ridges that look like old age. "Tell me something," I plead.

It's getting cold. I look up to the tree one last time, and one of the few remaining leaves falls down ever so slowly beside my foot. Picking it up, I feel a calmness like I do at my pond, and a smile crosses my face.

"Is this a sign?" I lean up to it and start to cry. It heard me. The tree almost feels warm, thus human. With my eyes closed, I can picture the people in my life that I have lost and try to feel them in my arms. I cry forcefully for quite a while, shedding a layer of sadness and grief.

When I finally relax my embrace, I feel better. I step back and fix myself: wipe my face, brush off the bark, and fix my coat. Okay, I am done crying. From now on, I am a woman who is going to take care of herself and be strong. Sitting around crying is not going to be very productive now, is it? I made my bed, move on. Crying time is over. Time to refocus my energy on the future. I will go to the cabin and plan my next steps. Cross the road, you damn chicken. I smile to myself.

I head back to the trail. The cardinals are still playing chase. I break off some pieces of my granola and sit on a fallen tree. While eating the rest, I feel a new hope. Best tree ever.

10

Kalamazoo is a big beautiful town. It looks bright and busy and vibrant, but I'm heading to the outskirts. I'm not going where people mingle. Finding the road that leads back to a secretive escape, I arrive at the cabin. It's down a long and private road, just like I remember it. I park my car off to the side and look around. Surrounded by trees, the cabin is a majestic sight. This is my paradise. I anxiously grab my bags and make sure I don't lock my keys in the car. Focus. I walk in, and it's a little musty inside. They must have not stayed here lately. I drop everything and get organized. I open the fridge which they leave on all the time. It has some cans and bottles of assorted drinks. I start to put away the yogurt I picked up at the store on the way, along with some chips. I move to the bedroom and make the bed with the sheets in the closet and get out some towels. I then turn the thermostat up to 68 degrees and look for the throw blankets. They're still in the chest beside the couch like I remember. There is no TV.

I'm not hungry yet after getting a milkshake on the way here. There used to be a diner about five minutes away. Hope it's still there. It had great food. Not sure exactly how to get there, but I'll find out later. I check my phone. As expected, there is no service here, so I just turn it off. I'll have to remember to send Hope's parents a thank you letter. This will be great; I needed a change in scenery. My yard haunts me, my basement haunts me, and basically my whole life. Not going to cry, remember? This is not a pity vacation. This is a planning vacation.

I grab a blanket and get comfy on the couch. With the lamp on behind me, it's very quiet. I get up and turn the radio on to have some background noise. AM radio WKMI 1360 is on. It's talk radio. I try to find some music but only find some old country which will be fine real low. Reading my book and pushing negative thoughts out of my mind is my goal for the evening. This new surrounding is just what I need. Before long, my eyes get tired, and I doze off on the couch. Waking up in the middle of the night, I use the restroom, and climb into bed. I sleep soundly all night long. No nightmares.

Hunger wakes me. After a late breakfast of yogurt and cookies with coffee, I get ready for a walk. I just started drinking coffee this fall. Dad told me it was time, and we laughed. He told me I use too much sugar and creamer, but that makes it taste good. Sometimes Dad would put saltine crackers in his coffee. That seems like a long time ago. Mom didn't drink coffee; she loved unsweetened ice tea. I don't remember what her favorite foods were or what her voice sounded like. Did she wear perfume? I think she wore makeup, but I don't really know. How different my life would have been. Time to get outside.

I'm not too familiar with this area, so I can't go far. Breathing in the fresh air and hearing all the animals scurry always brings me such peace. The trees are mostly pine, and the scent is rich. This must be a trail used by deer or something. My pepper spray is in my pocket. Hate to run into a bear or a mountain lion. That seems like a minor problem now, however. Could I live in the mountains? As much as it sounds fun for a while, I know I'd rather have a house with a family and lead a normal life. Is that possible?

Walking along, I see a rotting carcass of a deer. I think of the rotting bodies buried; innocent criminals just going about their daily routine of providing goods to the addicts. Should that be their fate? Will it keep the streets cleaner? As much as I want to forget it, I have to deal with the fact that dead bodies occupy my land. I still can't see my dad doing any of this. What am I going to do with the property? Should I confess? I know I won't; I would rather live hidden in the woods. A wood burning stove and my canned goods, that's all I would need. What other females live that way? Are there women in the hills hiding from their lives, spouses, crimes? Do they have no other choice but to disappear? How could I even find them to learn from them? I can't. That's the point; they're gone from society. Tears are starting up again. Nausea sets in, life sets in. What life, what possible life? Sitting down on a dry rock, I listen to the forest. I don't even hear any scampering. It is so still. No wind. This is not a little nature park or hiking trail. Those critters live the easy life. This is a real forest with multiple predators. The little critters are much smarter in these conditions. They don't let themselves be noisy. The real forests of the world accommodate all the bad. I'm about to cry again. I decide to scream a couple times. That helps. A couple more screams. Scream out the pain. Scream out the death. Get mad. Get up.

"Get up, remember why you're here." I walk and talk. "You're going to finish high school when you get back. Then you're going to sell off everything and disappear." That's your only choice. Whoever buys the property will hopefully keep it like it is and not know anything about its history. I'll visit Janna a couple times a year. No problem. Patrick. Will he go with me? Will he leave his mother? She's a capable woman. We can visit her, too. I wonder why she doesn't have a boyfriend. She's pretty and friendly. I thought once about encouraging Dad to ask her out, but Patrick said she doesn't date.

Patrick. I love him. He loves me-or did. I may never hear that again from him. I feel like we haven't talked to each other in weeks, like really talked. Where does all of this leave us? He hasn't told me about any definite plans he has. It's like he just goes about each day without a care. It will be his choice. I'll have to leave, too many memories and nightmares in Alliance. The woods are still silent, and that makes me feel uneasy. The animals are not moving. Is there a predator about? I better head back before I find out.

The cabin is in sight just ahead. It's so beautiful. Maybe I should just live around here. Close enough to drive back and visit family, and far enough away to be anonymous. Wonder if Hope's parents would sell me this cabin? Just as I am about to go inside, I am pushed in from behind, and the door closes behind me. Turning around, I am face to face with Ivan. We are silent at first, and he looks down on me with a smile.

"Hello, Libby, so nice to see you all tucked in here by yourself. This is a great place." My stomach has sunk and my legs turn to jelly. I reach for the back of the couch to steady myself. Show no fear.

"What are you doing here? How did you know where to find me?" My nausea rushes back and my body is going numb. Breathe, I tell myself. I stand up straight.

"Your aunt is so nice. I told her I needed to give you some items that were your dad's that would have sentimental value to you. Told her I wanted to see your face when I gave them to you and that I'm on my way to the west coast to live so I was in a hurry. She gave me the address and told me to tell you hello. What a special lady." He rubs his hands together and looks pleased. I sure don't see any sentimental gifts.

"Why don't we get comfortable?" He sees my cell phone and puts it in his pocket. No loss there. I remain frozen in place. He pulls the table in front of the door and checks out the rest of the cabin. No other doors. He closes the curtains and sits down on the couch. "You look terrified, Lib, what's the matter with you?" He talks slowly and calmly, like nothing in the world is wrong. I feel the tears coming out of my eyes and run down my face. My mouth starts to quiver. Do I dare reach for the pepper spray in my pocket?

"What are you doing here?"

"I just want to visit with you before I'm gone forever from your life. You know, I've always been fond of George's little girl. He talked so highly of you and loved you so much.

I didn't have any children, and I guess I never will at this point."

"Why did you move the table in front of the door?" I say not very calmly. Ivan doesn't know that I know what he's been doing. Right?

"You never know what's out lurking in the woods, Libby. I don't want anyone to disturb us." I need to think fast.

"Patrick is here. He's hunting for some rabbit and will be right back, and he won't like what you're doing."

"You're not a very good liar. Patrick's not here. I've been watching you, and you're all alone." He walks by me touching my hair and looks into the fridge. I sit down on the couch, my body tense. He takes out a yogurt and eats it standing by the sink. Then eats some of the cookies. I try to figure out what he's planning and how to get away from him. Stay calm. Patrick did show me some punch and kick moves. How did that go? I need to control my breathing, or I am going to pass out. Looking at the floor, my mind is not working too well. Hidden panic has set in. I can't swallow.

Ivan comes over and sits on the couch beside me. He places a hand on my knee and tells me how sorry he is that Dad has been killed.

"I need you to leave. I came up here to be alone," I say firmly and brush his hand away. Ivan is a monster, and he's here with me alone; this can't get much worse. "What do you have to give me?" He doesn't answer. He just keeps looking at me.

"I've wanted to get to know you better for a while now. You hide under all those drab clothes. How about we make a fire and get more comfortable?" I jump up and make a run for the door. He easily knocks me down and sits on top of me, holding my arms down. "This can be easy or hard. It's your choice. You might like it. Does Patrick really satisfy you?" He says that smugly. I struggle to get up and kick my legs up towards him. He takes my head in his hands and...

When I open my eyes, it's dark outside. How long have I been out? I try to lift my head, and shit, it hurts. What happened to me? I realize that I'm on the floor and one of my wrists is bound to the wood burning stove's leg, and a blanket is thrown over me. Damn, the back of my head is throbbing. As I start to look around, I realize what happened. Why don't I have on any pants? I am very sore between my legs, and I look down to check for blood. None that I can see. My arm hurts from being up for too long too. I suddenly vomit off to the side, holding my head with my free hand.

Trying to look around, it sounds quiet, and I seem to be alone. There's a fire in the stove and an empty bottle of vodka on the counter. I can now hear faint snoring coming from the bedroom. The door is open. Quietly, I try to loose myself. I am zip tied to a rope, not happening. Tears form. My mind cannot focus. My head hurts too much, and I am very scared. Ivan will wake up, and I need to figure out what to do. When I lift my head, I get dizzy. Trapped. I stare at the wall, unable to concentrate. Think Libby, think. Is he going to kill me? Again, I'm stuck with facing death. My head hurts, but I must force myself to think. I look around for anything to use, but everything is way out of my reach. What did Patrick teach me? Think, think. I come up empty-nothing. Nothing about being tied up and molested by your dad's buddy. Nothing about psychological warfare. Nothing about talking your way out of being killed. Nothing about being alone in a world gone mad. I can't even cry at this point, I'm utterly broken. Life was bad before. Now it's completely defeated. Death is close again. My head hurts.

He's awake. I don't even care that I'm lying here half naked. It really doesn't matter, does it? He comes out of the bedroom and walks right past me to the bathroom. I hear him urinating.

"Good morning, precious," he says. I close my eyes hearing his voice. Fear is somehow gone. I picture my mother, my sister. I picture us together as adults. We're driving on an old dirt rode listening to Little Big Town on the radio. The sun is hot. We're singing together and laughing. We have on sundresses, and we're wearing makeup because we do that kind of stuff together. Ivan kicks me a little.

"Wake up!" he yells. I remain quiet. He has proven to be violent, and I need to stay calm. "It wasn't that bad, stop it. If you don't talk, I'll have to punish you," he says with a smirk to his voice.

"Are you going to kill me, Ivan?" I look at him.

"How is your head? I am sorry about that. I'd prefer not to do it again. I'm sure that would be dangerous to your health." He's crazy. "I think you know the answer to your question. You know too much, Lib. I promise to make it painless," he says with utter ease, like we're talking about pudding. How can he know anything? I haven't turned him in. Patrick?

"Did you do something to Patrick?" Poor Patrick. Ivan is taking care of loose ends before he leaves town. I curl up into a ball.

"Caring for Patrick. How sweet. I'm sorry you had to get involved. I can take your mind off Patrick for a while." I can hear him walk towards me. "If you strike me, I'll be forced to hurt you again. I'm sure a smart girl like yourself can understand that." He takes his shirt off and starts to take his pants off. He's going to rape me again? This cannot be happening. Suddenly, I hear a blast and broken glass. I startle, and the tie pulls my arm. Ivan falls towards the stove then to the floor beside me. Very dead.

Patrick has to crawl through the broken window. He uses a knife from his pocket to cut the tie off my wrist. It's bleeding from the jerk. He then covers me with the blanket. I am shaking from fear but could not be more relieved. Patrick is here again to save me. I can't find words to express myself. He carries me to the bathroom. After finding bandages and getting me dressed, he speaks.

"Libby, I'm so sorry I got here this late," he apologizes. I look at him and he holds me. He then puts me in his truck, and we drive towards Kalamazoo till he has cell phone reception. He calls the local police and gives them the address, and we head back to the cabin. I turn to him while we're driving and look at this boy or, really, a man. He saved my life.

"How?" is all I can seem to say.

"I called Janna to see if she heard from you this morning. I wanted to check on you without bothering you. She said you were fine and that George's friend from the funeral was coming up to see you to give you some of your dad's things. As soon as she said that, I got in the truck and drove as fast as I could to get here. Thankfully, you gave me the address. I should have called the cops instead. I am so sorry." I close my eyes, trying not to imagine what would have happened had Patrick not called Janna. Ivan somehow knew I was aware of what he was doing, but how? We reach the house, and Patrick keeps the heat on in the truck while we wait for the police. My head still hurts.

"What was he doing?" Patrick asks with hesitation while we wait. I can hear Patrick asking me a question, but I don't want to respond. The trees surrounding us hold my mind in suspense. I picture an owl nestled in that tree right there. He's sleeping soundly, waiting for nightfall to choose his next victim. He's in the prime of his life and his claws are razor sharp..."Libby, are you okay?" Patrick startles me. Ivan, he was talking about Ivan. I look into his eyes, and I scream in terror as I see Ivan's face; I see blackness.

When I wake up, I'm in what looks like a hospital. No one else is here. My head still hurts. I close my eyes again, not caring about the world. My mother's face appears, and she's telling me to be strong. I see Dad's face and he is telling me to...

I'm woken up by a man in a suit. It's that detective, Jason Burkhart. I look at him, but words will not form. He's talking to me. What is he saying? Something about shooting, attack, and something about a cabin. I see his lips move. Now, I see my sister in the car. We're driving down that old dirt road with the wind in our hair again. We're in a convertible and I point to a beautiful waterfall far away, and we decide to go there. We turn off the road and pull up close to the edge of the river. People on a blanket relax beside the water. Casey and I get out of the car and stand by their blanket. They turn around, and it's Mom and Dad, but mom is crying.

"Don't cry Mom," Casey says, "Dad won't do it anymore." Casey and I laugh and run off towards the waterfall. We cross some rocks and stand under the cold water with our hands out. It feels good on this hot day. Then Casey says goodbye to me and jumps into the river. I don't follow. I just watch for her to come back up, but she never does. I just keep waiting for her to surface.

11

I wake up suddenly and feel aware of what's going on.

"He knocked me out. He attacked me, and he was getting ready to do it again." I just let it all out. My voice has come back to me. Surrounding my bedside is a doctor, nurse, and Detective Burkhart. Where is Patrick? He saved my life. "What day is it?"

"It's Wednesday. It's been four days since you were found at the cabin," the detective states. "You've been sedated for a while due to a concussion, Libby. You would scream out with delusions that Ivan was still coming for you. We had no choice." I nod. "Patrick filled us in on what he saw when he got to the cabin and what he did. You were very lucky. Do you remember what happened?" I do remember. Ivan the terrible. I can see his face looking at me. I'm elated that he's dead.

"Patrick shot him through the window. Ivan was about to attack me, again. It's been four days since then? Is my aunt here?" I ask. "Where's Patrick?"

"They were both here, but we told them to go home. We're going to keep you here for a few days to recover. You're now on a psychiatric floor, and we want you to stay as long as you need. You've had traumas no one should endure. Patrick told us how he found out Ivan was headed to the cabin. He had no idea Ivan would actually harm you." A doctor in a white coat is talking to me, and the detective is holding my hand. It's comforting. I look around the room and spot flowers in vases. My backpack is on the chair. I'm hungry. "You had a CT scan to make sure your head was not bleeding, but you were only experiencing swelling. So we used some ice therapy around your head." I don't want to hear any more.

"Can I get something to eat?" The nurse nods.

"Libby, how do you feel today?" the doctor asks.

"My head hurts a little, but I remember."

"We just want to confirm with you that Ivan attacked you, correct?" I nod yes. "Do you want to talk with anybody? I want you to know that a rape kit was performed on you confirming our suspicions. We have excellent counselors here to talk to."

I look at the young detective. "Why are you here?" I ask.

"I heard about this happening to you at the station. I feel partially responsible for not protecting you after your father was murdered. We're investigating any connection with Ivan and your father."

"Did Patrick tell you anything?"

"No, is there something you can tell me?" I look at him and wonder how much I should say. Am I thinking clearly?

"Ivan would come over on occasion to see my Dad. They were friends." He writes something down.

"How long have they known each other?"

"A few years, I guess, I didn't care for Ivan." I feel like that's enough information. "I would just like to go home and be with Patrick and my aunt now." The doctor and detective exchange glances. The doctor nods and states that I can leave after I eat something and can keep it down.

"I can drive you home, Libby. I didn't want you to be alone on Christmas, either. They already took your car home a couple days ago. The doctor had you sedated, and no visitors were allowed. Please call me Jason."

A tray of food shows up shortly after that. It tastes delicious. I'm ravenous. Later that afternoon, the doctor discharges me, and Jason and I walk out. I'm going to be stuck for hours in a car with this detective. Just pretend to sleep so you don't have to talk. Even through all of this, I don't want people to find out about my family.

I must have actually fallen asleep because before I know it, we're almost back in town. I look over at Jason. He has kind eyes.

"Does the media know about Ivan's death?" I ask.

"No, we kept it very quiet, due to the circumstances. You don't need more drama in your life. I want you to know that I'm still investigating your father's death. I'll still be around for a while, and I'll keep checking in with you." I wonder why that is.

"Okay," I reply. I suddenly see images of Ivan's face again. Ivan may have killed Dad. My real life returns to me. How did I not think of that before? Do I tell the detective this revelation? Will he discover why Ivan would have killed my father? Then all the sordid details might be discovered.

Ivan is dead. Everyone involved is dead. Should I leave it all alone?

"Does my friend know what happened at her family's cabin?"

"Patrick said he would tell them so they could contact the insurance company." The car is silent for a while as we sit in front of my house. Do I seem off? Am I acting normal? "What are your plans now?" he asks.

"I think I'm going to live with my aunt for a while and be around family. I don't have any desire to be alone anymore. I have cousins there to be with, and I need to get back to school at some point." He asks if there is anything he can do for me?

"No." I look at my house. "I doubt I'll stay at my house very much now. Too many memories."

"We're still investigating the disappearances in town. I want you to know that Ray Squire's dad, Earl, has expressed concerns about your dad, due to where he was killed. I'm sorry to say , but Earl is suspicious of your Dad's involvement. He's at the station everyday wondering what's been done to further the investigation. He is understandably frustrated. I just don't want him to bother you. Let me know if he ever does." I tell him okay. He shakes my hand and tells me I'm a very brave and courageous young lady. I thank him for the ride.

Once inside the house, I call Patrick and he answers right away. I tell him I'm home. He comes right over. I just want to hold him tight, forever.

"I'm so glad you're back and feeling better. I don't want to ever let you out of my sight," he says while he hugs me. I actually smile. "The doctor made us leave until you confirmed what had happened, I guess."

"I told the detective that Ivan and Dad were friends. I didn't see any way around it."

"I don't know what else could possibly happen, Libby. Are you sure you're feeling okay now?"

"Yes, no more Ivan talk." We cuddle on the couch and get a pizza delivered. We put on a movie, *Unstoppable*. I try to focus on that, but my thoughts drift to the cabin. My wrists are better now with just some residual bruising. Head feels fine. Looking around my living room, it feels bad. Something bad has been here, lived here, and is buried here. Does Patrick not feel it? How can he just sit here like nothing has happened? My life is no longer sitting on the couch. Tears form, and I get up and go to the bathroom. I sit on the toilet lid and hold my head in my hands. Patrick told me he was questioned twice by the police. Everything seems fine, but it is not fine. I still have a big problem. Bodies are buried, and someday they'll be found. It might be tomorrow or it might be 100 years from now. I need to sell this place and get out. I walk back out.

"Patrick, I think Ivan probably killed Dad." He's quiet. Patrick looks at me. "I didn't want to say anything to the police. I just want this all to go away."

"I don't know, Libby, maybe."

"Ivan told my aunt he was heading west. He might have been tying up loose ends and didn't want Dad to ever rat him out, or maybe they were fighting."

"We'll likely never know. I just want you to heal from all of this and get on with your life," Patrick says, making it sound so easy. He's still with me after all of this. What did he go through in his life that he's not rattled? Patrick doesn't like to talk about his childhood. "I love you, and I want to stay with you. You give meaning to my life. We'll get through this." He told me he loves me...one great thing in my life. I snuggle in close and try to watch the movie. Get through this. I keep trying to, but then then my thoughts startle me. My future still stretches before me. What did I want to do with my life? I can't seem to even remember now, but Patrick loves me.

Hope and Rashin come over to see me the next morning. I'm packing up my things to get ready to live with Janna for a while. I need family.

"Patrick saved your life?" Rashin asks. "Was that man going to kill you?" I wonder what to say. Keeping a secret while talking to your close friends proves difficult.

"I've always had a bad feeling about him, you know that. I guess he saw an opportunity to show his true self. He thought no one would know who killed this random girl in a cabin while he skipped town."

Hope says, "I don't know if I'll ever be able to go to the cabin again. My parents are thinking of selling it. I'm so sorry this happened to you. What can we do for you?"

"I just want to get past it. I don't see myself coming back to school for a while. I'll miss seeing you. Please tell me some gossip or something. I'm tired of talking about me."

"Most of the gossip is still about the missing students. So many stories are bouncing around. Who knows what's true or made up." I wish I didn't know, but I refuse to feel responsible. I'm living in a paradox world of corruption. How long can I keep this up?

"Please don't say anything about what happened to me. I'm trying to keep the news out of it," I explain. I wonder what they are not telling me. Does everyone already know about the attack?

"Of course not. Let us know if we can help." I ask them to just hang and talk with me, something normal to do. We make some lunch, grilled cheese. We eat junk food. They talk about the latest phones and jeans. The chemistry teacher got in trouble for having pictures on his phone. This is what I should be doing. Could this become normal again? My friends are laughing, joking, and talking about boys without a care in the world. I'm sitting here thinking about being alive, harboring secrets, where to go next, and that I'm no longer a virgin. My mind pops in and out of thinking everything will be okay and I just need to escape with my life while I can. The police could be one step from figuring it out, and then I think of Becka, too. I'm responsible for hiding her. Somehow, I keep the tears from flowing. My psyche is becoming numb. Is that it? Have I crossed over the line to a new dimension of darkness and impassiveness?

There's a knock at the door. My psyche shakes awake. Peeking out the window, I see the same car Jason brought me home in. Here we go; they found something out. I open the door to Jason Burkhart, young detective here to talk to me again...

"Hello, Libby. Sorry to have to come and see you again. I have some questions." Rashin and Hope decide this is a good time to leave. I hug them goodbye, and they tell me they'll check on me later.

The detective and I sit down in the living room. I wrap up in a blanket. "How are you holding up?" He asks.

"I don't think my mind has caught up with my life yet. I'm just trying to do normal things at this point," I reply. He looks around and comments on the house. "Is it hard to stay here now without your father here?"

"Yes, I plan on leaving later today."

"Glad to hear it. I need to ask you some questions. Would that be okay?" He is very polite and professional. He looks into my eyes. Will this be the person who sees through me and figures it all out? Someday he will come to my door and put handcuffs on me. "I know, Ivan, the man your boyfriend shot through the window was a friend of your fathers. Is that right?"

"Yes, I've known him for a few years now. He would visit my father, but I never liked him."

"Can you explain why that is? Why do you think he wanted to harm you?"

"He would look at me funny and talk to me in a creepy way. I guess he used to be a doctor but lost his license. I never thought he would actually hurt me." My lip starts to quiver, and the tears start to form. He gives me some time.

"Can you tell me why you went to the cabin and what happened at the cabin? Please take your time." He gets up and goes to the kitchen to get me some water and finds me some tissues. I wish I could just tell him everything right now and get it all out. A burden would be lifted, and it might turn out okay. But it wouldn't. It would be worse.

Bringing up the bodies and facing the consequences would be agonizing. I would not have any friends or family after that and would end up in jail myself. It's hard to retrieve good thoughts about my father anymore.

"I went there alone to clear my head. I'm used to being alone; it comforts me. After Dad was killed, I needed to get away from this house and all the reminders. Ivan found out from my aunt that I was there. He told her he had some things for me before he was moving away. She didn't know I disliked Ivan. He showed up out of the blue and started messing with me." I had to look away from the detective. "He tried to force himself on me, but I was fighting him off. Then he took my head and hit it on the floor. I woke up hurt and was tied up. I could tell by his words he was planning on killing me. He was getting ready to attack me again when Patrick showed up." The tears are flowing at this point. My breathing is sporadic. I don't want to think about that event.

"I am so sorry, take some deep breaths." Jason hands me some water. I take a drink and focus on the window.

"Does Patrick always have a rifle on him?"

"He hunts a lot, so it's in his truck all the time. He was checking on me through my aunt and found out Ivan had called. I guess Patrick drove there right away. Patrick knows Ivan creeped me out." I just realized Ivan took Dad's phone, and that's how he got Janna's phone number. He did kill Dad.

"You're very lucky, Libby. Your life was in real danger with Ivan. I'm sure he wouldn't have just let you go. Do you think he had anything to do with your father's death?"

"Maybe, but I don't know why he would want Dad dead." Did I make eye contact, should I make eye contact? Lying is not my strong suit.

"Maybe he was obsessed with you. Is that possible? He felt like he needed to get your dad out of the way. Unfortunately, I need to talk to you about some other troubling thing." My heart skips a beat or two. Slow your breathing down. "Your father, George, was dating a local waitress named, Becka, is that right?" I nod my head. "She has come up missing. Her son reported it a few days ago. This happened very close to your dad's murder. Upon inspecting her home, we found no suitcases, and it looks like her clothes and makeup were taken out quickly. Like she just took off and left most everything else there. Do you know anything about Becka's plans?" Her clothes were gone? Think about what you tell him. Patrick must have done that later on. That was good thinking. I shake my head no.

"I didn't talk to her much," I say. "I don't even know if she came to funeral. I have no idea if she had any plans." Stop talking so much, slow down. Between her and Ivan, I don't even know who did what. Maybe they were in on it together against Dad. My mind can't process all of this.

"There's also speculation that your dad was somehow involved with the disappearances, because of where he was found and how he was killed execution style. I feel he was led there, but we have no other indications he had anything to do with the disappearances." I close my eyes and feel the nausea rush in.

"I don't understand all of it," I respond. He shakes his head. I offer no other details, and he looks around again. "Have there been any more disappearances in the area?" I ask, this I do want to know.

"None that have been reported. We're still doing whatever we can, and tips come in everyday that the officers follow up on. I'm sure your father's killer will be found. With the disappearances ranging in the greater northeastern Ohio area, the task is challenging. The family members who do report anything are sometimes unreliable themselves. Several calls have come in about someone who disappeared, but most are found the next day, either overdosed or at a friend's house. It wastes a lot of our manpower and time on false leads." I can see the frustration on his face. He looks tired and defeated when he talks about the investigation. Jason stands up. "I have your aunt's address and phone if I need to speak to you again." He hands me his card again. "Please call if you think of anything. I hope you can get past this point in your life." He holds my hand and looks so kind towards me for a bit then leaves. If he only knew.

Relieved, I curl up on the couch. What else could possibly go wrong? Am I safe now? Surely, nothing else can go wrong. Everyone involved is now gone. The drug dealers are now safe to continue poisoning society. I wonder where those organs went. No doubt, Ivan's life will be investigated.

I can't even start thinking about that. I text Patrick. He tells me the detective visited him before coming to see me. I'm sure his mother wants him away from me for a while. I am trouble. She depends on him for so many things. Will he really stay with me after all of this?

12

In the morning, I feel better and stronger. So, I decide to shower and put on a nice outfit. I'm reminded of the clothes I bought to try and turn Patrick on. Cringing, I remember Ivan saw me in those. He was used to seeing me in baggy clothes. Was I asking for it or did I encourage him? I take all the new clothes I bought and bag them up. I never want to wear revealing clothes again. Ivan might never have done what he did if I wasn't showing it off. I just throw the clothes in the back of my closet. They can stay with the house. The feel of this house is changing; it doesn't feel like a home anymore.

I do my hair in my usual ponytail and without makeup then throw on black tights with a large long sweatshirt. Perfect, anonymous. I don't want any attention anyway, girl with the buried secrets. My aunt lets me know she has my little room ready whenever I want it, and I tell her that I'll see her later on today.

I stop by the high school and see the guidance counselor. I inform him I'll be living with family in Canton for a while. Surprisingly, he tells me I almost have enough credits to graduate, and states if I do some school work at home for each class, he'll gladly give me a diploma. Perfect. My assignments will be emailed to me next week. I thank him, and he says it's great to see me and wishes me well. I don't see Patrick's truck in the parking lot. How much school does he skip?

Before leaving Alliance, I let my dad's lawyer know where I'll be. Text my besties. Then pack up some things to take: clothes, books, hiking boots, laptop, and a few toiletries. I look around. Is there anything else I need to remember? I already cleaned out the fridge and turned the heat down. There is one more item to take care of. I walk down to the pond and sit on the bench that I never painted. That's low on my priority list now. My life a month ago was so different. I had a minorly-flawed father and knew nothing about a sister. Now I'm shielding myself from the real world of murder and madness. This could all come crashing down; I still have a bad feeling.

The water is calm on this cold day. All the days are very cold now. I suspect the pond will freeze up soon. Since it is deep away from the edge, we tossed a couple Christmas trees in it for fish habitat years ago.

While sitting and staring at the water, that big fish, Boggles, shows up again. It comes to the edge and stares at me, his tail slowly moving back and forth. This cannot be coincidental. Am I going mad? That would make sense. Anyone would be cracked up after going through my last couple of weeks. I wave at the fish, and it doesn't move. I wish I could separate this pond from the house. The house will have to be sold. I can't live here. Being around when someone else lives here is also not an option. What do I tell my family? Sorry, you probably won't ever see me again because bodies might be unearthed here someday and I need to be long gone by then. Knowing that the victims were dangers to society are the only thing keeping me sane now.

"Sorry, I won't be here to see you for a while. I have to go." He looks at me. I can tell he knows I'm sad. Tears start to form again. I was supposed to be done crying, but that was before Ivan made his mark on my life. "I love you, Casey, are you there?"

Behind me, I hear Patrick pull into the driveway. I wipe my face as he walks over to me and sits down, slipping an arm around my shoulder. The fish has gone now. We just look at the water without saying a word. He sits with caution; his movements are sometimes robotic. Patrick amazes me with his stillness and strength. His coolness.

"Are you talking to water now?" he teases.

"Does your mom want you to stay away from me?" I ask.

"Well," he clears his throat, "she does feel your life has become very complicated, but Mom lets me make my own decisions. You look very nice today. Are you getting ready to leave?" Funny he didn't compliment me when I tried to look nice. He tries to talk about nothing.

Honestly, I want to talk about Ivan, and I yell at him from deep inside to realize, wanting him to realize that. He does not hear it. I want to talk about what's going on before my life heads back into my shell.

"Patrick, did you go to Becka's house and get rid of her clothes?"

"Yes, it wasn't even locked. I went in late that night to make it look like she grabbed her stuff and left quickly. Thought it would look better that way."

"That was a good idea. Glad you thought of it. You didn't mention it to me."

"No reason, you had enough on your mind," he answers, "and I'm not sure you would have heard me." That is true.

"What did the detective ask you?"

"He wondered if I knew you were in danger, why I didn't call the police first. I said I didn't know he was that dangerous. Told him I peeked through the curtain and saw you on the floor naked with him over you, and my instincts took over," he explains. I feel myself back on that floor. "He said if I hadn't checked up on you by calling your aunt, that you would probably be dead." He says it slowly, and I shiver and look into the water to avert my eyes. I grab his hand that's around my shoulders and hold him tight to me.

"I feel like I'm in someone else's story. I want to close the book so I can resume my life. What am I going to do? You don't need this in your life. I understand if you want to take a break from being with me."

"If I wasn't with you, I would be wondering about you all the time. We're in this together."

"You're involved in everything, but you don't seem bothered. How are you dealing with it?" Patrick was quiet for a while until he spoke.

Patrick was quiet for a while before he spoke. "I feel like I was put on this earth to be with you and to protect you. Ever since I got to know you as more than just a school classmate, I've just wanted to be with you. We both have old souls. I really can't explain it. You're strong and independent. Love is rare and a person will do anything for someone he loves."

I look up at him. "You really love me?" My heart surges. "Through all of this you still love me?"

"I've loved you for a while. Just didn't say much because we're young and dumb, you know. Why do you think I'm still around? Your life is crazy." He nudges me in the arm and wraps me up in his.

"I love you too, and I have for a while. How about we plan something fun to do together. I'll get settled in at Janna's, and we'll do something fun." I look at him with a smile. Patrick will be 19 soon. "What would you like to do for your birthday?" I ask. He looks up at the sky and sighs.

"I would love to go to your favorite hiking spot, and we can have a picnic with cold fried chicken and macaroni salad after we talk with the trees and critters for a while," Patrick says.

"That sounds perfect. It's a date." It's something normal to look forward to. We look back at the pond for a while and let the sun warm our faces. He still loves me. Patrick is my future in the New Year.

13
COLA MASS

"Fuckin' gettin cold as shit out here. Parma blows in da win'er." I shove my hands in my pockets and pace back and forth to warm up. "Gonna be an early night tonight, too fuckin' cold," I mumble to myself. I hang by my usual spot a block away from my apartment and close to my alley. I can see up and down four blocks at one time, and I can get out of sight if needed by the bushes and trash piles. No panic tonight. Got new shipment in. "Just waitin' for da jonesing."

Too bad for Brad, he got jugged. Now I get his klingons too. Fuckin' Midget just left me here; brothers are supposed to stick together. Whateva, I rub my hands together with a grin. More dough in my pocket. Here comes that dumb fuck who always wants Mitsubishis.

"Hey, man, did you get clocked?" I ask, trying to sound concerned. This guy looks like shit with his face all beat up.

"Yea, just a lil family dispute. You got my poison?"

"Fuck yea, dis way to a great night, my friend." I start walking towards my office beside the shed. I have a large trunk on wheels stashed in my alley. A light comes on then the case is opened. In my pants is a Glock, and everyone knows it.

"You got da lettuce?" He flashes two twenties. I hand him the baggie. "Watch out for family, they da worst." The dumb fuck just walks away. I like to deal in pills and nails. Needles are bad news. I lock back up and head back towards my mark. Winters are bad for business. I look up to see a truck sitting across the block. Looks like a nix. Never seen that truck pass before. I keep my eyes down like I ain't holdin nothin. Fuck that truck.

Some well-known bangers of jack and june walk by, but they don't stop. "What's your hurry miss Amanda. Can't even give a man da time o day?" She doesn't answer. Just hurries on her way. Shit man, I gonna be out here all night.

The truck door opens, and a tall, skinny, white guy is walking this way across the street, silent determination. My hand reaches behind me just in case. Nobody else around to see my piece. Can't be too careful wi dis line of work. Damn, he jus' a pretty faced kid; yuts r easy targets. He walks up with his hands open by his side.

"I'm just looking for some ready-rock, no trouble."

"You too young to be no cop," I tease. I sense the situation. He seems too clean.

"Well, you got any?"

"God damn, hold on a fuckin' minute, I jus' standin here." The kid stands too still; I look around my four corners.

"I'm just a chicken crossin' the road, man, here to do some business." I ask him to show the cash, and he does. "Heard you had the spread."

"I ain't no cooker, but I got jack." The kid nods, and it seems like he's done this before. Not too many white guys come around, but his truck is old and his clothes are crap. I turn and walk to the office again, happy for another sale. I feel something stick my back. "Wha da fuck?" As I reach back, my legs quit working suddenly then my mind goes...

14
PATRICK

I have the deer in my sights. What a beauty. I like to use a bow most of the time. It makes me feel more primitive and one with nature. A rifle feels like cheating-I want to give the animal a chance. I've laid on the ground covered in dirt and had deer walk right past me. I don't let them know I'm there; I could almost grab their legs. Hearing their breathing and grunts make me extra sensitive to life itself. I become the landscape and in turn the animal's home.

I take a shot but it sails right over. Now it's running for its life. How many near misses has that animal ran from? Does it have any idea it's lucky to live another day? Life needs to be owned each day. My life is not how I want it to be. I want to get out of this town as soon as school is done. I used to have plans to live in Montana or Oregon and be a ranch hand, drive herds, and fix fences. Simple life with wide open space. I don't see that happening anymore. I am in love with a girl who needs me. She needs me for support, protection, and sanity. She thinks my life is simple now, and I don't have a care in the world. She could not be more wrong. I hope that someday, we can lead normal lives without looking over our shoulder. She has opened my eyes to a life I thought I would never have, to peace, and a bond beyond my world. Her genuine innocence enraptured me.

After my miss and half a nap sitting up, a doe walks towards me. I'll make this easy on myself for the day. This will be my third deer this season. Funny they've all been does this year. I feel my erection starting to form knowing I will succeed in a kill. I take aim very slowly. The deer is nibbling something now. I release the arrow and it lands in her right flank. I run towards her to find she's down. The blood is oozing out her side, and her breathing is hard. Her eyes are looking at me with such terror. I'm fully hard and aching. I slit the throat to end her suffering. Blood spills, and her breathing quickly stops. I pull out so not to make a mess in my pants. I hate myself. I sit by the deer for a while and listen with my hand on her back.

Wish my life was my own. Killing feels wrong now that Libby has been exposed to this side of existence. She is worried about me. Libby is so innocent and yet now wrapped up in a strange turn of events. Our relationship will never be normal or simple. I look down at myself. I want to perform with her, but my body won't let me. For so long I have associated hunting with carnal needs. It was one guilty pleasure in a world of turmoil. It would just happen. Nothing compared to it. I loved the hunt and so did my libido; it worked as long as I was alone. Which when hunting, I always am. But now my focus has changed. I want to be with Libby. My brain won't allow me to associate sex with love. I have associated sex with death for too long, been backwards too long, been a prisoner too long.

I need to refocus on the task at hand. I pull out the arrow, and then I feel for the bottom of the sternum and poke a hole with my dagger. Then cut down to the pelvis. Careful to pull out the gut sack and cut out the anus. I drag her to the edge of the woods and walk down the hill to get my truck. After loading up, I go home. I hang the deer in the garage for the night. Mom doesn't even notice hanging deer anymore. She likes the meat ground up for chili soup best. I give most of it to neighbors, because we have plenty.

I text Libby and ask if she wants jerky or steaks. She decides jerky. Libby tells me she's all settled in at her aunt's house. I'm glad she's finishing school and going to be around family. She needs to get back to her routine. We'll miss each other being further away, but she needs them. Janna is cool and Libby could use some family time. I'm not the best comforter, clueless really. How can I help Libby with all the pain and anxiety when all I know is death? This is me. Bury Becka in the yard; what's for dinner? Just a normal night.

Mom isn't working tonight. She opens the garage door and asks if I am hungry. I'm taking off the hide and head.

"Starved," I answer. She closes the door. Later, when I walk in the house, a warmed-up plate is waiting for me on the table. "Thanks, Mom." She sits by me and starts with the questions.

"How many deer did you see today? Did you get your homework done? How's Libby doing?" She loves questions. Mom likes to watch me eat. I suppose she gets lonely. She has never dated since Dad. I think she's accepting life as it stands. She enjoys her job at the dentist office and she helps out at a local diner frequently. Sally Kessler is a mother with a big heart but low self-esteem. She feels like she doesn't deserve to be happy. I tell her she needs to get together with friends and to get out more often. Men ask her to go out to dinner or the movies, but she never goes. This house is a curse on her.

"Well, how's Libby doing? Did she get moved?"

"Yes, she's fine right now. I don't think she could take much more happening to her. Sometimes I see her just staring at the wall. She's determined to get better though. It'll just take some time."

"You picked a strong girl. I hope she can recover. After your Uncle Ivan's attack on her, she's still vulnerable to a sudden break down. She probably hasn't dealt with that trauma yet." I hope Mom isn't right about that. Ivan was my dad's brother. He was very intelligent, but also very narcissistic. He thought he could do no wrong. Failing as a doctor was a blow to his ego. He then spiraled out of control. Ivan turned to the dark side to feed his twisted ways and his wallet. Thought he could get away with crime and come out clean. Guess not. Sometimes a man has to be put down. Family is a genus not an oath.

After Mom has asked all her questions, I'm free to roam. As I enter my room, I undress, shower, and crash onto the bed. I wonder what I should get Libby for a late Christmas gift. There hasn't been any good time lately to exchange gifts. Mom thinks she needs girl stuff like jewelry and lotion. I think she'd like binoculars or new boots. Libby is not typical. The first time I saw Libby on her property, she was talking to herself. She was in the woods, laughing. I didn't know back then that she was conversing with trees. If she knew I saw her peeing, she would have been so pissed. I watched her. She got down on the ground and threw nuts at squirrels. She even hugged a tree. I had seen her at school before, but never heard her voice. After that, I made it a point to run into her from time to time. She's the one thing I can thank Ivan for. I hope I never screw this relationship up. I'll get to see her at our birthday picnic next week. My birthday is January 2.

I keep myself busy attending school in the mornings. I have early release for farm work, which is really a lie. Our 12 acres are all overgrown, and we no longer have any animals. We used to own pigs. Hated the smell and the butchering, but Dad liked his pork.

I like to work on old tractors and trucks when I'm not hunting. I have an old mutt, Pete a hound mix, that lays around all day. I pass him on the way to the barn-my private getaway. We all have our issues to escape from. My life is a prison, but now I hope it gets better. With Ivan gone, life should be looking up.

In general, I need time away from people. When I start imagining arrows going through them, I know to separate myself. Most of my life, I went to school to be away from home and to have peace. School was bad enough, but being around Dad was worse. I was an easy target at school, always being alone. Girls wanted to get to know me, and the boys wanted to kill me. Now that Libby and I are together, school life has been easier. I feel more typical; not such a recluse. A lot of girls at school still pass me notes about getting together. The boys know I get attention, and sometimes my truck is messed with, like a broken window or eggs all over it. They know better than to mess with me though. When I was a freshman entering high school, a group of three boys started to push me around in the parking lot because the girls all looked my way. Since I showed no interest in them, it was all the more challenging. Two of the boys ended up with broken faces and the other a broken arm. I never wanted any friends; I never cared. I have too many other issues to worry about. Some of girls do look good, but my sex complication needs to be worked out first. But, I now feel a strong devotion to Libby. If she ever finds out about the lies I've told her, I would surely lose her forever. I may also lose my life. Some people choose the wrong path and can never escape from it. Others are forced onto a path and have to live with it. I want the ability to hide from my past and forget it. Wipe my memory clear. Start fresh-far away where I'm too far for anyone to care.

15

It's my birthday, and we're together. Libby came back to Alliance for the weekend. We both needed to get away and be one with nature, so to speak. She already visited her friends, and now she's all mine. Mom insisted she stay in our house in the extra room. I notice Libby doesn't talk as much as normal, but I'm not surprised; she has been through many ordeals. While we hike, Libby is quiet and her face flat. Her sparkle has faded. I feel defeated, not knowing how to help.

We don't talk about the past month at all. I know she'll need time to process her life. She doesn't even look at the trees or talk about that little squirrel that crossed our path. Before, Libby would pick out very unusual trees and study their form. She would guess as to why it was crooked or split. Or she would watch where the squirrel would go and see if he has a buddy. She would always be very concerned about each animal not being alone. It was so cute. I hope she'll someday be able to enjoy those little moments in life again. Is she scared? Is she sick? I'm not sure. We hold hands on our walk, but the eye contact is fleeting. I'm losing her.

When we're nearly back to the parking lot, she turns to me. "Thank you, Patrick. I would be dead if it wasn't for you. I'm getting better and better every day. Just be patient with me. I know you're worried. I want to feel better, and I will." She squeezes my hand and we walk on. I wish I could comfort her like she deserves.

We arrive back to her car and grab lunch. Sitting at our old picnic table, we soak up some sun. Wish we could Deja vu back to the last time we did this and then change everything since.

"This is just what I needed," she says.

"I want to do whatever you need from me, but you might have to tell me. I'm not the best at comforting."

She shrugs. "I feel like the same person inside, but I also feel like I have signs up all around me that read: murderer, molested, liar, and death. I feel that people can just read these signs and judge me. Like they all know somehow."

"I don't know how to help you." I look down into my hands. I can't fix this. She looks up at the sky with her eyes closed. "If you're ever ready to take off, just say the word. I'm ready," I say.

"I know." We sit in silence for a while. There is no need to talk. "I got a call from that detective, Jason, yesterday. He wants to see me. I told him that I'm in town for the weekend staying with you. I wonder what he wants to talk about. I didn't want to spoil your day talking about that earlier." So that's another reason why she's quiet. She is worried about what the detective wants. Say something comforting.

"He probably just wants to check on how you're doing." I wonder if the detective has something significant to talk about. Hopefully, it will help the situation, but it could also cause more problems. He might have found out that Ivan was my uncle and inform Libby. That would be bad. My mother changed our last names back to her maiden name after my father was out of the picture. That way there was less correlation to the Sipos family. If he tells Libby about that, I could see her leaving me forever. I guess I could tell her we didn't have any ties with him and that I was embarrassed to tell her.

"I don't care what happens to me at this point. I'm tired of hiding the crimes of my father and myself," she announces. I am shit, I think to myself.

"Libby, I'm sure everything will be fine. In the end, you didn't do anything wrong."

"I killed a woman and buried her body, Patrick!"

Luckily, there's no one around us. I scoot closer to her and hold her close. "You were under stress. Her gun is still with her if it all comes out. Just claim temporary insanity. I'll be right by your side and I'm a witness." Or we'll be half way across the country.

"I don't know what good it'll do to drag you into this right along with me. That's why I haven't confessed yet. I don't want you to have to deal with this and get in trouble." This girl does not deserve me. She deserves a man who is honest and unbroken.

We head back home. Mom is working at the diner tonight. Libby's room is ready with a smelly candle burning. She's quiet again. We make popcorn and watch a movie. Sometimes I catch her staring at the wall instead of the TV. She isn't really here; she's lost. I have to figure out a way to help her. How far away is she willing to go? Libby falls asleep in my arms. A tear rolls down my cheek. How can I make this right?

The next morning, Mom makes us pancakes and bacon. It is more cheerful with Mom around. She can keep the conversation going and get Libby talking. Those two talk about school. Libby will get her assignments all done by next week and get her diploma. They talk about where she wants to go after that, and Libby looks at me for help with that answer. I tell her I have to wait till school is out, which I don't really-not a concern to me. Just need to stall for a while longer. I think Mom wonders if we will move away soon. I know that Mom shouldn't stay here by herself, too many memories. In fact, I wish we weren't living here now. Libby is the main reason we still are. With Ivan gone, changes can now take place.

After breakfast, we all move to the couch. Libby and I sit close at the far end. It is quiet. I guess no one has any good memories or events to share. We all have pasts worth forgetting. I reach behind the couch and bring out Libby's late Christmas presents. Mom gets up to leave to give us some privacy.

"I'm going to do some errands. Will I see you two later on?" she asks.

"Someone has to make dinner," I smile and say. She smacks my arm and gives Libby a hug before she leaves.

"I hid your birthday and Christmas presents in your room. Be right back. I knew you wouldn't expect them to be hidden in your own room." She gets up to leave, and I watch her go into my bedroom, leaving the door open just a crack.

I'm so excited. I have her big tin full of jerky and a new pair of hiking boots waiting for her. I thought she might like a new robe too. She doesn't come back out though. Then suddenly, my stomach sinks down to my feet. The realization of what might have happened almost stops my heart with alarm.

I quickly walk back towards my bedroom and look through the crack of the door. I see a portion of her face. I freeze. This is it. Thank God Mom isn't here. Then she shuts the door. I need to make sure she isn't climbing out the window or something. I listen by the door. Sure enough, I do hear her opening the window. I open the door and pull her back in. She screams at me to leave her alone. I shut the window and give her some space. When I look towards the closet, she has the boxes of Ziploc bags and my bag of darts on the floor.

"What are those for?" she yells and cries.

"Just stay calm, Lib. I'm not going to hurt you." I keep a safe distance.

"What's going on? Why do you have these? Are you killing people?" She hides her face in her hands and cries uncontrollably. I'm finished. This will not go well.

"I'll explain when you calm down." I hand her a box of tissues, but she hits them away. Oh my God, she is not going to let me explain. "Please, just listen to me. I'm not proud of what I'm going to tell you." She sobs into her sweatshirt and curls up into a ball on the floor. "My life has been a mess, and I have been forced to do things I didn't want to do." I take a deep breath and sit down on the floor a few feet from her. I don't want to be standing over her like Ivan was. She looks at where I am and closes her eyes again. It's time to tell her the truth. I have no choice. I messed up, careless-just like I was with Ray Squires. She is still and quieter. That must be my cue to begin. "Ivan forced me to do this. He's my uncle and has been using me for years in this atrocity to make money. Libby, your dad never murdered anybody." That was the hardest thing to say. She's going to hate me forever. I let that statement sink in. She looks at me with hatred and disgust. The crying has stopped. She sits up against the wall.

"You had me believe it was my dad this whole time, and it was you!" She is suddenly hysterical again. She tries to get up to leave, but I block the door.

"No, you have to hear me out then you can leave." I try to remain calm and composed. She falls to the ground again in a ball and hides her face. She is hyper ventilating. I give her time to cool. "I know, that was horrible of me to do, but I didn't want to lose you. When you figured out about the organs, I panicked." I take some breaths in and out. "It was either tell you it was me or that your dad was working with Ivan. I'm so sorry. I wanted to tell you the truth, but when your dad was killed, it seemed easier to use that story. I'm such a coward, but I didn't want to lose you." I know she's thinking about how to kill me right now. I want to just kill myself, but her life is now in danger, and I have to fix it. She has given me life and I have taken hers away.

"So, Ivan did kill my father?"

"Yes, he told me after he did it. I didn't know he was going to. I swear."

"How did he force you to do this? That doesn't make any sense."

"Ivan had some information on me that would put my mother and me in jail. He used that to manipulate me into his little puppet. I'm a trapped animal." She sits up against the wall and blows her nose. She can hardly look at me. I wait for another question. Her breathing has calmed down. She is red, and her eyes are frenzied. She's in a room with a monster who will not let her go.

"Please understand what I'm telling you. I had no control over my life, and then you came into it."

"What did your uncle have on you to make you kill human beings?" She is at least listening to me. I know she has to hear all of this to understand. My shame, my past, my first.

"Growing up, I had a terrible childhood with my father, and Ivan knew it. Ivan knew my dad beat mom and me. He came around to see us, occasionally. To visit. Never tried to help or take Dad away. Ivan would find me out in the barn or somewhere. I was troubled and had a lot of aggression. I would occasionally hurt animals. Not like dogs and cats but rodents. My hunting skills turned violent. Ivan thought it was funny. I guess he saw I had an ability, and he took advantage. I was tall at 15, and I had to grow up fast. Libby, I swear I wouldn't have started this if I could have done anything about it. My mom doesn't know, and I have been trying to protect her all this time. You know Ivan. He was horrible."

"Answer the question! How did he make you?" I can't answer her nor can I look at her face. How will she ever understand my reasoning? She grew up in a happy home without violence and despair. I will have to tell her; I'm sure I've already lost her anyway.

"I killed my father," I answer. I look at her. "Ivan figured it out and told me if I didn't do these jobs, he would tell the police, and Mom and I would be arrested." She is pleading to herself and shaking her head for none of this to be true, but it is. Her father is innocent, and I've been the one causing the disappearances for over three years now. "The beatings had to end."

"Why did Ivan kill my father?" She looks overwhelmed.

"Ivan told me that George was starting to notice his equipment was being moved during the night. Your dad was planning on putting up security cameras so he could see what was going on. I swear I didn't know he was going to kill him. I thought we would just change our body location. I realized later that Ivan was trying to make it looked like your dad committed the murders if it got out. I know he put the candy bar wrappers on the ground, even though he denied it. I know he killed George close to a crime scene to make it look like your dad was involved. Ivan only cared about himself and his bank account."

"Why didn't he plant more evidence so they would blame Dad?"

"Ivan didn't really want the bodies found. He just wanted to keep suspicion off himself, and me, I guess. Didn't want production to stop."

"Do you know that is wrong? Why do you still have these bags and these darts? Isn't it all done now?" I don't know how to answer this question. I don't want to lie anymore. I shake my head a while looking at my hands. I see stains that never completely come off.

"No? It's not done?" The disgust oozes from her face. "I need to get out of here. May I please leave now?" I nod yes, and she walks by me and out my front door. Her car starts up and peels out of the driveway.

I saunter to the front porch and sit. I have on a T-shirt and it's 23 degrees outside. My pain is so deep that I can't feel the cold. That was it. She's gone. The only reason I have any happiness in this life is gone. I'm sure she'll call the police. Will I go to jail? I should be in jail. What will happen to my mother? This killing needs to stop. I'll be safer in jail, I think. I could still be hunted down in jail. I'm always under the control of someone else: my father, my uncle, my supplier. I don't want to end up like Ivan. Cremated and sitting on a shelf in the morgue because no one claimed him. If my mother finds out what I have become, she'll be devastated and trapped just like during my childhood. I don't want her to feel responsible because she will blame herself. She tried so hard to keep me safe.

Once when I was around ten, Dad was in a bad mood after drinking, which happened often. I moved my dresser in front of my bedroom door, which happened often. I could tell he was slamming Mom around. I had a small picture of me and a cousin riding our bikes together. It was a rare moment when we would visit with family. I would play with my cousin, Poodle he was called. He had curly blonde hair. We would ride our bikes up and down the dirt road. I had such a great time with him. I would hold that picture of me and Poodle tight and think about that day in my mind. Just look at the smiles on our faces. It was always sunny when playing with Poodle, always the best times. Poodle and his mom moved to Texas, and I never saw him again. I frequently wondered if Dad had anything to do with them leaving. I don't remember even getting to say goodbye. I hated my dad, and I had no one to help. The abuse got worse each year. Something was bound to break.

My life without Libby in it-bleak. She allowed me to be a better person with her. When I had to recover from a bad night, she wouldn't ask. When I needed to contemplate my next job, she could stare at trees for an hour. When I couldn't be loving or affectionate, she would just hold my hand. No questions or demands The perfect mate. I needed Libby to accept me beneath my silence, and she did; what a gift I had in this simple girl. Total acceptance.

I decide I have to get away from here for a while. I grab my coat and head out. I need to drive and think. Glad I don't have to do a job tonight. I'm such a freak and a monster. Can I fix anything in my life? When can I have some control? Libby is gone, and I'll have to get used to it. I'm still a puppet in a show unable to break the strings, and I'll have to tell Libby she's tied up by strings now, too. She could be at the police station now. This could be my last night as a free man. A man, am I a man? I am a child who has never been able to grow up and live his own life. I am tethered by ropes. I'm yanked in directions no person should ever have to go, still a child that is helpless and forced. A child trapped. I may be a free man, but I live like a prisoner. I will never get the opportunity to be free and live on my own terms.

So, what do I want to do with my possibly last night as a free man? Pleasure. What else is there at this point? This one aspect I've been working on, trying to control. The last time Libby snuggled up to me in her tight sweater and jeans, I actually got somewhat aroused, finally. But when I thought about her seeing me naked, the moment stopped. I want to actually have sex with a woman. I don't want to go to jail and never have that experience. I fear what will happen in jail, but I doubt that will ever happen until someone dies first. How can I test this-sex.

I drive towards Cleveland and pull into a strip club. I need to remedy this problem. I need to train my brain. I can't perform with Libby because she'll not only know the lies in my head but see the scars on my body as well. Maybe my mind will let me get an erection with a stranger, as if I'm on the hunt. I'll think of these girls like animals for the taking. That does help. I don't care about them, playing the field. I watch several girls dance around with some string on. I do enjoy looking. Don't think about Libby. Not getting much reaction though. Then a girl comes out that makes me take notice. She looks alert, prepared, and smarter. She knows she's better than what she's doing. Blonde and lean but not weak. When she's close to my section, she looks right at me. We make eye contact. This happens often with females, but I usually don't hold my gaze. Then we both lock in.

I try to think of her as prey, and I just sit back and watch real quiet. I'm not swinging my arms, hollering, and grunting like the men around me. Then something starts to take shape. I walk into the bathroom and into a stall to picture myself-wanting a woman. I picture a naked female and what that would feel like: warm, soft, smells good. No blood or arrows. I orgasm. That's a first time without something dead in front of me. My mind can be taught new tricks. Maybe I'm not completely broke. I need this diversion thinking. I need to feel like there is something normal about me. I want to play sports, have sex with females, and drink beer with the guys. All those things are foreign to me.

I find my seat again and watch a red head dressed up like a cowboy. Terrible dancer. I decide it's time to go, and then that girl finds me. The one I liked.

"Hi, handsome, I've never seen you here before. I'm Natalie," she says. She stands right up against me. Her smell is a mix of cheap perfume and sweat. Not bad. Her makeup is mostly on her eyes and lips. Her skin is clean, and her aura is hot. She's wearing some skimpy shorts where half of her ass checks are exposed with a bra to match, hot pink and sequins. Her legs are athletic and long. I like that. Not even thinking about Libby. Libby. I'm sorry, Libby.

"First time here. I'm Patrick." No use hiding my name.

"Do you know we have private back rooms here? If you want some special treatment, I would love to help you out." This is way too easy. Do I want to do this? Can I do this? That is why I'm here, right?

"Show me the way." I follow her down some hallways with some big dudes standing around. She leads me into a room and tells me it will cost three hundred dollars. I look around for cameras on the ceilings. None that I can see, but I'm sure they're somewhere. A couch and an oversized chair occupy the middle of the little room with condoms scattered about. It smells even worse than it looks. I consider what I'm doing, but I have nothing to lose. She's getting impatient with me and walks over and puts her hands on my chest.

"Is something wrong, Patrick? I'll do whatever you desire. It would be my pleasure to have a handsome stallion like you overpower little ol me," she says with a smile. That word overpower sticks in my brain. I like it. I picture myself dominating her or wounding her a little. That makes me stir. It is working. I decide my life is going straight to hell now anyway. I get out the cash and hand it to her. "What would you like me to do?"

"I want you to run around the furniture for a while, so I can chase you. Please try your hardest to keep me from catching you."

16

On my way home, I feel sick. That was not a perfect scenario, but it did work. She did a good job keeping away from me, but I decided to take her down and proceed on the floor. After ripping her little pants off and taking her from behind, she may have become a little frightened. Or possibly when I had my hand around her throat. I thanked her afterward and gave her more money for the pants. She did not seem as friendly anymore. That was more like a scene right out of Hunters Bizarre. I did accomplish what I set out to do though-I usually do. As much as I've been controlled, I have a knack for getting the job done. Power and money do talk. I'm good at what I do. Unfortunately, what I do is very wrong. Over the years, I've grown accustomed to the process and I like the money. I plan on using it to help me escape, but Libby is my weakness and now also my liability.

Libby was the first person to make me want to become a better man. Her innocent nature was hypnotizing. I already miss her and her little ways: talking out loud when she thinks no one is around, not caring what others think of her, being independent, her strength over turmoil, and her love. She is truly gone. My body hurts more than ever before. I've never felt the pain of heartbreak. Physical pain, sure. Physical pain can be controlled to a degree. Just picture pain as growth and development into a stronger human. Heartbreak has no alternative benefit. Death would be easier. Knowing she is now gone, my good side will inevitably fade away. My mother is not enough to save me; she is weak. I'm on my own, alone.

I arrive home. It's late, and Mom is in bed. All I can do is stare towards the dark wall all night and wonder what Libby is doing now? So many questions swirl around my head. I keep waiting for the door to bust open and the police to haul me away. If those bodies are dug up, it will be national news with Libby dealing with it. Libby will have to turn me in. The wait is tiresome to reach the end of a tormented life, all due to repeated generations of tyranny. It will end with me.

By morning, nothing has happened. I'm still staring at the wall and wondering what to do next. I decide to text her. Just checking in, nothing to lose at this point. No response. I try calling just so she knows I tried, but I know she won't answer. I sit up on the bed. Her presents to me are still on the floor. I put the Ziploc bags and darts back into the rear of my closet. Ivan got me the drugs in the darts. Just one little blow from the tube, and they stick right in. It only takes seconds for the victim to drop. Glad Mom didn't see these, but things can't get much worse anyway. I open her gifts to me. A guide to the national parks and two new flannel shirts, perfect. I can't fight the tears anymore. They stream down my cheeks. I lie on the floor, waiting for the world to engulf me. Please just swallow me up so the wait is over. I could shoot myself, but I know I wouldn't be able to. I've had to deal with worse things than this, and I have an innate drive to overcome. I try to picture a future of freedom and hope for my life-like it could actually happen someday. Dream of rolling hills and water trickling by. A small house with an Australian shepherd keeping watch. Eager for another day of the primitive life. I now picture that scenario alone. I will see that vision every day in my jail cell. I should escape now, but I can't make myself go. I'm too tired to run from the police or the suppliers that will come for me.

I get some cereal and crash onto the couch. My mind is elsewhere. I think about what I did last night. Will I ever have a normal sexual encounter? If I do, I want it to be with Libby or never at all. Of course, then she'll know I lied about that also. Lies make up my whole life, but I'm not a monster. I've been forced to perform these acts. However, I do kill.

I wait on the couch to be taken away. Thinking of my father, hatred surmounts. He molded me into a person who can do unspeakable tasks and walk away. Poodle and his family probably moved to get away from us. My cousin didn't even say goodbye. One day, Mom just said they moved away. She knew. What did Dad do to them? Mom had a look in her eyes that said we are stuck here with him. I had no other friends after that point. My abusive father made sure we were isolated. If he were here, I would kill him again and again.

Days go by and I am still waiting for the knock at the door. I'm a vegetable, trapped in limbo. Unable to move forward or reverse course. Where to go from here? I'm waiting for life to affect me. Can I fix this? How could I ever prove the details of my life? My dad beat me so much I finally had to kill him. My uncle blackmailed me to kill or my mother would be put in jail. The supplier is now in contact with me directly and encourages me to continue in their convincing way. I can't prove any of this. Where can my life go from here? What did I do to deserve this existence? I don't believe in past lives or God or Hell. But Hell has been my shadow. It fastened to my soul, and now I can't run from it. It is always there, my hell. Without Libby, my Hell is not only there, but I feel the pain and burn all the way to my core.

Mom and I spend and evening together at home. I tell her Libby is with her aunt and cousins. We eat dinner and sit in mostly silence. She can tell I'm restless and knows not to ask. She can tell when I don't want to talk. I can't look at her face or carry on a conversation. She tries to keep the evening easy.

"I know you're getting too old to spend all evening with your mom, honey. If you want to go, I'll be just fine."

"I'm sorry, Mom, I do have things on my mind. Libby and I had a fight. I'm not the best communicator." That she will believe.

"Please, don't hang around here for me. I'm going to enjoy this fire and read my book. I just want to put my feet up and drink hot chocolate and eat all these cookies we made." She smiles and heads to her room. Then she turns around. "Make your life great, son. You deserve it."

I don't know what that is anymore. My former plan was to go wherever Libby wanted to go. What will make me happy now? No idea. I get in my car and leave so Mom thinks I have somewhere to go. But I don't. The snow is falling slowly, and the town is quiet. Nothing is open.

I decide to drive by her house. No cars and it's completely dark. I know she's at her aunt's house. I park out by the equipment yard, the very familiar yard. I walk over to the house and get right in with the electric key code. It's cold in the house but bearable. I go up to her room and stand in the doorway. It smells so nice. Just like her. I find extra blankets, strip down, and settle in for the night. I need sleep, and I sleep soundly.

The light wakes me up. It's 9:08 a.m. I haven't slept that good for a long time. As much as I want to stay here and feel close to Libby in this creepy way, I need to get my mind occupied. I decide I need to get a job. I have way too much time on my hands. I'll contact the school and tell them I need to graduate early. There's no way I can tolerate classes without Libby there. I know I have enough credits. I need to change my life and get a legitimate job. I drive to Jafri's gas station to grab a breakfast sandwich, an orange juice, and a job listing paper. Rashin isn't here, thank goodness. Don't feel much like talking, feel more like hiding. Perhaps it is time for us to move. Nothing is keeping me here now. I can perform my forced job from other locations.

I drive home and the house is nice and quiet. The job listings are full of nurse aides wanted and care givers for disabled persons. Concrete workers are also needed. The thing is I have plenty of money in my safe deposit box at the bank. Cash. Ivan cash. Death cash. As much as the job was perverse, it did pay well. I'm surprised Ivan gave me that big of a cut. It makes me wonder how much he made and where his money will go. He had no other family. I don't want his dirty money anyway. The problem is the company, S.I.F.T., that Ivan dealt with are now contacting me directly. They demand my services will continue or there will be problems. The big problem is they know who I love. They know where we live. If we move, will they do something to Libby? Nothing stops. I have always been imprisoned. My life cannot be my own. I may someday have to tell Libby that she's in danger, but she has dealt with so much already. As long as I keep providing for them, everyone is safe. Trapped. Always trapped. Even though I feel like this is all my fault, I must remind myself that it isn't. My father and uncle were a pair of deviant beings that ruined my life. Glad I never met their father. He must have been pure evil to spawn those individuals.

A couple more days pass with no word from Libby. She hasn't turned me in. When I drive past her house, it still looks empty. Should I text her or give her some more space? I wonder if she has blocked me. Need to keep myself busy. I haven't pursued the job market yet. Still busy staring at walls. I helped Mom out at the dentist office yesterday. There were two call offs. I learned how to package the instruments and sterilize them. I handed Dr. Messerly some tools while he worked on some kid's braces. Strange and mundane work. It passed the day along, and Mom was thankful. She asked me about Libby. I may have to tell her we broke up, but I don't want to admit it to myself. Most of the time, I have my emotions turned off now. Nothing is wrong with me from the outside. I smile, I look at faces, and I try to move my limbs with ease-normal.

The weather is a little warmer today. The sun is shining in the bright blue sky. If I was with Libby today, we would be hiking somewhere for sure. Stop! I need to think about something else. Good day to work on my tractor. This will be the day I tackle that water pump on the Farmall. I have put off this job for a while. I open the barn doors and start taking off the muffler and the hood and the nose off the tractor. Only two scratches so far. Then the radiator and fan. My wrench slips when I go to loosen the fan belt and I bust my damn knuckles on the frame. Finally to the water pump. Mundane work. I go inside to find some Band-Aids and eat some lunch. Pete is basking in the sun, sleepy old mutt. I warm up some meatloaf and mashed potatoes. My appetite has not been affected much. Like I said, I've been through worse things than waiting for jail or losing a girl. Dad holds the spots for the worst days. He made life not only suspenseful, like now, but terrifying as well. Will he kill Mom tonight or just break her? How many whips will I get if he finds me? Is it a three-whip night or a twenty-whip night? Those were the worst days. The day I killed Dad was not my worst day. I should've taken care of Ivan when I had the chance. I should have not taken out Ray Squires though, too close to home. I should've moved from here long ago with Mom. All the "should haves" get me nowhere.

Mom comes home after work, and I am covered in grease.

"What are you going to do with this thing when you're done fixing it?"

"Buy another one."

"You could sell it to support your life of leisure," she says. I already told her I'm not going back to school, so I guess she would wonder why I don't have a job.

Mom doesn't know much about my real life just my optical life. Maybe I'm more like my elders than I care to admit. I can easily separate the calculated kills from my every day self. That realization makes me feel like I'm worse than they were. I have an amazing capability to flip a switch from charming boyfriend and son to merciless executioner. I don't even bat an eye about it. Libby is better off without me in her life; yes, better off.

17

By the next day, I'm tired of working on this tractor. I'm tired of feeling like a prisoner waiting for my next obligation. Libby is gone. I need to get all this out of my head. I know of only one way to do that right now. I need to drink. I told myself I would never drink after growing up with my father, but I can't think of any alternative. Another influence I'm doomed to develop because it all runs through the veins. I drive to a convenience store on the other side of town. I watch for a likely individual. It doesn't take long to find a prospect. He walks right towards where I'm parked. I get out. He looks at me.

"I'll give you 50 dollars, and you can keep the change, if you get me a case of Miller light." He looks at me, and without words, he takes the money and goes back into the store. I get back into my truck. After about five minutes, I see him put the case in the back of my truck. I head home. Mom won't be home for hours. By then I won't care.

I decide the barn will be the perfect place to begin my decent into the abyss. I sit on an old tire and open my first beer. Doesn't taste too bad. The second one goes down quickly. By the fifth one, I'm getting very loopy. I go in the house to get some chips or something salty. Pretzels. Mom always has salty snacks, thank goodness. She's the best mom ever. I have a hard time walking back out to the barn. This drinking thing is working-I am not thinking about anything right now besides trying to walk. I sit back down on my favorite tire and open beer number six. I start to fall off. "I don't think the chicken is going to get across," I say to myself with a chuckle, trying to get back up.

My head is starting to feel like a tornado. Maybe I should...

"What the hell are you doing?" I drop the beer and choke at the same time. I can hear Libby. Jumping up, I look around. Am I drunk already? Am I hallucinating?

"Libby?"

"I'm up here." I look up towards the loft where old bales of hay are still stored. I see her face as she peeks down over the ledge. "I've never seen you drink before. Is this your new pastime?" My heart is full of life, and the smile on my face is euphoric. I can't even think of any words to say right now. I stumble towards the back of the barn and go up the old wooden stairs built into the wall of the barn. I discover a makeshift camp. She has a couple blankets and goodies. I suddenly see myself as a child. I would bring my supplies up here to hide: food, picture books, blanket, and a jug of water. Mom knew where I was. She would tell me to go camping for a while. Sometimes I stayed up here for days. I would pee out the small hole in the barn.

Then my head comes back to the present. Libby looks different. Her hair is half out of her ponytail and straw is in it. Her clothes look stained. She looks thin in the face and pale. Wrappers and empty bottles of water are strewn about. Like she has been up here for a while.

"What are you doing? I'm so happy you're here!" I say without slurring.

"I decided it was time to spy on you for a while. You have a few Band-Aids on, and you can't drink. It doesn't look good," she says, while she looks me over. I go in for a hug, but she puts her hands up. My heart sinks. Just give her space. She does look like a wild animal.

"I'm not ready for that, Patrick. You need to answer some more questions first. Let's go down before you fall off." She grabs her blankets and bag and points for me to go down first. I offer to help. Not going to happen. "I need to tell you that I talked to the detective on the phone recently. He wanted to tell me that Earl has been hanging around the station daily, and he feels that Earl is obsessed with finding his son to the point of being unstable. Earl is convinced that Dad, you, and Ivan had something to do with it. The detective told me Earl overheard Ivan call Dad on the phone to invite him to the town meeting, and then he was killed. Dad was doing a job for Earl's neighbor that day. Earl thinks there is a big conspiracy. The detective wanted to warn me about him. I guess you picked a kid that someone still loved." I thought about Earl. I've seen him drive by the house on occasion. He goes by slow and stares at the house. I was lazy in picking Ray. I didn't want to drive far. I remember thinking who cares, another bad seed.

"Where is your mom?"

"I don't remember, working or out...working."

"Do you want to go in where it's warmer?" I nod yes. I still can't believe she's here. My buzz is wearing off from the shock. I close up the barn, and we walk inside. We both sit down at the kitchen table.

"Why are you drinking?" Libby asks.

"Why do you think? I need to stop thinking about you and my screwed up life. I'm sorry, that came out mean. I miss you so much."

"Patrick, I want to know more. What was your life like? How did all this start? I don't understand how this started." Libby wants to hear all the sordid details. The best thing is to tell the truth, I know, but where to start?

"I'll tell you, but I don't think I can handle it if you leave me again."

"I can't make you any promises. But if we're going to have a chance, I need to know everything." I get up to make a sandwich. I need to be more clear headed. Water also tastes good. She watches me eat and drink. I offer her some, but she shakes her head. She is being patient with me. That's a good sign. I sit down.

"Okay, well, growing up, my father was a drunk. It progressively got worse. He would beat us. He always hit where it wouldn't show. Occasionally, Mom would have to hide me in the rafters in the attic. She was just like many other battered women; she thought he would get better with her help. I always hoped he would kill himself somehow, leave, or my mother would take us away, but it never happened. By the time I was 13, he was still beating us both and Mom was living in hell. She was never going to get us out of it." Libby sits with her hand close to her mouth hiding behind her fears of hearing the truth.

"What happened when you were 13?"

"Ivan knew what was going on all along. He knew there was violence and didn't try to help. I had a tendency for aggression because I was living it." I have never told another soul about that day. Libby is watching me, and her eyes are tearing up. This must mean she still cares for me. My heart starts to beat again with vigor and hope. "One day, I'd had enough. Dad and I were in the backyard, and he was looking for a fight. He was drunk and unsteady and yelling about the bills. I saw the shovel and decided it was time. I took it and hit him in the head as hard as I could. While he was down, I hit him a few more times." No reaction, I go on. "Then Mom came out of the house. We both stared down at him. She showed no emotion; she was free. The problem was he was dead. What were we going to do then? Neither one of us had ever made a formal complaint about him, so we figured it would look like murder. I walked out to the edge of the yard and started digging a hole with a shovel. You know where that old wooden fishing boat is laying upside-down with the brush and trees growing around it, he's buried under that spot. Mom and I then got in his truck and she drove it to Columbus. We ended up on Cleveland Avenue dumping the truck and taking off the plates." Libby now knows that I have done that before. "Mom grew up in the Columbus area. I never forgot how to get there. Same place we dumped Becka's car." I waited for a reaction from Libby. She folds her head down, and her hair is falling all over in a ratted mess. She has a stronger odor than usual.

Libby isn't doing so well. Her face is thin. Look what my family has done to her.

"Then what?" she asks.

"We just acted like nothing happened. If anyone asked, we would say he took off with some woman. He was working at a factory in Canton, and they never even called to find out where he was. They were probably glad he stopped coming in. A few months later, Ivan showed up to visit. He asked where Dad was. We said he left us. He didn't believe us. He knew Dad would never leave. Dad was weak. He looked me in the eyes and asked what I did to him. Ivan didn't care about his brother; he just wanted to hold something over us. He walked right outside, looked around, and went directly to that boat. He started to dig the ground up; it was the exact spot." I will never forget thinking, how did he know? He was smart. He knew his brother, and he read my face. "I thought he would stop if I didn't say anything, but he didn't. He eventually found the blanket we wrapped Dad in. He found his brother. Mom started crying, and I asked him to leave it alone. Ivan just left. We didn't know what he would do. The police never showed up, so that was it. Soon after that, we heard Ivan lost his medical license. We read about it in the newspaper. 'Previous Alliance resident physician faces felony drug charges.' It was almost three years later that Ivan showed up at the house. He asked if we were staying here to watch over the body. He took me out to the barn for a little talk. Told me he had a little business he needed my assistance with. Ivan knew that I hunted and butchered meat. He told me I would be perfect for the job, and if I refused, he would turn us in. Mom and

I would then spend the rest of our lives in jail. Of course, I would protect my mom to the end of the earth." She tried to take all the beatings from Dad, but he got me plenty when she wasn't home. Libby is still looking down at the floor at this time. She is silent.

"I'm so sorry I didn't tell you it was me and not your dad, I panicked when you figured out about the organs. I'm also sorry about your sister. When you thought he did it because of her death, I just went with it. I didn't want you to know about my life."

"This is a lot to take in. I can see that you had no choice. The consequence is both of your freedoms. You seem so normal, and yet you must be fighting back the urge to leap off a cliff. "

"I grew up with that feeling most days."

"Now I know why your mother doesn't date."

"Ivan wanted me to ask your dad for his permission to hunt on your property so we could have a dump site, if you know what I mean. The equipment came in handy. That way we both could keep an eye on what was going on at your house. Ivan visited your dad to watch over things. I wasn't supposed to talk to you and fall in love. It's the one bright spot in my life. You were different and perfect for me. Then Ivan took an interest in you when he knew I liked you-such a great uncle. Between protecting you and your father, I was always a little too late." Tears are running down her face. Libby starts crying into her hands.

"So, what about Becka? She wasn't involved?"

"No, she just wanted his money, apparently."

She contemplated that. "Is there anything else I need to know about?" I can't answer her. She looks up at me with pleading eyes. "There's more?" I get up and walk into another room. I have to tell her it's not over.

"Patrick, what is it?" She is crying more and breaking my core.

"The men that Ivan dealt with selling the organs are from Detroit. After Ivan was killed, they contacted me directly and told me nothing stops. They told me they know who I care about and know how to find them. I'm still trapped in this sick game, and I don't know what to do. I can't tell my mom I'm the one causing these disappearances. Now they come directly to me and pick up when I call them. Two guys come, and I'm sure they're armed. I have to produce once a month or people will get 'hurt' as they say."

"Oh my God, Patrick, they're talking about me and your mom, right?" I nod yes. She sinks to the floor and covers her face again as she cries. I can't comfort her because I'm the reason she is hurting. I suppose if I were dead this would all go away for her, but I'm not even sure of that. I wonder if we need to worry about Earl. I don't think he'll ever find the bodies, so the police won't have a case. This killing business will never go away.

Libby sits weeping and still. She takes in all that I've said.

"I've never felt a connection with anyone other than Mom. I've always had to adjust my emotions to the circumstances I was dealing with. With you, I can actually be happy. I can laugh and do fun activities that never happen in my world. I can forget my life for a while," I say.

"How do you find the ability to do this?"

"First off, I'm forced, and second, I tell myself they're all bad people. That's how I get through it. I pick a population of people who cause harm. Makes it a little easier."

"What are we going to do?" she asks.

"Now that you know, I don't know. I was going to keep doing this until I found a way out. I want to be with you. If you can't be with me now, I won't blame you." I have a sudden realization, so I hold my fingers up to my lips and give Libby the shush motion. Then I say, "I better get you home before Mom gets back. Let's go." We walk outside, and I take her towards the backyard.

"Libby, for all I know, these men could be bugging the house. If they are, they already know you are aware of me doing the killing because you found the bags. We need to act like I've never thought of them listening to me. These people could have our cars tracked. If we're ever to escape, we'd have to leave everything and change our names. Do you understand? I don't really know what they're capable of, but as long as the goods are delivered, they don't seem to care that you know. They always stay anonymous. These people need to think they're in control of everything going on here."

"Patrick, you think they're listening to everything we're saying?"

"It's possible. We need to keep talking like we don't suspect. But if we make plans to leave, we need to do it secretly." She hugs me close, and we stand there for a few wonderful minutes. I never thought I would have her in my arms again. She came back to me. I owe her a life without all of this mess.

"What are your plans for tonight?" I ask.

"I was going to stay at my house. Is it bugged?"

"I don't know. Just do whatever you were going to do." We walk around the house to the cars. "Do you want me to stay with you?"

"Yes, I don't want to be alone." I follow her home in my truck, and we go inside. She turns the heat up.

"I feel like I can't talk now," she whispers in my ear. "Are you hungry?" She says openly. I can't believe this girl is with me. After all I've told her, she accepts me. "I love you, and yes I'm hungry." I shake my head no.

"I love you, too." Libby says. "Maybe I'm somehow relieved I'm not the only one who has committed a crime. I thought I had the bad family. Finding out it's your family changes my whole concept. I can't hate you or judge you or blame you." I put my fingers up to my lips again. She realizes she may have spoken too much. Her wild eyes look around the room. I'm just afraid she'll say something damaging.

"I'll take care of everything. I just want you to be with me. As long as I know you're going to be there, I can deal with the demands." I hold her face and kiss her. She kisses me back. There is urgency and fear in the kissing. Like it could be our last night together. Our bodies are pressed together. I can feel myself react to the situation. I am hungry now. She senses the intensity.

"What is that I feel?" Libby is aware. "Did you lie to me about that also?" She's now getting fired up and very mad. She walks around the kitchen in circles scratching her head.

"I couldn't be with you for many reasons."

"I'm listening."

"First off, I wasn't comfortable with intimacy. I felt like I didn't deserve it. I'm also ashamed of the scars."

"Scars?"

"Dad knew to beat me where it wouldn't show, and it's not pretty to look at." I'm going to have to show her so she at least partially knows why I lied about that. This has been a secret shame for many years. I turn away from her and lower my pants and briefs. There is only silence. I know she can see all the lines and ripples of skin on my butt and upper thighs. It is horribly jagged and irregular. "This is another reason why I hunt. I have never been able to run a lot or do any sports. The scars still hurt when pulled or stretched too much." She is crying again. I pull my pants back up and try to comfort her.

"I'm so sorry, Patrick, for all you have had to live with and still have to. I can't imagine dealing with your life. I guess since you have been honest about everything now, your body will let it express itself." She may be right about that.

I then realize Libby is taking off her clothes right now. I do the same thing. The clothes are thrown onto the floor. We embrace each other and enjoy the feel of skin on skin. The raw smell of her excites me further. I want to get deeper into her skin. Without an invitation or hesitation, I enter her. She seems at first uncertain, but her need must also be strong. We both scream out and grab and hold each other with raging fury. The daunting situation we are in has turned us into people who may only have one night left.

Humans who have to live day by day or hour by hour to survive. Libby has crossed over to my life. Libby is feral. Her personality will change to hiding out and acting on impulse. My job now includes making sure she eventually will be herself again. Someday, the running, hiding, or burying will end. We hold each other tight all night.

18

When morning comes, I open my eyes. We are still entwined together, keeping warm. I can see her now with the sunlight coming through her window curtain. Her hair is a mess, and she smells like a sweaty hayloft. I wonder how I can begin to fix our situation. Protecting my mother is another factor.

"Are you staring at me?" she asks.

"Yes, how are you?"

"Good, considering the circumstances. Hungry. How about we shower and hit the Waffle House?" I let her go first. While she's drying her hair, I shower. I put on the same clothes. I then whisper in her ear.

"Change your purse out to something else in your closet." She understands and grabs her backpack. I may be a bit paranoid. We take her car to get some breakfast. Not much conversation in the house or car. We sit down in a back booth.

I start, "I want to feel like we can talk freely, and I don't know how long you have had that purse, and it could be bugged." I look around for people too close to us. "I feel the only way out of this is to leave everything behind, move away, and change our names," I explain. "I have around $150,000 in a safe deposit box, all cash. I know we can have realtors take care of selling the houses. Papers can be faxed. I'll talk to a lawyer about all of that. I just want to do whatever it takes to keep you safe and escape this life. Are you willing to leave your remaining family and friends?"

"I don't really have any choice. I don't know if I'm ready to just leave and disappear forever though. I feel like I need more time to just absorb this for a while. Patrick, last night only confirmed that I want to be with you. I want to give you love and comfort that you have never been able to have. This is all happening very fast. I received $300,000 from Dad's life insurance. I have it in the bank. There's also thousands in the safe." She shifts in her seat. "When do you need to make another... delivery by?"

"I've got a couple more weeks yet. I know you always wanted to live by a National Park. I keep thinking about a place I've been. When I was around 10, Dad took me to Montana to hunt. It was one of the few good memories. It was the last hunting trip we went on. We went to a town called Billings. It was by the Crow Reservation; lots of people to drink with. I got to see bear and elk-it was amazing. Dad was always on his best behavior around other people. We even laughed together. I made a friend that was the same age as me. His name is Kull Meadows, and he's a full-blooded Indian. He's the only male friend I ever had, and I would like to see him again. I got to see where Custer's Last Stand was, and we roped horses at a little cattle ranch. I don't know why my dad was so mad at home. I guess he didn't achieve what he wanted in his life. Our little house on a small piece of land reminded him of being a failure. He was greedy like his brothers. Mom and I were not enough." Libby listens to me, her eyes focused and intent. She's still in there. Her hair in a ponytail, she looks more like herself. I still can't believe she's with me. Last night was the best night of my life. I feel so full of promise if that's possible in this situation, until I have to turn my switch to someone else. We order eggs and steak.

"Tell me more about that trip."

"We drove around the area. It's just south of Glacier National Park. Another town we saw was called Kalispell. It was beautiful. Dad said it's full of rich snobs. Thinking back now, he was just jealous. It had museums, culture, beautiful homes, and mountains surrounding it. I'd like to be in a little house surrounded by those rich snobs." I know just the place. "There was also a park by Flathead Lake. I wanted to stay there forever. The most beautiful place you could ever imagine. What do you say I go up there soon and look for a perfect place for us to be? We'll make it sound like Mom wants me to take her to see her sister in Kentucky or somewhere. There is no sister. Mom can take her car and trade it in for a new car and go to her favorite state which is North Carolina. Then I'll trade in my truck and go to Montana and find us a place to live. You'll love Kalispell and being beside Glacier National Park. I'll get a job doing something. We both will have our diplomas. When I have a place bought, you can trade in your car and come up. A realtor can take care of our properties and auction off the equipment. What do you think?"

"You seem to have this all planned out."

"I have thought of that town many times, and I think it's time to go."

"When and what are you going to tell your mom?"

"Soon. I'm going to tell her we need to disappear because of Dad's body. If it's ever found, we don't want anyone to find her or me. She'll understand that. I'll tell her to keep all conversations private and have her get a new phone. She'll need to change her name legally. She can come up and stay with us during the summer time. She'd like that. I'll get her a new purse, too. Can't be too careful."

"Will she want to live away from you?"

"I think if she gets away from that house, she'll become a new person. She's been tied down by staying there. She can always live in Montana if she wants to, but she's always wanted to live in North Carolina. She won't want to intrude on our new life together. Mom needs a new life-just like us. All new things and a new identity. I doubt they'll try that hard to find us. We just can't make it easy for them."

"So, you're going to do one last job, get your mom off safely, and then head to Montana to find a house in the woods for us. How's it going to look buying a house as an 18-year-old?"

"Parents died and family in the area, money talks." We try to eat breakfast while we contemplate the next couple weeks. "It'll look better if we don't disappear at the same time." I don't want that nosey detective to become suspicious any more than he probably is. Libby is the center of so many recent events.

"What do I tell my family and friends?"

"Tell them you need to get away for a while and you can't be reached. Tell them Ohio holds too many sorrows or something like that. You'll keep their numbers, and when some time has passed, you'll see them again. This is not forever, Libby. I'm sure after a few years, we can do whatever we want again." Libby's eyes are looking at me, but she's not looking out her eyes. Her mind is picturing a different life. A shimmer of a spark shows in her face thinking of a different life.

"Right, okay. I'll get a job as a waitress in a ritzy restaurant. Good tip money."

"We can reinvent ourselves. Not many people can do that. The craziness of our lives has provided us with money, unfortunately at a cost."

"Why are we all trading in our cars?"

"Might have a tracker on them." Her eyes look worried now.

"I don't think they really do, we just need to be as cautious as possible."

After breakfast, we both drive to her house. We close it up again, and she heads to Janna's for a while. If there's a tracker on her car, fine. I go home and order Mom a nice purse online. She would never buy it for herself. I think of any details I might be forgetting about. Where will I hunt for my last job? Cleveland would be easy pickings, but small towns are much better due to fewer people milling about. The thought of one last job makes it seem bearable. Flip the switch one last time, and then turn it off forever. Becoming my own man, living an ordinary life, and having common day-to-day tasks sounds unreal. Can that really be me? I'll have to throw in some crazy occasionally; it's in the blood.

I'll have to instill in Mom somehow a sense of urgency to her moving before the house sells. That will be easy. Well, Mom, you don't want to meet the new owners do you? She will not. Mom will love that Libby and I are getting out of this town too. She feels it is toxic. I hope she never finds out how close the poison really is. I'll get them both a new phone, and hopefully Mom will embrace her new life.

I think about long, cold nights in front of a fire with Libby. We're wrapped up together in blankets. We're living the lives we've always wanted. I'm reacting to these thoughts, a good sign. We need a life where things grow and flourish not die and dismember. To be in a life that is not dictated by others. Freedom. Please let this plan work.

The doorbell rings and I jump. It's an infrequent occurrence. I glance out the window to see an older man in a blue suit. I answer the door.

"Hello, my name is Dominic Welsh. I'm Ivan Sipos' lawyer. It took me a while to track you down due to the name change you and your mother had done. I didn't have a phone number either. Hope this isn't a bad time to come?"

"No, come in." I stretch my arm towards the living room.

"Are you Patrick Kessler?"

"Yes, I am. Unfortunately, Ivan was my uncle."

"I'm very sorry about the situation with his death. I understand you shot him."

"Yes, he had abducted my girlfriend, and I shot him through a window."

"Right," he says while pulling papers out of his folder. I'm sure the police must know he was my uncle if this guy found out. "Patrick, let me make this clear for you, Ivan left everything he owned to you. He must have had strong ties to you before that event." Ivan's money; here it is. Could this link me to him in other ways? Or be a trap set up by Ivan? I don't speak. Does this man wonder where Ivan's money came from?

"Ivan's estate was sold to pay the bank, and after my fee and the government's take, the rest is yours. His house sold quickly, and since no one ever came for the belongings, they were mostly donated to charity. I thought you would show up at some point, but you never did. The final check isn't ready yet, but I wanted to get in touch with you now that I found you. It's looking like you'll receive around $173,000 and change. If I could have your number, I'll call when it's ready, and you can let me know what account to use for the deposit...are you all right, sonny?"

"Yes, thank you for letting me know. Here's my phone number." He jots it down. "I may be moved by the time you call me, so can I have your number too?" I'm wondering if taking Ivan's money is a good idea. He ruined my life for the most part, so yes, sounds good. I picture the most beautiful cabin tucked in beside a lake. Libby and I go out on our boat and fish for our dinner. We live a life of freedom and simplicity.

"Thank you, son, sorry about the whole situation. Here's my card. It might be a few weeks yet. I'll get out of your hair. This seems like a fitting reward for you under the circumstances. I hope you and your girlfriend are getting along all right?"

"We are, thank you." I stand up and Mr. Welsh follows.

"By the way, could you handle the selling of this house should we move away soon?"

"I don't see why not. I guess we'll be talking again. Goodbye for now." I shut the door behind him. Ivan left everything to me. I didn't want his money, but why not. I can get Libby a much nicer place than I ever dreamed, and this will help Mom. Something good comes my way. Then why do I feel like it's bad? Because this money was from the slaying of living, breathing people. It's another reminder of what I am, but soon it will be what I was. I'm going to be free of this prison, and I get to keep the girl. I deserve this. I do I do I do.

19

What I know now is I have a plan. I know where we're going and how we're going to do it, and I have the funds. To be this young and have this kind of money might throw up red flags-my abnormal life. Unfortunately, I have to deliver again before my plan can start; that will allow me some breathing time. I text Libby to say hi and how are you. Today, I'm going to go to the library after school to do some research on the town of Kalispell. I don't want any searches on my personal computer. Libby texts me back. She's spending time with her cousins.

In the computer section of the library, I find a quiet corner in the back and look up job postings, a particular real estate property, and town facts. The town offers plenty to do and see. It runs along the Continental Divide. Peppermint and spearmint farms sound interesting. I look at images of Glacier National Park and note that Kalispell is southwest of the park and perfect for Libby. Neither of us want fancy, just practical. Hopefully room to grow; however, I don't even know if Libby wants kids someday. We just don't want them now. I want to give her whatever she wants-trees for her to talk to and animals to watch. I zoom in on a secluded place, 2965 Haywire Gulch. That's where we'll be living soon.

I decide to put some of my funds from my safe deposit box into my bank account so I don't have so much cash. I wonder what they think when I've never have a paycheck to deposit. Don't over think it, just get it done and get out. If anyone asks, I won in Vegas. I should check my bags for trackers. The day I leave, I'll unload the truck and trade it in. This will all come together. Just need to talk like normal at the house. Okay, you can do this. You have been dreaming of an escape your whole life. Just another couple weeks.

Mom and I have dinner together a few days later. I catch her looking at me. She can tell I'm acting different. I decide to ask her some questions before she starts asking me.

"How's the diner, been busy? You haven't called me for help lately."

"We have some new people who are good workers. I thought you were looking for a job. How's that going?"

"I guess I'm waiting 'til I'm out of school so I can work full time somewhere," I say very convincingly.

"Do you need money? You never ask for any. How do you pay for gas?"

"Tractor money. I saved most of it, and Libby doesn't ever want anything."

"She's a special girl, you know that, right?"

"I do Mom." I feel it's time to tell her. "Show me that tire you said was low."

"Oh yes, let me get my coat on." We go outside. I turn on the compressor and pump up a low tire. As we start to walk inside, I tell Mom I want to meet her at the diner when she's done working tomorrow night. She agrees. I tell her not to talk about us getting together in the house. I look her straight in the eyes so she understands this is serious.

"Okay, is something wrong, Patrick?"

"I'll explain it all tomorrow. Don't worry." She will worry. I know as we go inside. "I'm going to see a man about a '55 Oliver for sale. That'll be my spring project." Need to make it look like we are not going anywhere. I kiss her on the forehead and get into my truck and drive to Jafri's station. Feeling like some junk food, so I grab some candy and chips. When I turn around, I see Earl staring at me from across the store. He doesn't approach me, just stares. He looks at me like some crazed individual. Yes, I was lazy and took someone close to home. I messed that up. Ray had a father who loved him, lucky kid. Earl is my biggest problem right now. If I could only go back and tell Ray that he better clean up his act before the reaper gets him, but he wouldn't have listened to me. He was dead inside. He didn't care about life. I could see it in his eyes. What really got me was that he sold to the younger students, and he was one of the few dealers who also used. Most dealers are smart enough not to use the drugs they push, but I got to him early while his organs were still in good shape.

Earl's eyes follow me. He looks tired and thin. Wish I could go back and pick someone further away. I pay and leave the store without looking rushed. When I get into my truck, I look to see if Earl follows me. He's at the window looking out. I drive away. I was going to go to Libby's house again, but I don't want Earl to find me there, so I decide to just go to the library again and do more research. Planning my next life is the only thing I want to focus on.

The next evening, I eat dinner while watching Mom work and talk to customers. Will she care about leaving this town? Does she have close friends she won't want to leave behind? Mom is a caring and giving person; I can hope I got more of my mom's qualities, but I fear I didn't. That's why I'm in this predicament-the capacity for evil. I want to protect Mom from having to know everything about her sinister family. I help her fill up some empty bottles on the tables when the place is nearly empty. She doesn't meet my eyes, since I can tell she's worried about what I'm going to tell her. So am I. Her purse is in a locker, so I don't have to worry about that.

When she's done working, she gets some coffee and sits down with me. Her eyes are watering. She stammers, "I knew this day would come. You need to leave me."

"Mom, yes, Libby and I want to get away from this town. We're going to move to Montana for a few years. We want to be close to a National Park, and I remember going there once. It was beautiful." Mom knows what I'm talking about.

"Well, I should be fine. I'm happy for you." She relaxes.

"I want to tell you something that is critical. You know I don't ask you to do anything you don't want to, and I love you very much, and this is very important. Do you understand that I'm serious right now?"

Mom looks at me with worry starting to fold down her face. I hold her hands in mine. She nods. "I'm listening," she says.

"You know what I did years ago. It's time to put that behind us. I need you to move away at the same time. I need you to leave most of your belongings and car here in Alliance. You can't tell anyone that you're leaving or where you're going, because if the new owners find the body, the authorities will come after us. Do you understand?"

She ponders my request. "No, I don't need to leave Alliance. I'm fine staying at the house. It's my home, Patrick, and if I stay, we don't have to worry about anyone finding him."

"Mom, here is the thing. I only want to tell you this one time. I've had to grow up very quickly in my life. I feel like a 35-year-old man in an 18 year-old-body. I NEED you to move. I'm not going to tell you why, so please don't ask. We can't talk about this at home in the house ever. You don't need to know all the details, and that's for your safety. This will need to happen next week. You can't tell anyone until the day before you're leaving. I need you to tell your employers we're going to Kentucky to help your ailing sister; however, you'll be moving to North Carolina instead. I'll be giving you money to start your life, and when the house sells, you'll get more money. I'll get you a new phone and the day you leave, you need to trade your car in for a new one. Please don't ask me any questions, because I can't answer them. Just tell me you understand and will do this for me. I know it's a lot to ask." Tears are streaming down her face.

"Patrick, you're scaring me. Is this about more than just your father?"

"Mom, just tell me you understand and will do this for me. I need you to do this for me."

"You're also saying that I won't see you for a while, right?"

"No, I'll be able to visit you. We just have to leave this life behind. I don't know if the house is safe or not, so we can't talk about these plans when we're in it. Please understand." She covers her face and tries to stay strong. I know this is hurting her to not know what's happening to me. "I hope that by getting out of this town, you can move on with your life and not feel tied down. You can't spend the rest of your life tied to that house. This will be a great adventure for you, and I need you to be strong enough to do it."

"Well, I can see that this has been decided. I understand you're serious. All I care about is you and your well-being. I can do this for you. As long as I can talk to you and see you, I would move to the other side of the Earth." She runs her hands through her hair and wipes the tears off her face.

"I love you, Mom. It'll all work out. I foresee the day when we live in the same town and you will have grandkids to babysit."

"I'll hold you to it." She doesn't want to talk any more about it. Mom is good at pushing feeling away too. "Right now, I'm going to go home and take a hot bath."

"Just remember, act the same. One last thing-you will need to change your name when you get out of town." We hold each other's gaze as she gives me a contrary look. "The chicken will make it across, Mom." She tries to smile.

"I'm going to assume that Ivan has something to do with all of this, and I'll be glad to be rid of that family completely." Mom walks out with her head high. That went well.

20

Tonight is the night. One more criminal will be quietly escorted off the street. That's how I see it. Heading to Youngstown with my coolers, ice, bags, carver, and darts. Wonder how long it would take them to realize if the parts were from a deer and not a human? It probably wouldn't take long. I don't think they'd find any humor in that, either. There would be no time to escape. This last job has to be done. We need breathing room. Libby would probably like to come with me when I go to Montana, but I need to take care of something first. I also think it will look better if we don't all disappear at the same time. Earl is no doubt watching. And that will mean she'll get more time with family and friends. We'll just stick with the plan. One more job, one more job. Time to turn my switch.

This looks like the kind of neighborhood I'm used to picking from: dark, poor, occasional passing car, and stinks of desperation. I park the truck a little ways down the street and crouch behind a garage. I see a group of people outside a barely standing house. I hang back and observe for a while. Scarcely any cars go by and few walkers out. Most of them leave, but a female sticks around. I can hear their lingo and problems from my hiding place. Like everyone in the neighborhood wants to hear about your sperm donor boyfriend. Then I see a couple walk up to her. A quick exchange takes place. Yep, she's the ticket, a female. Never took out a girl before. Should I do this? She would be so easy to carry. I decide to watch a while longer. Maybe she's a prostitute and a drug dealer. Moving my position, I'm now squatting behind a bush between two abandoned houses across the street. This job is easy in a dark, quiet neighborhood; time for hide and seek. With her big coat on, I'm guessing she isn't a prostitute.

I hear a baby suddenly cry loudly from the house behind her. She walks in, and the baby stops crying. Then she emerges again and stands on her porch looking in the house. Is she taking care of a baby while pushing her paraphernalia? That baby would be better off without her. I get a dart ready to shoot.

Then a man emerges from the house and is yelling at her. He's shouting that she isn't working hard enough. He smacks her across the face. My focus has completely changed. Medium build, no fat, and obviously strong lungs. He struts to his old rusted up Jeep and yells one more time. She's left standing on the front porch, trapped. He drives off slowly while yelling more, and my only desire is to follow him. I beeline behind the houses to my truck and catch up to the poor fella three blocks down. A smile is on my face. Luckily, he sticks to these deserted neighborhoods. At a badly lit stop sign intersection, I politely rear end him then, sitting contently and eager for him to get out and come to my door. That's it, buddy, bounce on back here. I glance around, no one.

"Hey, you white mother-fucker. You're goin' to pay big for that!" I roll my window down and dart him in the neck as soon as he's close enough. He had his gun out but not using it with any authority. His eyes go wide. He reaches up to aim it, but it drops instead. Ketamine is cool. I open the door and haul him right over my lap across the front seat. Front half of him crumbles onto the passenger floor. I pull over and move his Jeep to the side of road with gloves on. I start heading back home. This guy gives me an idea. I usually drain them right away into the gutter with a slit to the wrist and an arm out the door. No pain or suffering, but I want to play with this one. I should've thought about wife beaters long ago although they would be harder to find. What is your name? I reach into his wallet and find plenty of cash. Wonder who made this money, her or him. Warren. Well Warren, you picked a really bad time to hit a girl.

Another idea comes to mind. I pull out most of my cash and add that to his wallet. I drive back by the house and throw the wallet up on the porch. The woman is back in the house now. Your prayers are soon to be answered, girl; I'll get rid of him for you. I drive the back roads instead of the highway. I usually have to get busy quickly after I drain. Ivan told me that organs deteriorate quickly, especially the lungs. That won't be the case this time. No need to hurry as I drive back towards Alliance. I look at satellite maps to find a secluded area without many houses. Trees and fields are also needed. Middletown Road, you look perfect.

This road is quiet and secluded. I find an access road into a corn field and drive along the edge towards a wooded area. Well off the road, I park and get out of the truck and just listen for a while. Stillness. Not much time left; Warren is starting to stir. I drag him out the passenger door and strip most of his clothes off. Just to get them out of the way. Rope is thrown over a big tree branch and tied to his ankles tightly. I tie the other end to my bumper and after taping his arms together behind him and shoving his balled-up socks into his mouth, I drive the needed amount to hang him three feet off the ground. He sways there upside-down. That would suck. I call the pickup crew and tell them to meet me in New Albany NOW. The pickup crew is always the same two men. I don't know their names, and there's never much need for conversation. One is tall and thin, and the other is short and squat. In my mind, I just call them Bert and Ernie. Bert is usually an asshole, but Ernie almost seems nice. Ernie shouldn't be in this line of work.

This new position makes Warren wake up quicker. Eyes are wide again. He struggles some and starts to turn around. He sees me standing there and becomes very still. His breathing is now labored and fear has completely embraced him.

"Hi, Warren, don't worry, I'm not going to kill you. I just want to teach you a little lesson in life. Boys aren't supposed to hit girls, you pussy. Didn't your daddy teach you that? No? If your daddy taught you how to hit because he hit, I'm sorry, but you should've been a stronger man. I just like guys that are not fat, much easier to manage. Whoops, did I give too much away?"

Warren tries to scream through his sock and thrashes around. I'm not into the long drawn-out torture game, so this is getting old fast. I reach out and spin him around. This will take his mind off dying.

"Round and round Warren goes, where it cuts nobody knows." Wow, this rope can really spin. He moans aloud and gasps for breaths. I take off my coat and shoes, don't want to get them messy. I take the blade out and hold it close to his neck while he is still spinning, and move in slowly. Blood squirts out in a fanning motion for a good 20 seconds. Then the night is quiet again. I stop the spinning and cut the rope. I strip my clothes and point my headlights toward the work site to give me plenty of light to see by. I can almost do this in the dark. Gloves on and Y incision made. Each organ cut out and the main vessels flushed with sterile water. It keeps the clots out. Bags are filled one by one. Then packed in the coolers with ice and into the back of my truck. His clothes and my clothes are placed into a trash bag. I always have wipes, new clothes, rope, water, and trash bags in my small toolbox locked up. Coyotes should take care of the rest of him. Doubt if anyone cares anyway. Last one.

I see the dead eyes and the empty cavernous torso. Can I ever forget what I have done? Ten years from now, I won't dream about people chasing me down and shooting me in the back. It's not me, Warren. It's survival; it's a job. I can tell myself it's just like a deer, but it isn't. The deer all look alike. Seeing a human face with scars, tattoos, and hair makes it personal. Warren has good teeth and clear skin. His hair has been recently trimmed to perfection. He has an appendix scar. His fingernails are all bitten off. In the light of my headlights, I see a good-looking man. He may have been a nice kid growing up, but he was not nice anymore. Warren should have made better choices.

I drive to New Albany and find a gas station and park behind it. I use the restroom to freshen up, and grab some pizza with a drink and wait in my truck. I text Bert and Ernie my location. When the big black SUV arrives, they follow me down the street. Need to get away from any cameras. I stop two blocks down and pull off. They get out and take the coolers out and give me two empty ones. Bert hands me an envelope full of cash from the last hit. I know they have guns under their coats. No words are needed. Ernie smiles and waves hi. I wonder how many people they pick up from. I would love to say "last time fellas" but I get in my truck to leave. Not sure why they need me, these guys look like they could get their own parts. Some people just can't get their hands dirty. I turn my switch back to good son, sweet boyfriend.

Driving home, I'm thankful that was my last time. Now I have a safe stretch of time to escape my life before they realize I'm gone. Oh yea, no erection that time, making progress.

21

Mom and I have been like silent business partners: eating the food we have in the freezer, getting important documents together, cleaning out closets, while talking about everyday mundane tasks. We turn the radio up loud on occasion so we can still talk under it. She loves her new purse, leaving the old one in the closet. We make lists of important numbers so we can later change insurance companies and cancel utilities. She seems excited for this adventure. I know she wants to ask me questions, but she realizes she doesn't really want to know the answers.

I ask Libby if she wants me to come there and see her this weekend or if she's coming here. She responds that she'll come here. She wants to spend some time cleaning out her house before the big shift. I can't wait to see her. I feel so hopeful about my life for once. I feel like I'm partially free already. No Dad, no Ivan, and no quota. I hope I can be enough for Libby to have a happy and fulfilled life. I know there are times I should be a better boyfriend and talk to her more or just hold her. She might truly be better off without me, but I just cannot let her go. Libby has a special beauty and light few people have the ability to see. She makes my life worth living. She is always on my mind. But does my mind even know right from wrong at this point in my life? I seemed to enjoy that last job a little too much. Am I actually a monster and don't even know it? No. No, I've been manipulated and forced. I'm not an evil person. We'll be a perfect match, and I'll cherish her every day for the rest of my life.

She seems sad when I arrive at her house. Her clothes still hang on her small frame, and her hair is wrecked. Those fancy clothes she started wearing must be long gone. I wonder what her aunt thinks about her mental status. Her smile is rarely seen, and she mumbles to herself. We talk for a while outside.

"It'll be hard to leave Janna, Cody, and Regina. They've been so great. It's nice to live with people who laugh, play games, and talk about normal life. If my mother was still alive, I would have grown up to be a totally different person." I contemplate what she's saying.

"You mean someone who wouldn't be interested in me. Someone who would've spent more time with people and not out in the woods." She doesn't answer. "I'm sorry about all the changes in your life recently. If I could take it all away I would. I just want to make you happy and keep you safe."

"Patrick, do you really think everything will turn out okay?" She looks towards her pond. I put my arms around her.

"Yes, I don't think they'll hunt us down. I'm sure other people are fulfilling their needs for that kind of income. I haven't told you yet, but Ivan left his entire estate to me. His lawyer came to see me, and I'll be getting a good bit of money in the next few weeks." Libby doesn't like to hear his name. She turns and walks into the house, and I follow her. I turn the thermostat up and open some curtains. I signal for her to be quiet while I ask her if she's hungry.

"No, I just ate before coming here. Are you?"

"I can wait a while." It's hard to talk when we can't talk about what we want to. She grabs my arm, and we go back outside.

"So they might know about Becka, right?"

"Possibly, I don't know, but they're in the business of killing, so what are they gonna do about it? The house is probably not even bugged. I just don't want to take the chance."

Somewhat appeased, she leads the way back inside. She sits down on the couch with her hands on her face. Coming here must be like coming back to her reality. The reality that her life isn't her own anymore. She has committed a crime, and she has to run away from dangerous people. I turn the TV on a little loud and whisper in her ear.

"Libby, are you still with me on this?" She looks up at me and nods her head yes with a forced smile. "Picture yourself at Glacier National Park every other day, taking a little stroll." She still holds a forced smile. Then as she thinks about the park and the pictures she has no doubt looked at recently, a real smile forms. I hold her hands and stand in front of her. "I want that life for you every day; and I'm going to go get it," I whisper in her ear.

We make sure her papers are in order. She has a bag big enough for the guns in the safe. She has already donated her dad's clothes. A list with important phone numbers goes into the safe. Libby has her suitcase for clothes and documents. They didn't keep much food in the refrigerator so that will be an easy clean up. We look at each other. She looks pale, but it's winter time now. We don't talk about the night we had sex. I don't even know how she feels about it. I guess too many other complications are on her mind.

"Have you been feeling okay?" I ask.

"I've been tired. That's all. Let's snuggle on the couch and order a pizza."

"Sounds great. I love you, Elizabeth Jane Simon."

"I love you, Patrick Brian Kessler."

"I haven't told you that the school has decided to let me graduate after this semester. I told them I would have to finish up online because I have to help my mother out. They determined that I have enough credits and will mail the diploma." I'm not telling her that my last job has been completed. She doesn't seem to want to know any details about that, but I feel the need to fill in some silence.

"Have you seen Hope or Rashin lately?"

"No, they're in school. Hope is playing basketball now. I'd like to watch her play, but I know people will ask me where I've been. I don't want to deal with that. Rashin and I have talked on the phone. She plans on going to Ohio University to study communications or something. Rashin is dating Darren Mast, remember him? It's her first real boyfriend. They're both busy with their lives. I will miss them..." Her hands go up to her mouth and she looks at me with big eyes. She forgot to be careful about what she says. I try to remedy her mistake.

"I know you'll miss Rashin when she leaves. She'll be back for holidays and summers, though. We're all growing up; times will change." I may not be helping. The doorbell rings.

"Let's eat. Pizza is here," she calls out. We walk into the kitchen and sit at the table to eat. I turn on some music because we have a hard time having conversations now. We both feel on guard. I hope Libby isn't wishing we had never met. I'm afraid to ask her that question. She hasn't made a motion to be close again. She has too many obstacles to face.

"Are you drinking any more beer?"

"No, you're back in my life, no beer needed." I hope I never have the urge to drink alcohol again. I want to be on alert, no surprises. I have so much to protect and consider. I need to do some research on finances and property ownership, since I'll have so much more to take care of. I need to research winterizing a home, so I don't forget anything before we leave. I look at Libby while she eats a couple little pieces. I hope I can make her happy.

After the pizza, we decide to bundle up and take another walk outside. I know it's so we can talk freely. We walk past the equipment yard and notice the weeds are growing up around the buildings, scrap, gravel piles, and buckets lying about. Everything looks abandoned. I'm sure this is sad for her to see.

"My life is so different. You're leaving next week, right?"

"Yes, mom is getting organized, and I think she's excited for a change. She doesn't ask any questions. She's telling people the day before that she and I are going to Kentucky to be with her sick sister. She knows exactly which town she wants to live in in North Carolina. And I have new cell phones for all of us."

"Do you think we'll be able to come back?"

"If bodies are never uncovered, sure we can. If they find the bodies of those boys, we'll have to disappear forever. Your aunt's phone might even be bugged by police if bodies are ever found. Let's just hope that never happens. You know, since we're changing our names legally, do you want to get married? It might look better in our new town." Libby looks at me in surprise and then looks at the road we are walking along.

"I don't know. If we are changing our names, couldn't the 'parts department' find us anyway with the name change?"

"I doubt they search every state for evidence of where we are. I also plan on installing an amazing security system. We'll be prepared. I can even build a safe room. Let's try to be happy about this change. I want it to be a new start of our amazing journey together." Libby looks both excited and apprehensive.

"I'll have so much cash and guns in my car."

"You should put some in the bank then transfer it later. Open accounts at different banks so the amount doesn't look suspicious. Just keep enough in the car for food and gas."

"Okay." The wind starts to pick up so we turn around and head back. "What all do you know about these people?" She's curious. I do know a few details.

"Just what Ivan told me. The organization is called S.I.F.T. It's black-market organs for the wealthy and powerful. It has a lab and operating room run by surgeons. Many of these physicians are still practicing, but they work for this company to make big money and not have to pay for malpractice insurance. It's how they recruit physicians. A rich client with organ failure is contacted out of the office by his physician. Any way they can live and enjoy their riches longer results in big money exchange. The organs are antigen tested and matched within the hour to a recipient on file. The transplant is done that very day within hours. These people are desperate to live longer and can pay. Kidneys and livers go for the most."

"Do drug dealers have decent organs?"

"Most dealers don't use the stuff themselves. Not much anyway. They wouldn't be able to work being high, so their organs are usually young and usable. I only had one person who I couldn't use. He was full of puss, and his lungs were overinflated." We're talking about this like it's a walk in the park. She has accepted this dark side of me. I hope she isn't going to change her mind, but I don't want to admit that she might be better off.

"How did you decide on drug dealers?"

"Who else would you take?"

"Good point. You're staying the night with me, right?"

"I would love to." I hope she's open to more sex; I'm high on life right now. Stop being selfish. "The little chicken wants to come across the road again." She smiles and hits me. I grab her hand tighter and hold it to my chest. I picture the Libby I knew three years ago. She's just coming of age, not quite a woman, and she was walking through the woods to her grandmother's house with her basket. But the big bad wolf got her, changed her, and is keeping her. Her life may seem like a prison now, while mine feels free. The big bad wolf can't let her go.

We shower separately. Then go to bed stripped down right out of the shower. Skin to skin warms us up. We just hold each other. I can tell that tears are running down her face. My shoulder is getting wet.

"Libby?" I ask.

"I'm fine," she squeaks out. "Just scared sometimes. I hate to complain after all you've gone through." She's still worried about me.

"I'm scared sometimes, too. My biggest fear is not having you." She wraps her leg over me, which I take as an open request. I easily slide into her. We were both ready for this instance. We heat up quickly, and the result is spontaneous. Made for each other. The fact that we don't use birth control does not come up. I guess a pregnancy would be easy compared to everything else in our life.

22

Tomorrow is the day Mom and I are leaving. We have paperwork and belongings ready to go. I told the school to hold onto the diploma for me. The fridge is cleaned out, shut off, and left open; anything we still want cold we leave outside on the back porch. I winterize the toilets. New cell phones are ready and programmed with a few numbers. Old ones will be cleared and left here at the house. The deer meat went to neighbors up the road with four kids. My safe deposit box is cleaned out. Pete is coming with me. Dad is staying in the yard.

No one mentions Dad. We decide the boat will just stay on him. We got rid of the shovel a long time ago. He, in his truck, just took off one day and never came back. It was an easy story. Mom took off her wedding band the day after the incident. It might also be in the yard. She has been a happy person since that day. My life forever changed; some good, some bad. I can't blame Dad as much as I blame Ivan for my life. He was the real demon. He knew Mom and I were being beat, and he used my psyche to his advantage and hurt all the people I care for. We all are born with a capacity to do harm, but unless something happens to a person to bring it out, it may never surface. What you do with your dark side once it's unleased is up to you. Dad and Ivan gave themselves to it. Mom blocked it. Libby has accepted it. I let it roll along like a roller coaster. I get on and off the ride with a push on a lever. I've been exposed to sinister acts all my life. I'm reminded of it every time I sit down on my scars. I just try to live for the good side, knowing I'll remain on the ride.

I have Ivan's lawyer's number to contact in a couple weeks. I decided I'll gladly take Ivan's money. He owes me so much more. I thought stopping Dad from his drunken beatings was going to solve my problems, but little did I know, new circumstances would arise that would be even worse. I'm ready for a normal life with normal problems: out of milk, muddy boots, flat tire, or lost hat. Unfortunately, there could still be problems. Being found by organ smuggling mafia-type assailants is just one. What if the bodies are found? They were buried quite deep. Hopefully, whoever buys Libby's place leaves it the same. There are over 28 bodies rotting in their own personal holes. Rest in peace boys and Becka.

Libby felt so bad about involving me with Becka's death, and I just led her to think her Dad was involved. Sometimes my dark side picks the wrong solution. Libby could be completely rid of me and this whole problem. I could have just moved and continued my job. My deepest part does not ever want to let her go-I am selfish. The rest of my life needs to be spent making it up to her. New place with a new reality.

Libby is going to a basketball game tonight to watch Hope play. I hope she really is doing okay and not hiding the fact that she's falling apart. I believe she still plans on coming to be with me. She understands it's for her safety, but she could easily take off and go somewhere else and not tell me. I would never blame her. Her future is all in her hands. We said our goodbyes. She had me take all her guns out of the safe because she's now thinking of flying to Montana. It's over two thousand miles to drive.

As of yesterday, she has been given the necessary instructions on shutting down her house. She has her new backpack and phone. Her bags are ready to empty the safe, and the keys to the equipment are labeled and organized. The grass won't need be mowed for a long time. We don't plan on seeing each other in the morning before Mom and I leave, too hard to say goodbye, and we can't talk anyway.

Morning comes. Mom and I hug and quietly cry. Outside, we stand in the frigid air. It's getting cold faster than usual this time of year.

"I'll see you soon, I promise. Let me find a place to live and get organized while you're doing the same thing. Then I'll come see you," I tell her. We have our titles ready to trade in our cars. She has several thousand in cash on her. Don't know what she thought about that, never even asked. She gets in and heads south, while the dog and I head north. I won't miss anything about this old house, except maybe my tractors. Goodbye Alliance; goodbye Patrick, the puppet. Hello, Patrick, the handyman or mechanic or lumberjack. It will be nice to have an answer when someone asks, what do you do? I can see the house now, down the winding drive, each detail. Once Libby shows up at the door, all will be complete.

I stop at a car dealership in Canton to trade the truck in for a new Jeep. They don't care what my name is once they see the cash, perfect. Here I come, Montana and freedom. If there's a tracker on my truck, good riddance. I hate to leave Libby behind, but she'll be coming soon. I have to take care of a few things first, and Libby needs some healing time. I hope her aunt can help with that. Glacier National Park will do wonders for her. I predict a positive future with no problems, along with an impressive security system and a new dog or two. I look over at Pete. Always asleep. Pete sure could tell some stories from growing up with our family. He knew when to hide too; finally escaping. A true smile is on my face, along with a tear or two.

23
MIDGET FINSTER

I have temporarily settled into a little town in Indiana when I get a call from Paco. He tells me that my stupid brother, Cola Mass, has been missing for a few weeks. I told that kid it wasn't safe. I thought he'd join me like old times, but he said he was making more coin on his own. Paco is a regular customer. He brought me plenty of business. It would've been nice to have been notified earlier, but my crowd isn't very reliable.

I pack a bag, load into my Range Rover, and head back to the neighborhood. I told that stupid muther there was something going on. I knew he wouldn't listen to my warning. Now look, Spark and Cola are both gone. This has got to stop. Cops don't waste their time lookin' for no drug dealers. It's up to us to protect ourselves.

I was thinking about heading down to Louisiana to start a little business there. I decided Louisiana would be a perfect place for my gig. A very short man standing on his case of valuable commodities, wearing his fancy polyester gigs in the heat without sweating. I just don't sweat. I would be cool as a cucumber in the hot months. All suited up, I could just see it now. My hair slicked back smiling at all the half-dressed babes. Girls would just love to undress me for a look at dat package slightly emphasized. My tongue is also a little thick. Maybe the sweat is absorbed by my tongue. The girls will like that, too.

I only make it as far as the eastern border of Indiana when my Range Rover decides to drop its transmission on the highway. Have to pay for a tow and several nights stay at the Super8. Transmission cost me over two thousand. But then I meet Mindy at a little diner. She's a very short waitress with a terrible overbite that found me very appealing.

I stayed a couple extra nights to see her and find out she goes to church every Sunday. I tell her I'm an entrepreneur. She doesn't even ask anything else, just smiles and giggles. Mindy likes my tongue, but that's all she'll let me do, because she's a church goer. It just won't work out with Mindy in my life. I'm the man with the plan, but instead I'm heading back to the greater Cleveland death area. This isn't moving on with the big plan. Poor Collin.

I arrive back in Parma and go straight to Paco's house. "It was about four weeks ago last I seen him, then nuttin'," Paco says. He hands me a cell phone. Ronny's youngest kid found Cola's cell phone at the edge of the street. Cola and I had started to tape record our little drug transactions once we found out about the disappearances happening. We would push record and place our phones in our shirt pocket close to our faces. Cola's phone must have fallen out. Like he was turned upside-down or sumpin.

"We've listened to the recording several times. Just sounds like a white guy." I sat down in a chair to get comfortable. I hit the audio button and I hear talking.

"I'm just looking for some ready-rock, no trouble...You too young to be a cop...Well, you got any?...God damnit, hold on a fuckin minute...I jus' standin here...I'm just a chicken crossin' the road, man, here to do some business...heard you had the spread... I ain't no cooker, but I got jack... Wha da fuck?"

Then nothing. I listen to it over and over. He sounds young, must be why Cola knew this person wasn't no cop. No gun or painful stabbing sounds. No blood. Just gone. Very creepy. That voice is tattooed into my brain. It doesn't have a southern drawl or foreign tone-just white boy. I don't even know any other dealers or white boys in the area. The dealers are all gone now; the neighborhood will really go downhill now.

I head out to grab a few more items out of my abandoned apartment, but it looks like it has already been ransacked. My secret wall was never found, but nothing's left here for me. I look around my neighborhood. Up and down the street. Kids on tricycles, but anyone older than eight is holed up inside. Sad place. Empty. At night, the craziness comes alive.

I ask Paco if he wants to leave this town and go with me to Louisiana, but he declines. My brother is gone forever-no doubt about it. I decide to keep Cola's phone, might come in handy. Course, who else would care? Nobody cares in our world. It's an open prison, my neighborhood. Fend for yourself or get gone. I don't even let grandma know I'm back in town, because I have nothing good to say to her. I just leave as quickly as I came.

24
LIBBY

Sitting alone at this basketball game is unnerving. I see all these people I know, but they look so foreign to me. It's only been a couple months since I was at school; however, my eyes see the world differently. I don't see what some girl is wearing or who is dating whom. I see people smiling. I see families together. Their lives appear to be without danger and risk. Out of place, that's how I feel. Could anyone else be hiding anything? A secret life, a secret sin. Surely, I'm not the only one here with secrets. What's behind her walls or hidden under his floor? Will I be able to look so innocent someday? Will I get used to our life of discord? Patrick said we weren't supposed to fall in love. He was just there to hunt and do his job. Our lives' colliding was meant to happen. We became a pair because of our unusual circumstances-his abuse and my solitude. We clung to each other out of a need to be understood. I fell hard, and life revealed its fury.

Life throws you a curve ball, and you either have to hit it or it hits you. I hit mine. I will not sink to the floor and melt away. This life chose me for a reason...the buzzer goes off and startles me out of my trance. Am I even watching this game? Where is Hope? There she is, the star of the show. Is anyone looking at me up here? Do I look like a changed person, a changeling? I can smile when I need to. Right?

I see Rashin sitting with her boyfriend. I don't think she has seen me. Do I want to go over and talk to her? My mind is telling my legs to stay put. Just sever the ties. Look at them and bank the memory. I don't remember how to carry on a conversation. What would I say? I think about what I'm wearing. Large drab clothes with my hair hiding most of my face. When was the last time I even washed my hair? Not good. I'm an animal poised to attack. Hiding at the top of these bleachers, I look upon these people with wild eyes while I fidget and stir.

I'm also unsettled from another bad dream. Drowning in the cold water, and struggling to surface. I think of Casey; she's with me now. She was the one struggling, and she's now living inside me. I feel her picking at my heart, tugging it. With Casey so close, I feel full. I don't need any of these people. Just Patrick.

There's no room left for more to happen to me. My body has reached the level of enough: enough secrets, enough lies, enough crime, and enough near death. I'm scared to go to sleep, but I'm always tormented awake. When I'm with Patrick, the world feels tolerable, but when I'm away from him, I feel crazed. Hopefully, when I leave this town, I will leave my demons as well. Patrick is my salvation and my misfortune. I have to remind myself that none of this is his fault. He was placed in his life just like I was, and suffers for it.

I can't just sit here, and it's getting hard to breathe. Why did I want to come here? This is not my life anymore, and it never will be. I'm not part of a society that goes to games and cheers for a team. My society is blanketed in a shroud. I have crossed over to a side that can't be reversed. Move on. My legs get up and carry me down the bleachers and walk me toward my car. Not one person approaches me or says anything to me while passing. I'm a distant memory of a girl who once went to this school.

Patrick is leaving in the morning. He will make his escape. He told me what new name he picked out for himself, but I can't even remember it. I drive back to Janna's house in the dark. I'm preparing for my escape. When Patrick finds a place, buys it, and gets in, he'll let me know. Then will I just leave my life behind and go? Since my boyfriend is breaking away from contract killing, I don't have much choice. I just hope he's right about these me, that they won't care enough to find out where we're hiding. They have other hit men to do their dirty work, right? Sure.

My life has been mainly sitting around lately. Janna has been very patient with me, but I'm sure she wonders what my plan is. I told her when winter breaks, I'll get a part time job and start going to the local college. She liked that answer. That gives me breathing space.

I wonder how cold it is in Montana. Do I need to get more warm clothes before I go? I can get stuff up there. Don't want to pack too much. I've decided to sell my car and fly there, too long to drive. Detective Burkhart will not be able to call me after that. I'll miss talking to him. He has almost become a friend to me; he genuinely cares. I pray he never finds out anything. He has always been on my side and talked nice about my father. His frequent calls will be missed. It'll disappoint him that I disappear and don't tell him where I'm going. Another necessary evil.

I'll soon be leaving this life. My mind is getting prepared for this, so I must be going through with it. I do love Patrick. I loved him, hated him, and loved him again. We need each other. How could I be with anyone else? Jason, Detective Burkhart, wonders if Patrick and I are doing okay. I tell him we are. Does he want to make sure I'm not alone since the Ivan attack, or does he think Patrick is off somehow? He's glad I'm living with my aunt. Damn, I'm thinking about the detective again. My mind goes to him often. Am I falling for him? Noooo, he has just been so good to me, how could I help but like him? I do like him.

Everyone is in bed when I get to Janna's house. I sit at the kitchen table in the dark to unwind. Patrick is leaving, leaving, yes leaving. Breathe in and out, in and out. You will be fine; you can do this. The good thing is, you can just leave a note here on the table when you leave. That would be best. No crying or hugging and WHYS!!!!!!! A clean break will be easiest for all. I'm worried about tomorrow. Patrick will be gone. I know I'll drive by his house tomorrow. It will be empty.

In the morning, I watch everyone move with their daily routines. They make coffee, eat breakfast, gather phones, and pack lunches. I just sit on my chair and put a happy smile on my face. Do they feel sorry for me? Poor Libby. I don't feel pitied, which is why it will be hard to leave this house. Janna is great and my cousins took me in like a sibling. I'll never be able to tell them the truth. Very sad. Cory will be going off to college, and Regina will start to date boys. I'll miss all of it.

Now the house is empty, and I sit here looking at the wall. Patrick is gone. I could use my new phone and call him, but he might be trading in his car now. I'll wait a while.

I need to be productive today, get my mind occupied. I eat some cereal, put on some clean clothes, and stick my hair in a ponytail. Most of my clothes are in a suitcase on the floor. None of these are my new fancy clothes though. I left them in the back of my closet at home. They got me into trouble.

Time to leave. I'll eventually go to my house today and clean more of it out. Before I do, I drive to Patrick's house like I knew I would and park the car. I get out and look into the windows. Dark and quiet. Furniture left all cleaned off and the fridge door open. My stomach is in knots. He has really left; this is really happening. I didn't want to believe it. The loneliness of the house draws me to it like I crave emptiness. I want to feel closer to Patrick somehow. I creep around to the back of the house and instantly walk towards the overturned boat. The back yard is surrounded by trees. There is no wind or sound just cold stillness. Peace. I stand beside the old rotting wooden boat. Weeds are overgrown around it with some old lawn chairs leaning up against it. So this is where, as a boy, Patrick buried his abusive father. He thought his tortured life would be better, only to find another tortured life around the corner. A big tree grows close to the site. It's a maple tree. It has empty limbs and an empty heart. This tree has had to slowly soak in the residue of an evil and immoral being. I look up at it. You were once happy, I'm sure. Then one day the fluid in your veins started to burn, and your happiness ended. I bet you wish someone would cut you down and put you out of your misery. Stuck here and sucking in more and more foulness over the years till you are now wicked yourself. Do you even remember when you were happy and your leaves fluttered with joy? No.

I look back down to the ground. You are the cause of all of this. Ivan could never have used Patrick if he wasn't already broken. My dad wouldn't be dead either. We would not be criminals and have to run and hide. I hear a limb crack and break off the tree. As I look up, it falls right beside me. No time to even react. If that was a sign, I'm going to take it. I run straight for my car to get out of here. I nearly back up into a car going by. I stop to gather myself. Calm down.

While driving, I wonder if the tree was trying to warn me or kill me. Then I remember the nightmare I had the other night, my drowning one. Down, down into the water. I could not scream. It hurt without air. I remember feeling like my cells were bleeding. It's just like the Joyce Carol Oates book, breathing in the black murky water. That is what I kept saying to myself. "I can't breathe!" Maybe that tree feels like its cells are drinking in sinister water and it can't breathe. The tree was telling me yes, that is true. I'm suffering here. Now I think about my sister. Could she be warning me? I've always felt a presence at the pond, but can she be with me all the time now? I arrive at my house and go inside. It is so empty. I need to get a hold of myself. Am I spending too much time alone?

I want to see Patrick. He is the only one I can talk to. Perhaps I'm not dealing with the traumas as well as I think I am. I was attacked. I do think I would be so much worse if I were awake during the rape. Thankfully I have no recollection of Ivan's vulgar act. I probably would not have been able to be intimate with Patrick. It is comforting to be with him though. Knowing what he has done has not swayed my love. I know he was forced, and he is protecting his mother. I do wish I had known Dad was not the killer from the start. I let Patrick bury Becka's body thinking I was protecting Dad, and in return, I also became a monster. We both had our reasons, and now we have to live with them. I go to the freezer and open the door. There are the boxes of 100 Grand bars. These are one of the reasons I suspected Dad in the first place. Ivan sure liked to play his little games. I get a trash bag and start throwing them all in. These need to go.

Not much in this house is left from Mom. Janna came and got some things after she died; I was very young then. The rest we donated. Nothing in this kitchen is special to me or can't be easily replaced. The furniture is dated. I will miss my bedroom though, but I'll enjoy sleeping every night tucked into a warm, secluded home away from this town. With Patrick, with Patrick? I did not give him an answer to his marriage question. Was that on purpose? Do I want to marry him? I can't think about that. I just need out of this town and house. I sometimes forget there are bodies buried here. How horrible to have this knowledge. Maybe it's the dead coming to me in my dreams and not my sister. Will they haunt me forever? It is not my fault. Good thoughts, good thoughts. Breathe.

25

While anticipating a new life, I decide what to do to fill my time. I drive to the Alliance Dog Shelter. Volunteering to help walk and take care of the animals would give my mind some rest. I can even look a vagabond. They tell me to come anytime, so I start right away.

I first take several dogs for a walk. Five leashes at one time is as hard as it sounds. None are really big, but all together they prove to be smarter than expected. They work as a team to go as fast as they can. I can't help but laugh most of the time. We must look ridiculous. This is just what I needed. Honest laughter.

When I get back, I play with some frisky kittens using feathers on sticks. And then I wash and brush out a German shepard/retriever mix that just came in. His name is Archie. He has a quiet calm demeanor and doesn't wag his tail at all. Archie watches everything around him, very aware. I feel he has secrets to tell; his eyes are piercing. He is now my favorite dog here. I take Archie for a walk-just him and me. It's our private time to be ourselves. Archie isn't like the other dogs, and only I can see it. The staff tell me he's approximately four years old. His owner had to move, sounds familiar. After a long walk, he's happy to eat. I wonder how this dog would like Montana. His ears lay down, and he now wags his tail at times.

I tell Janna I'm going to stay at my house for a few days and work with the shelter dogs. I know she doesn't want me there by myself too much. She worries about me staring at walls. But she is glad to hear I have a new interest though.

My new phone rings just as I walk in the door to my house. It's Patrick calling me. I sit down so I can soak up everything he tells me.

"Hi. Libby, I'm driving through Minnesota now. I bought a gray Rubicon Jeep, love it. How are you doing?"

"I'm good, so happy to hear from you!"

"Libby, I can't lie, I'm very happy to be leaving everything except for you of course. I feel like a new person. A weight is off my shoulders. I'm on a mission to find a perfect place for us. I can't wait till you're on your way."

"I'll be ready. My mind isn't here anymore. I started volunteering at the dog shelter. It's helping me pass the time." I don't mention my sad, emotional upheaval.

"That sounds great for you. I have an appointment in two days with a realtor. He already knows what I'm looking for and will be ready for me. I'll try to look older." He does sound good. I can hear happiness in his voice that I haven't heard in a long time. I hope when I leave this town, I find my happy voice.

"How do you think Pete get along with another dog?"

"I think he would be fine," Patrick snickers. "Did you get a dog?"

"Thinking about it." We laugh and talk about some of the sights he has seen along the way. I don't mention the awkward basketball game or the tree in his back yard. Why would I?

"Talk soon," I say.

"Just take care of yourself for me."

"You too." We hang up. I feel a sense of renewal. He has a new quality to his voice, so inspiring. Patrick has a lot to deal with. I wish him a safe and happy life. I wish *us* a safe and happy life, us, us. What was I thinking there? Where else would I go? I can't stay here. My life could be in danger. Libby, you'll be okay. Just stick with the plan.

I turn up the heat some and look around. What is there left to do? I know, I'll go through all my drawers and closet to pack just the things I really want to keep. I'm only taking one big suitcase on the plane and a carry-on holding my important papers. I have my diploma. Guns are with Patrick. Most of the cash is at different banks. Nothing else of value left to take. I search my old purse I was using for any signs of tampering. Nothing. Ivan would have been the only person I had been around to bug my purse. Patrick could have a problem with paranoia, but I can't ignore the dangers. There are bodies buried on this property. I don't want to know any more about that. How could Dad not have known about this or seen anything? I guess he did start to notice which is why Ivan killed him. Tears quickly form thinking about this awful situation.

I always wondered why Dad was Ivan's friend. They did not seem to have anything in common. Ivan just came around acting like a friend to check on his private dump site. I think about Dad and the life he had, the life that doesn't exist anymore. I miss running equipment and joking with Wayne. That was another lifetime ago. Seems like killing Dad was not the only solution. They could have just found another place to dispose. Patrick should've stopped using our land when he and I got close. Maybe I feel like Patrick should've made better choices, even when forced. They could've found another place for disposal. Some other another solution.

Do I harbor some bad feelings toward Patrick I don't want to admit? Is that why I didn't answer the marriage question? Is he broken, and I don't want to see the truth? NO, I still love him. He was practically just a kid. Look at all he's had to deal with. He's not defective or ruined. We will be fine...

I get up to walk around. I go to the garage. Oh yea, all the camping gear. This all might come in handy in Montana visiting the parks: tents, camping dishes, lanterns, and blankets. But this can't all go on the plane. I could box it up and have it shipped to the address Patrick gives me when he buys a place. That's what I'll do. Then I acknowledge the coolers sitting around. I open one up slowly, and look inside, afraid of my own thoughts. It looks clean. Then I open another one. Clean. I take a deep sigh of relief. I look around the garage at all the stuff. Maybe nothing is actually worth packing up. This can all get sold with the house and equipment someday. Forget it. I go back into the house and sit in a kitchen chair and stare at a wall again. I'm done here. Nothing else for me to do. I head to the dog shelter. I hope Archie is still there.

26

Three more days have gone by. Patrick and I have talked a couple more times about his drive. He has sent me some amazing scenic mountain pictures to my phone. His time in Bismarck sounds lovely. He stayed in a hotel overlooking the Missouri River. He met some fisherman, and they showed him their array of fish. He said they were very friendly and were surprised he was traveling alone. He told them he was starting a new job. He ate at a restaurant named Marcello's or Nardello's-something like that. The food was great, and he feels like a king being around a new environment. Life opened up for him. Will I be the same way? He should be in Montana by now and checked into a hotel. He contacted some realtor and has an afternoon appointment with them. I can't wait to hear about some of the places he looks at. I hope they don't look like Hope's cabin. That might be a problem for me. I wonder if the isolation I think I want will be the worst thing for me. Maybe I should change my name and go to New York City, the city where a person is never alone. I could lose myself among people. I have the money to get started. Would I be better off alone or with Patrick? I need to think about something else; my mind is getting scattered. Then I think about Jason, the detective. Libby, he's a detective. His job is to talk to you and check on you. Probably not someone you should continue to see or talk to under the circumstances. I think I will miss him. He is so easy to talk to, and he listens to me.

I take myself outside. I don't want to be alone, but I don't want to be with anyone either. Perhaps a dog is what I need. I think dogs can be flown on planes. Archie and I have become best friends. I would hate for anyone else to take him, so tomorrow I'm going to start the adoption process. He has been fixed and Janna has a fenced in back yard. I'll have to buy a dog crate to take onto an airplane and find out what paperwork I need for that. Might be easier to just drive to New York, stop, stop. Why do you keep thinking this way? You love Patrick...

I feel I'm done with all I'm going to do at my house. Other than coming back to winterize it and get my bags, I'm ready to move on. There is one last item to attend to though. The pond. Before going back to Janna's house, I need to say goodbye.

It's still cold outside, but not as bad today. The sun is trying to come out. It's a good day to spend some time on the bench. Walking down to the pond, I can start to feel that old sense. The sense is different for me now; it means so much more. This pond will always be where my sister died and where Dad should've woken up. I love you, Mom and Dad and Casey. I'm sorry our lives didn't turn out at all how we expected.

I won't see my fish since a layer of ice covers the pond. I sit down but see no rippling water. Very quiet. Are you there, Casey? It feels dead to me. It would be great to think that her spirit can come with me. I'll find another pond or lake to sit beside, and a new fish will show up and look back at me. Then I'll know it is you. Casey, I wish I would've known about you all along. Dad kept you a secret. I would have loved to grow up with a big sister to watch over me. We'd have done everything together. I hope you can find me in Montana and let me know you're there somehow. I'll be watching for you.

I suddenly feel like Kate Winslet. She had been rescued from the lifeboat, and she's on the dock among all the grieving, cold people, sitting alone. Her fiancé is yelling for her, and she doesn't know what to do. Does she go to him or start a life on her own? She knows she would be better off without him. She ducks down and hides, and he is gone forever. She was saved from the sinking ship, from the cold water, from the lifeboat, and from him. I don't know what...I hear footsteps behind me, crunching snow and before I can think, Earl is right beside me.

"Hi, Libby, who are you talking to?" He sits down right beside me. I feel my body tense up. This doesn't feel like a friendly visit.

"You caught me. I do that a lot, you know...talk to myself."

"I guess we all do that." He is silent for a little bit. "What's new around here? I haven't seen much of you except when you almost hit me the other day leaving your boyfriend's house. Seemed like you were in a big hurry."

"Oh, I'm sorry. I don't remember being in a hurry." It was Earl I almost hit. What does he want with me? I start to feel trapped like I did with Ivan. Maybe I should get up. He puts his hand on my arm to keep me down when I start to rise.

"Hey, let me ask you something." I sit. "Did your boyfriend go off and leave you here? His mom told her friends she was going to Kentucky. Sounds like it was such a sudden thing. Hope everything is all right."

"She's helping her sister out. She's sick," my voice cracks a little.

"Well, that's too bad. Hope she doesn't die too. So many people are either dead or gone around here. You're the only one left. It makes me think you might know what's been happening."

"Earl, I have no idea what happened to Ray. It's a mystery to all of us."

"Well, I don't believe you or your pretty boyfriend. Ivan and your father were up to something, and I want to know what it was. If I have to hurt you to get it out of you, well, I'm willing to do it." He pulls a gun slowly out of his coat pocket. "I don't want to have to use this, but I want some answers. The police can't find anything, but I know something bad has occurred. I demand you tell me now." I'm frozen with fear. This man is threatening me and I'm alone here. Jason warned me about him. What am I going to do next? I think about some of the survival tips Patrick taught me. Drawing a complete blank.

Then I get a feeling or pull of what to do. Here it goes. I stand up quickly and take off running across the pond. I can hear Earl starting to chase me. Please don't shoot me I pray while I run crouching across. The snow on the ice is enough to get traction. Is Earl crazed enough to shoot me? No gun fire yet. Then I hear some cracking. I'm almost to the other side, and I look back. Earl is standing on the middle of the pond, and the ice is breaking under him. I reach the bank while hearing him feet slapping against the cracking ice. He tries to shoot me when he knows he is going down, but he misses. The ice breaks under him, and then he's falling in. While watching, I see him grab the edge of the ice with his bare hands, but his heavy clothes pull him under. His screams are urgent and fierce. Then he's suddenly gone. I see bubbles coming up and waves in the water. I'm frozen with the realization that I was nearly killed, again. This is like my dreams, sinking in the cold water. Earl just lived my dream, my nightmare. I stand stunned and dazed without anyone else around. What do I do? Looking at the hole in the middle of the ice, there's just stillness and silence. No waves. No cars. No witnesses. Are you crazy? You have to call the cops. Make your legs move.

I go back to the house and call the police. I tell them Earl Squires tried to kill me and fell through the pond. I hang up and collapse on the floor. I start to cry. Cry for my life, cry for my death, cry for my sanity, and cry for my family. How much more can I take? The tears just keep coming and I cry harder. After some time has passed, my door opens. It's Jason, here again.

PART 2

MIDGET FINSTER

After finding out my brother Collin, Cola, was among the missing, I went back towards Indianapolis to the city of Greenfield. I was staying there on my way to Louisiana, and then I got busted. As I was getting back into my gig, an undercover cop tricked me out. He was trying to preach the Bible to me with his little "wife" you see, and when she went over to another group, he told me he actually wanted some reefer, he called it. Said he wasn't really into this Bible stuff and needed some to make preaching bearable with the "little woman," you see. He was good, and I totally bought it. After the exchange, he had me face down on the ground before I knew what was happening, and the little woman was straddling and cuffing me. They treated me like I was some big 6-foot, 295 pound giant, while I am only 4 foot 11. The little woman could have taken me down with her Bible.

I don't have to be locked up for long, because this is my first arrest. Three months is all. It will give me time to think. I mostly think about that recording on Cola's phone with the man who is making my job undesirable. The man who has changed my life and who I'm determined to find someday. Cola and I had a good thing goin', and now I'm stuck in Indiana State Prison with no brother or foreseeable future. If I get busted again, it will be 5 to 10 years.

Mindy came to see me once. During the visit, she broke it off, because she is a real church goer. Too bad her front teeth couldn't tunnel me out of here. It really isn't all that bad except for the part where I'm Tommy's little bitch. It was looking like I was going to have a very bad prison experience, which I always feared being a little guy. Then Tommy came along right when three guys had me in a corner. Tommy is huge in all dimensions but one, thank God. He told me he would take care of me as long as I'm his. What choice did I have-one guy versus the whole gang.

Tom, as I now refer to him, has proved to be essential to my safety. He's in jail for beating up his mother's boyfriend. Apparently, he has done this several times before. I don't ask what's happening at his mother's place. All I know is, he seems to be a gentle giant unless provoked. I just smile and agree. Thank God, his unit is not proportional to his body, for some reason. He tilts back and lifts his stomach after he puts me up on a table in the machine shop. I can hardly even feel it now. I guess I'm no longer a virgin, I think. He's very polite about it. He is able to reach up and turn the light on and off with his bare hands during the act. The light must be over eight feet high and very hot, but Tom wants the lighting to be just right.

Tom would be an interesting addition to my team once we're out of here. I would have protection from the drug dealer killer. But I'm guessing he would still insist on violating me, so I'll just have to survive on my own. My main goal when getting out of here is making my way to Louisiana and hoping someone finds out who is killing off my livelihood and my street family in Ohio.

2
JASON

I feel responsible for this. I knew Earl was getting more and more agitated and frenzied, but I didn't see this coming. Now I'm here with Libby Simon going through another tragedy. This investigation brings me to this girl and this house over and over again. Am I missing something right in front of me? Libby is the center of so much sadness and pain. I also now struggle with the fact that when I look at her, I want to stay here and take care of her.

It's hard to believe Libby is facing another terrifying experience. First, I meet her after her father is murdered. His killer hasn't been caught. Then she's attacked and violated by her boyfriend's uncle, which is shocking and horrendous. Now she's nearly killed by a man tormented by his son's disappearance. These factors focus around Libby, her boyfriend, Patrick, and this place. And where is the boyfriend? Funny he's not around. Does he have reason not to be here? Did they break up? Do I want to know because I actually want them to be broken up?

Earl has fallen though the icy pond with a gun in his hand, Libby said. It will take a while to find a diver or two to retrieve him. I see his footprints in the snow where he also came down to the pond beside Libby's footprints. His car was found parked behind some back building. How long was he watching the place? I know Earl felt that her father had something to do with his son's disappearance because Thomas was killed near the scene of Ray's disappearance, but to pull a gun on George's daughter seems unfounded. She seems to just be left here. Staring down at the icy water won't give me any more answers. Nothing else to see outside, so I'll go back in and see if Libby is up to talking some more.

She's on the couch wrapped up in a blanket. Her hair is a mess coming out of her ponytail, and her face is blotchy from crying. Her brown eyes are lost in anguish and suffering. She is so alone. I just want to go over and wrap my arms around her and take the pain away. All of this is so much for a young woman to deal with. I sit down beside her, while two other officers are hanging out in the kitchen. They're making calls to find divers and getting ready to go back outside. They'll see if they can find any stray bullets in the snowbank close to where Libby made it across the frozen pond. She heard two or three shots, she's not sure. I put my hand on her shoulder.

"Libby, how are you holding up?"

"I don't know." She looks up at me and tries to remember to breathe between whimpers. "Not sure how much more I can take."

"Can you remember what he said to you?"

"Earl wanted to know about Ivan and his son again. He felt sure I knew something about it because of Dad. I wish all of this would just go away." She looks at me again, so lost and so vulnerable.

"Libby, where is Patrick? I'm surprised he's not here with you."

"He went with his mother to Kentucky. His aunt is sick and needed some help. I'll call him later on. There isn't anything he can do here now." That seems weird for her to say. He should be here with her. He could comfort her and do what a boyfriend is supposed to do, yet she says there's nothing he can do here now.

"Are you going to go to your aunt's house then? Do you want a ride there?"

"No, I'll just stay here for now. I may go later on." Does she feel like she isn't worthy of comfort or love? She has lost a part of herself. With so much trauma, she doesn't know how to take care of herself. She needs people, support, but she stays alone. I'll worry about her even more now.

"We'll get Earl out of your pond as soon as we can, but for now, can I get you anything?" Her backpack sits beside the door, old and unzipped. I can see a sweatshirt and a water bottle in it. A little purple bag is tucked in the side, probably her wallet. This house is sparsely lived in. Not your typical home with decorations sitting around and pictures on the walls and warm cozy items. This is a shell of a house with a lost girl living in it. An empty girl. A beautiful girl caught in a troubled world with no answers. I fear she's already lost in herself.

"I need to get something out of my car," I stand and say. I go outside and see cars driving by very slowly, stopping even, to see what's going on. Hard to believe a news van isn't here by now. I get into my car and pocket a small GPS tracker and find a phone number to a grief counselor that is local. At least that's what I'm going to tell her I came out to my car for. Then I head back inside. She's not on the couch, and I can see she is in the bathroom. I quickly hide the tiny tracker in one of the small front pockets of her backpack that has nothing in it. I sit back on the couch.

She comes out with her hair brushed back into her ponytail and her face washed. Her baggy sweats hide the rest of her like always. Not the typical girl her age who wears clothes too tight. She walks to the kitchen for a drink of water, so small and frail yet so resilient. I join her in the kitchen.

"Here's the number of someone you can talk to if you need it." I hand her the card. "You also have my number. Please call me anytime." She takes the card and thanks me. I offer her a hug, and she takes it. I feel her weight lean on me for an instant then pull away. I don't want to leave her, but I have to pay a visit to Earl's wife, Nancy. Not what I want to do now. I'll also drive by Patrick's house and take a look around since they aren't home. Just to check on it and make sure Earl didn't do anything there before coming here. "I'll give you a call later on and check on you, okay?"

"Sure," she says. A small smile forms, but it's forced.

"I'm sure I'll see you soon. The officers will be around to make sure no one comes near the pond." She nods and shuts the door after I leave. I worry about her. I worry she will just take off, and I'll never see her again. There are many reasons I cannot let that happen. Back at the station and in my office with the door shut, I need to decompress. After telling Nancy that her husband pulled a gun on Libby Simon and then drowned in the middle of their pond, she took it rather well. Nancy told me that Earl wasn't sleeping, and he was out of control. It was almost like a relief for her. He must have been making her life difficult while she just wanted to mourn her son. I gave her my condolences and left.

Now, Libby is all that's on my mind. I don't know where else to look for answers. I'm sure Libby's dad wasn't involved in Ray's disappearance, but why was he shot? Maybe it was a mistaken identity. But then to find out that Ivan Sipos was Patrick's uncle is also crazy. He must have become obsessed with Libby. She does have that effect on people. She hides her beauty behind plain clothes, no makeup, and ponytails. She's a stunner, and every time I see her, she is vulnerable and somehow alluring at the same time. She is also about five years younger than I am.

I became detective quickly after four years as a police officer. I passed all the tests the highest in my class and worked very hard. This town is my first actual assignment, and I haven't uncovered anything yet. It's a major letdown to my psyche. The lack of progress on this case makes me feel young and unprepared. There haven't been any reports of missing dealers for nearly two months now. Could the perpetrator be done, dead, or moved on? I have no idea. I would like to be pulled off this case, but then I may never see Libby again. This is all a mess.

My parents had a normal meeting, marriage, and life together. They met in high school. I grew up outside of Toledo. Dad is an insurance salesman. I needed more excitement in my career than that. Dad knew this, so he introduced me to his second job which was very profitable and fit right in with my policeman role. I like action to a certain degree. My mom is a nurse. She works in the ER. She's probably what made me want to become a police officer, people coming in after some horrible abuse or crime happened to them. That's where Dad's side job came in. I worked as an orderly with Mom a couple summers during high school-intense. I wanted to help these people and myself.

I also learned patience from my mother. It would take her one to two hours to eat a meal. We hardly ever went out to a restaurant to eat because she would take so long. She said it was good to eat slow, chew your food, and enjoy each bite. We would have to take magazines or puzzles to restaurants. She was a great cook at home. On the weekends, she would make all finger foods so we could eat whenever and not have to eat a meal with her. During the week, however, we had to sit down and eat together. My sister and I didn't have to stay the whole time she ate, thank goodness. That was how I learned to be patient. A detective needs to sit back to think, analyze, and wait for results. I'm not very good at being a detective. I feel I eat at a normal pace.

My sister lives in Logan, Ohio. She is also a nurse, and I think she eats like a normal person. She works in the maternity ward, I think. I'm not sure, she bounces around jobs. She's dating some guy named Drew. She wanted to live near the Hocking Hills area. I visited her once, and she took me to some beautiful waterfalls and hiking trails. Both of us can cook. Mom taught us to enjoy food, life, and love. Those thoughts bring me back to Libby.

I gather myself together and drive to Patrick's house. I step up onto the porch. I can see in past the curtain. The house looks uncluttered, almost empty. The refrigerator door is open. Another house with no pictures or warmth. I walk around back to see nothing that looks disturbed. No footprints in the snow but mine. There's an old boat overturned in the back yard but little else. I walk over to the barn. It's locked up, and all is very quiet. If they were just visiting a sister, would it look so empty? I don't think so.

3

It's been a week since Earl went through the water. His body was recovered along with the gun. I tried to call Libby twice since then, and she has not picked up her phone. According to her tracker, she has not left town or gone to her aunt's house. She's keeping her car in the garage, and the one time I stopped, she didn't answer the door. I was sure she was there, but I had to let it go. I never left a message because I don't have any police business or news to tell her.

I stop at a diner for lunch. Alliance seems to be getting back to normal. Less talk about the missing high school kids and more chatter about the weather and politics; I'm no longer asked any questions. As I get ready to leave, I'm stopped by a man asking about George's property. He wonders if it will be going up for sale. I tell him I have no idea. That's a strange question. Why would he ask me if Libby's place is for sale? I go online and see that Patrick and his mom's house is now for sale. I knew it looked empty.

I also check on Libby's tracker location and see that it's untraceable. That man must have known Libby and Patrick are together, and since one is for sale, maybe the other will be, too. Where are you, Libby?

Her phone goes right to voicemail. It no longer rings. She does not respond to texts. She has left. Is she okay? Why won't she answer me? The thought of never seeing her again scares me to the point of being frantic. I could contact the aunt and act like I have important police work that I need her for. That is plausible even though completely bogus. I have nothing. The missing will remain missing, and her father's killer will remain a mystery forever.

I get up the next morning, having not slept for wondering about the whereabouts of Elizabeth Simon. Will she be on the news again, and this time will she be the dead one? I check her tracker again and again. Finally, I get a ping. I stand up quickly while my chair shoots out behind me. I calmly walk around my desk to shut my door. I don't want to look like I found out anything. It has pinged in Montana. *Montana!* It's moving slowly. She's in a car. I cannot believe this. She must have been on a plane, and that's why I couldn't trace her. I whisper to myself out loud to try and think more clearly. Is she alone? Was she taken by someone else? Is she running? I'm terrified and sick over her.

The door opens suddenly. "Hey, Jason, do you want to go with me to question Janet Hines about her missing husband?" I'm startled out of my private agony.

"No, Brock, I am sure you can handle the preliminaries. Just let me know what you find out, and we'll make a plan after that."

"Sure, you okay, you look spooked, sir?"

"I'm fine, thank you." I cannot even think of an excuse for my expression. He leaves while shutting the door again. I don't care about any missing husbands or wives or kids, for that matter. There is no way I'll be able to think straight now. I have to know if Libby is all right. My job here has become stagnant. I know that my detective abilities are flawed because my focus is not actually on this job. It's more of a cover. But all of my thoughts are now on Libby. She would be perfect for me. I need a resilient, beautiful mate. I think she needs me too.

I find out later on that Janet Hines' husband is sleeping with the barmaid and didn't plan on going home. Brock said that her house smelled like sauerkraut and fish. I look at the files on my desk to process. I have three thefts and a manslaughter domestic case to investigate, but I don't care. It will be hard to investigate when I don't care. I just want to know where that tracker is going.

"Libby, what are you doing? Is that where Patrick is?"

It finally stops. The tracker has landed. I whisper the address excitedly as I write it down, 2965 Haywire Gulch, Kalispell, Montana. Time to get your gun?

4
PATRICK

Libby arrived a couple days ago. I picked her up at the airport. She used her new phone to call me for the first time. She flew into Glacier Park National Airport, and we embraced for several minutes. She felt even smaller than before. I meet her dog, Archie, still in the crate. Libby doesn't seem to have much to say. In the car, she stared at the mountain ranges before she fell asleep. I wanted to show her some of the sights, but she had no focus. Once we got into the house, she washed up and went to bed with her dog right beside her. She has hardly been up for two days.

I'm concerned about her, but I don't know how to help her. She doesn't seem to want my close company. Libby seems a bit different than when I left her. Could that be the problem that I left her? I thought it would look better, and I had to leave first. We couldn't disappear at the same time. People wouldn't talk as much, but then again, what people? Who is really watching us? The police have not questioned Libby about her dad for a while. I made a delivery, so S.I.F.T. should not be concerned yet. Was it too hard on her to be left behind? I wanted to have this place ready for her. The plan has worked perfectly. I know that Mom seems fine. She found a job easily at a nice restaurant, and she's renting a condo. She wants to come and visit me soon which would be great.

I guess Libby just needs some time to adjust. While looking out the window towards the driveway, I hear her getting up. She is quiet, keeping to herself, almost acts shy. I suppose we haven't lived together before, and having sex was something that recently started before I left her. I'm anxious to rekindle that part of our lives, but obviously, not too soon. Archie is sitting here with me this morning. He doesn't stay outside too long-smart dog.

She emerges and looks at both of us. She comes out smiling and looks ready to interact. She looks like herself, hair in ponytail and baggy clothes. But there's that feature Libby has, the one where when she looks at you, she really looks at you, and when she looks at you, you are in her world. Libby makes life special just being with her. Her spirit is a gift, and her beauty is baffling. The last few months has taken some of her spirit away. I hope together we can bring all of her essence back and get beyond my past life.

"Can I make you some breakfast?"

"No, I just hope you have my favorite cereal." I let her look around herself. She finds her Honey Nut Cheerios and then finds a rather large bowl and takes a surprising amount.

"Libby, I was starting to worry about you. You seem better this morning."

"The plane ride was long, and I didn't get much sleep the night before." She starts eating with an aggressive appetite. I almost laugh, but I don't want to distract her.

"I have so much to tell you and show you. You'll love it here. I started a job a few days ago in a town over called Columbia Falls. I work for Cedar Creek Lodge. I'm the outdoor maintenance guy. I work with one other older guy named Jake. So, I do stuff like plowing snow, removing downed trees, and animal control. It's an easy gig, and I even get to work on tractors." She seems happy to hear that while she continues to eat. "I'll start getting benefits in 60 days. I want to show you what I have set up so far with security here. Oh yea, and I haven't told you my new registered name, William Noble Cantwell, or Bill, now. I thought it sounded like it came from money. I called that attorney from Alliance about Ivan's money and my name change. The inheritance should be transferred soon to my account. He also has my house for sale." She looks less happy now. Perhaps it was too soon to even bring up the name of Ivan to her.

"Patrick, I haven't told you all that has happened to me lately." I'm stunned silent. What could she be talking about? I stay silent so she can tell me in her time, while my stomach twists into a knot of fear.

"A couple days before you called me saying you were ready for me to come here, Earl Squires surprised me at home and tried to shoot me." Her eyes are tearing up, and I feel so helpless. Why didn't she tell me? I look away, knowing I let more danger into her life because of my life. She has been dealing with this alone. "I was sitting down at the pond, and he snuck up and sat down beside me. He wanted to know what happened to Ray again. I tried to get away, and he pulled a gun on me. I started running across the pond, and he chased me. He ended up falling into the pond when the ice broke under him." I can't believe what I'm hearing. She's telling this story like it happened to someone else-so calm and reserved.

"Oh my God, Libby, why didn't you tell me?" I stand up and have to walk away holding my head. All of this time, I'm thinking everything is great and we can live here now together and then to find out she was recently attacked, again. "You said he had a gun..."

"Yea, he um, fired at me but missed." I grab my coat and flee out the door. I can't believe I'm hearing about this now. I walk down the trail I have painstakingly made for her, which leads down the hill to a small stream at the bottom. I stand at this spot where I've cleared out a small area where she can come and enjoy her outdoor talks or spiritual times, whenever she's alone. I used to watch her, which she isn't aware of, over the past three years. I watched, even studied her behavior when she was alone. Her stare changes, along with her mannerisms. Libby becomes like a chatterbox or animal whisperer. I haven't seen that side of her for a long time. Will she ever be that Libby again? I stand at the spot I couldn't wait to show her, but I don't see this Libby enjoying it-I see this Libby sinking into a hole. She holds all the hurt in and absorbs it. I take some deep breaths and try to conjure the best way to help her. This is all because of me. I head back up the little trail and go back into the house and drop down in front of her. I need to be there for her.

"I'm sorry, Libby, all this happening to you is because of me, and I hate it. I am so sorry. What happened after he went through the water?"

"That same detective, Jason, came over along with a few others. They got Earl out of the pond. Jason wondered where you were. I told him you were in Kentucky with your mother. He wanted to take me to Janna's, but I had already told her goodbye. I didn't want to do it again."

"You have just been home alone?"

"I knew you would call soon. Archie kept me company." He's right by her side now.

"Didn't your aunt hear about Earl?"

"No, my name was not aired because of the ongoing investigation with Dad, so she never knew. The detective has tried to call me a couple times, but I didn't answer. He never left a message, so I think he just wanted to check on me. That phone is just sitting at the house turned off." She followed all her instructions and came to be with me. Even with all she has gone through, she still came to be with me. I know I don't deserve her love. I am a little worried about that detective, Jason.

"Libby, I want to promise you that I'll do whatever it takes to make you happy and keep you safe from now on. I love you so much." She holds my hands and smiles. "What do you want to do right now?"

"Show me the house, first. I've only seen parts of it, and then you can take me outside for a big tour." I'm happy to show her around and point out things I bought.

"I decided I needed some nice clothes to blend into this town when needed, which did help during my interviews. I landed the second job I applied for." The house has two bedrooms, and I put her in her own for now if she wants it that way. She's impressed with my new clothes. She seems puzzled by some of the items in the house, but she doesn't say anything about it. The security system is easy to explain. Then we go outside. Archie is happy to be outside sniffing around. The little trail catches her eye right away, which I knew it would. She follows it down with her dog right at her heals. The snow is mostly cleared off the narrow path. The stream is frozen. I tell her about the wildlife around here.

"We can't keep any food outside, stuff like that, because of bears and cougar. I'll show you the spray and knives that are all for you." She laughs. "The woods are way too boring in Ohio." She starts looking around now for evidence of the much bigger game. I hope she loves it here. "You saw the national park beside the airport. We can go there on my next day off, if you want. I got us year-long passes." She looks happy. "I do need to go back to work tomorrow. They were nice to give me some days off already. I told them family was coming up to visit. They must be desperate to keep someone for that job."

"When is your next day off?"

"Wednesday," I say. "You could work there, too. We could ride together even. I won't have to worry about you out on these snowy roads by yourself." I hug her to me and slowly angle down to kiss her. Our lips meet, and I can tell she's shy about it. That's okay, we'll rebuild our lives together. I'm still overjoyed that she came here to be with me. I want to ask her more about what happened with Earl, but she seems happy right now. "I have more to show you at the house."

We walk back up the trail. I can tell she's cold. Her teeth are even chattering.

"I hate to say it, but this is a warm day. A blizzard is expected to move in soon. We're all ready for it. Lots of wood cut, if needed for the fireplace. Canned food is stocked up along with toilet paper. Here, walk around the back side." I lead her. There's a door to a cellar. It goes under the house. I turn on the light. "This is the biggest safe I could get down here. I have all your guns and a bit of cash here. Whatever you want to do with your money is fine. You can put anything in here or use a bank, whichever you want."

"This is great." She looks around. The shelves are covered with tools and old paint cans, but mostly dust. She sees the bag of dogfood. "Where is your dog?"

"Pete, well, I think something got him. He was old, and he decided to go explore and never came back." She looks at me with those eyes that bind. "We can get Archie another friend if you want."

"That sounds great."

"Okay." I hold her again and hug her tight. I think it will all work out. "The chicken made it across the road, and here you are, with me. I love you, Elizabeth Simon."

"I love you, Patrick Kessler."

5

The following week, Libby seems more at home. She's attempting to do some cooking. We've been sleeping in the same bed now, but she doesn't seem receptive to sex. When I start kissing her, she stops and just holds onto me. I told her yesterday that Mom wants to come up soon for a visit. This excited Libby, and she moved all her things to our room to get the guest room ready for her.

The snow is falling hard over Glacier National Park, so we haven't been able to visit yet. When the weather breaks, I promise her we'll go first thing. There is something I've been meaning to do on a day off, but I was too busy getting everything ready for Libby to come. Today, I'm going to find my friend.

"Libby, I'm going to drive over to the Crow reservation. Remember me telling you about going there with Dad and how I made a close friend?"

"Yea, sounds good. Archie will be here with me."

That makes me think of something. "Libby, where was Archie when Earl snuck up on you?"

"Archie liked to run around the yard and back behind buildings chasing rabbits and feral cats. He'll be with me here today. I think he can smell stuff outside that makes him stay close." Archie looks up at us from his nap. He is a nice dog. I'm glad he's here with her.

"Well, I should be back by five. Do you want me to bring back some pizza for tonight?"

"Yes, I think I'll take my knives and spray outside for a little exploring."

"Be sure to take the dog with you."

"I will." I don't want to tell her that the dog will get attacked first then she can get away. Hopefully, she'll never have to find out. "And no food, I remember." I kiss the top of her head, grab my drink and sandwich, and hope I can find my friend.

While driving along the south edge of Glacier National Park on Interstate 2, I first think about Libby's dog. Neither of us mentions the fact that Archie might have found something interesting buried back in her yard. I know I buried them extra deep, but you never know. Once a dog gets a smell of something, it could cause a small problem. Well, she didn't mention that the dog ever brought any surprises. Hopefully, chasing rodents really is what Archie was doing.

Now I think about my friend. I hope I'll be able to find him. I have no phone number or address, but I remember his name. We both knew as soon as we met that we had something special in common. Kull Meadows and I were severely beat by our fathers. We were close in age. Dad had always wanted to hunt for some big game and fish in the cold clear waters. This was the one time he got to do what he wanted to do. That's what I heard, anyway. We flew to

Great Falls and rented a car. Dad had found this area because it was cheap, someone would help him navigate the hunting spots, and he could drink it up afterwards. It was all he wanted. This trip probably started my love for the hunt, but it also started a friendship that held a lasting impression.

Kull and I would escape together along the edge of the Cut Back River and talk about the few fun aspects of our lives. It was hard to come up with good stories. By day two, the bad stories came out. I showed him my scars on my back side. Back then, they were not nearly as bad as now. He showed me his burns. Kull's dad beat his mother, too, just like Dad did. Sometimes, while telling stories, we would both cry and yell. I never had a friend like that ever again.

We were so young, but we were strong. Then we made the pact. The pact that would change my life forever. We both said that if we still had these father's that beat us when we were 13, we would kill them. We would have to find a way and do something about it. No one else would be able to help. Our mother's wouldn't leave for some reason; I still don't know why. We swore to each other to be strong every day, and we talked about ways we could do it-the tools that we could use and how to hide it. During the last day together, we knew we would carry out the pact if needed. I told him that someday, if I lived through it, I would come back up here and find him. Today is the day. I plan on finding my friend. I want to hug him and cry with him. I just hope he made it.

I arrive in the town of Blackfoot. It has changed, or I was just too young to remember. I stop at a diner and sit up at the bar. I order some lunch. The waitress gives me lots of attention. She all but pushes her boobs out of her uniform for me when she talks.

"I've never seen you before. Where are you from?"

"Just here to find someone. You wouldn't happen to know someone named Kull Meadows would you?" I ask without looking down.

"Um, no, but do you want to see the phone book?" The phone book. People still use those. I look for Meadows. I find five different ones and snap a picture. I keep looking at my phone just to look busy.

"Thank you for the phone book," I say when I get up to leave.

"Come back again before you leave, or if you need anything else," she says with a smile. I leave a good tip. Her boobs were very nice. I start with the first name and google the address. Then I notice that three of the Meadows are on the same street. That makes it easier. I knock on the door to a cute little white house with a metal roof and a loud yappy dog inside. An older lady comes to the door. She even looks Indian.

"Hello, ma'am, I'm looking for an old friend, Kull Meadows." She looks all around, up and down the street, and then at me directly.

"Kull is probably at the Suds Bucket. A few blocks that way." She points down the road.

"Thank you," I say. I was going to ask if she was related, but she shut the door too fast. I drive to the bucket place. It's a very run-down dive of a place. I am not even 21 yet, but William Noble Cantwell looks old enough. I walk in. Four guys are sitting at the bar, all too old. It's dark and smells faintly of vomit and mold. I ask them if they know Kull. They all look at me, waiting for someone else to talk. The bartender finally speaks.

"Go check on the step behind the bar, kid." Kid? I walk around outside to a step that faces a house next door to the bar. A young guy is sitting on the step. A half-drunk bottle of Jim Beam is in his hand.

"Kull, is that you?" I squat down and look him in the eyes. He tries to focus on me. I can see that young scared boy that was my friend in his eyes. They still look scared. His face is drawn, and his dirty clothes hang on him. He looks at me harder.

"It's me, Kull, Patrick." He drops the bottle and grabs for my shirt.

"Help me up, man." I help him stand. He is several inches shorter than me, and he can't seem to even stand up with a straight spine. "Is it really you, man. I can't believe it." He starts to cry which makes me cry. I pull him into me, and we laugh and cry and examine each other's faces. "You sure turned out a hell of a lot better lookin' than me!" he yells.

"Kull, what are you doing out here on the step?"

"I hurt myself on the job, so this seems to be what I do now." He reaches for his back. "I can't believe you're standing here!"

"I told you I would be back someday. Do you remember?"

"I do remember, but we were just kids, man, I never really thought..." Tears are still streaming down his face.

"Can we go somewhere and catch up, buddy. It's great to see you." I say that knowing he doesn't look so great, but I'm still happy to see him.

"My trailer is just down the road here. We can talk there. Just leave your car here. There isn't much parking." He starts down the sidewalk.

"Okay, sounds good." I fall in beside him. He limps and his back seems twisted. "What happened to your back?"

"I was driving a truck and hit a patch of ice. That sent my truck head on into an overpass cement wall at about 65 miles an hour. I've had three surgeries, but there isn't much more that can be done. My bones aren't so good. You sure look good. But hey, you sure look good. Where are you living now?" By now we're to his place. He motions for me to go in, and we sit at the built-in booth, him much slower than me. His trailer is actually a camper.

"I just moved to Montana from Ohio." I'm not ready to tell him exactly where I am. "I'm so sorry about your accident. How long ago was that?"

"Almost a year now. I don't take any more pills, but I do drink when the pain is bad enough or if I want to. I just can't drink in the bar, so I sit outside." He chuckles a little. "It isn't much of a life. No girl or anything. I don't think I have anything left to give to anyone, Patrick."

Just then, two guys come right into the camper yelling and laughing.

"Hey, Kull, we need some of..." I stand up quickly and face the sudden intruders. They freeze in their tracks. They look around 30 years old, but it's hard to tell with the missing teeth and dirty appearance. They look at me and step back. "Oh hey, we didn't know you had company, man." They retreat back out. I turn towards Kull.

"Who were they?"

"Oh just some guys I know." Kull looks down at his hands. His back and posture make him look so weak and small.

"What do they want?" I look out his little window. "Kull, I'm here to help you, not judge. Just tell me."

"They stop by for money sometimes. They need beer or smokes. They know I get a disability check. It goes a lot easier if I give them some." I look at my friend. He is deteriorating before my eyes. His life may not be living in a world where you are forced to kill people, but he is living in his own hell here all alone. "It's okay, Patrick, I don't need much." I am so sad to see his life. I pictured him strong and with a good job. Why did I assume he would be fine?

"Did you remember our pact?" I wonder if his dad is still around because he didn't follow through with our deal. Kull looks up at me finally and I see a sparkle in his eye.

"Did you remember our pact?" he asks me.

"Why, yes, I did." I put on a small grin also. "Is your dad around here now?"

"Well, no, he isn't. He took off a few years ago. How about yours?"

"Mine took off a few years ago, also." We smile. Kull stands up and tells me to follow him. We walk outside and start walking up the street further away from the bar. We pass a couple houses ready to fall apart and another trailer. Then he turns down an alley, and we walk into a back yard. He stops.

"This is where my family used to live. You only saw us on the reservation. That was all for show." The house looks abandoned, and the small snow cover probably hides the ugliness underneath. "Mom died three years ago, cancer. I moved into the trailer because I couldn't afford all the repairs the house needed. I remember when we talked about the ways to take the fuckers down. I was 14, and I used a shovel. He's buried somewhere in the yard here, but I could not tell you exactly where. If you had a metal detector, we could find him. I laid the shovel right over his body and filled it in by hand. Then I got Mom some tomato plants. She loved tomatoes." I look at the yard-eerie quiet. Just like I did, with a shovel. "How about you?" He asks while he looks deeply at his old life. He stands a little taller, and I can tell that must have been a good day for him.

"I used a shovel, too. I should have buried the shovel. Instead, I looked at it every day. I put a boat on top of mine. Did your Mom know? Mine did."

"No, I never told her. She seemed sad for about a week, then she realized what bliss could be like. She had two happy years." We walk away from the scene and back towards his place. When he is about to go in, I hand him some cash.

"Kull, I'm going home. Take this and don't share it. I'll be in touch with you soon." We exchange numbers, and I tell him to use the lock on his door. He looks sad that I'm leaving, but I want to get back to Libby.

On the drive home, I wonder what to do about my friend. I can't leave him in that place. I know I can't bring him to live with me and Libby either. I'll have to figure that out later. The weather report is calling for another big snow storm to hit tomorrow. I think about the snow covering the bodies of our beloved fathers. We both went through with it. The pact of two young troubled boys.

6

When I arrive home, Libby is sleeping. I watch her, still not believing she's here with me. She was nearly killed again. I have put her through so much. She usually sleeps on her side with her hair a mess. It covers most of her face, but the parts of her face I can see are literally dreamy. Her little chin swooping down to her delicate neck. She will need time to recover from all that has happened to her since Becka. That seems like such a long time ago. I wonder if Becka's son is still looking for her. Becka would be a surprising find-the only female in a vast array of males.

I am so happy to be living my new life and soon with my new name, and the only person I would ever want to be with is here with me. I hope we can really be free of my past. While she sleeps on, I go get pizza and bring it back.

The smell must have woken her up. She comes out with her beautiful, dreamy face.

"I guess I took a nap," she says as she grabs a slice. We sit by the fire I just made. "How was your friend?"

"Not as good as I would have hoped. He was in an accident which left him half crippled, and he drinks. He seems lost."

"I'm sorry.

"It's okay. I'll work out something for him."

"I've only heard you talk about him once, and now you're going to help this person. Do you really know him?"

"Yes, he's my friend..." She lets it drop.

"When spring gets here, I want to get my own Jeep. Then I'll look for a job. I was googling jobs at the park, and maybe I can do walking tours or something."

"That sounds perfect for you." I love that she's thinking about a future here. It will turn out just how I planned. "I work tomorrow. Do you need me to pick you up anything?"

"More breakfast foods sound good-cereal, eggs, bacon, that kind of thing."

"Done. Now come over here so I can hold you." She moves over to me and tucks herself in. She smells just like Libby, like the first time her scent came across my nose. It was out in the woods behind her house. I was hunting that day, but spying on her became my favorite pastime. I'm getting excited thinking back to when I used to watch her.

I start nuzzling her neck, hoping she feels the same way. She's not shying away this time. My desire reaches full bore very quickly. I pull those sweatpants off her before she can even react. I lean over her back and bring myself to her. Her heat and desire is confirmed, so I waste no time. I bury my face in her silky mess of blonde fur, hair. We are like animals, animals that live for the day, animals that don't know what tomorrow will bring.

Early the next morning, I leave for work, but I hate to leave her all snuggly and warm beside me. After last night, I feel our connection is solid.

Arriving at the lodge, I park off to the side and notice that Jake's truck is already here. He's always early, but I am never late, I make sure to point out to him. We get along well. Other maintenance people work inside, and they all get together during breaks and lunches. I usually go do my own thing. I find it hard to talk about mundane things or kids all the time.

Today, Jake is showing me how to maintain the roof gutters when the snow gets too thick. After the trash run, he has me carry an old wooden ladder all the way to the far end of the building so it doesn't look unsightly.

"There's hardly anyone here, Jake."

"We don't want guests to think anything is wrong," he explains. Why do I get the feeling he's pulling another prank on me. The last day I worked, he had me use the very small snow blade and plow for an hour with it before he showed me the large one they normally use. He laughed about that one for a while. We finally arrive to where he wants to put up the ladder. I extend the ladder, and he has me climb up to see over the gutters.

"Now, Bill, I want you to look really close at the roof and the gutters." I'm still getting used to that name. "What do you see?" I don't actually see anything. There happens to be no snow on the roof.

"Did the sun melt the snow off because the roof is dark?" I ask.

"No, the roof is actually heated, so the snow always melts off." Then he belly laughs, bent over and completely amused with himself. He had me carry this ladder and look up here just to tell me that. Looking down at him, I want to be mad, but I can't be. This guy is what I always thought a father should be like. He's almost falling on the ground laughing as I descend. I stand with my hands on my hips waiting for him to get done with his hysteria. Jake is someone I want to take home and meet Libby. I feel lucky to have this job with such a goofy old guy.

"Hey, I'm going in for lunch now," he says.

"I'll catch you later then." My lunch stays in my truck which is where I usually eat, especially today. Jake will be telling this story over and over. I watch Jake walk back in without the ladder, and he is still laughing. Climbing into my truck, I eat some cold leftover pizza. After a few minutes, I see a family walk out and get into their minivan. It makes me wonder if Libby and I will have any kids. That conversation is for another day.

As the van drives away, I suddenly hear and feel a powerful force and see the van utterly disappear. I jump out and run towards it. It must be some sort of sinkhole. It's the size of a small house, and the van is on its side down in it. They're screaming and opening windows, but the earth is still shifting under the van. They're approximately 20 feet below the road and almost that far away from me. I don't know how to help them. In a flash, I think about the ladder and run back for it. The idea of the van falling deeper into the earth is terrifying. I run with the ladder over my head while still extended, figuring I'll need it that way. It bends slightly with my steps, but I can keep it up. I reach the hole and they're now standing inside the van with the side door slid open. When they see me, they are screaming for help.

"Get on top of your van!" I yell. They scramble up as I extend the ladder to rest on the top of their van. The kids look young, maybe 10 and younger, I have no idea. "Have the smallest one get on top of the ladder and crawl to me!" The ladder has a small incline and luckily some bend to it. I lay my body down along my end, and the little boy comes across on his hands and feet like a monkey. If the earth falls in more, I'll still have the ladder held tight. He reaches me, and I tell him to lie on top of me. "Now send the girl!" She looks older and thicker, but she makes it across the same way. I have her lie on top of her brother. The mother knows she's next and is in position. As she crosses, the earth makes a breaking noise, and the van tips a little more the other way. She screams. "Just keep going!" I yell to her.

It takes her quite a long time to climb and has to be on her knees to do it. The husband is very anxious for her to hurry up. He and I lock eyes. His face shows signs of doom, but he knows his family will be safe at least. She makes it across. I tell her to lie on me and the kids to get on her. We need all the weight we have to support the husband across if the earth caves in more. He fumbles trying to get on, but climbs with some speed. By the time he reaches the middle juncture, the old ladder develops a slight bend. His wife is screaming in my ear. Just hurry up, fatty, I want to yell. He's breathing heavily, and his face is beet red. Finally, he makes it out of the hole, and I quickly herd everyone away from it.

A couple on the other side of the vast, empty lot are looking our way, but they have no idea what we're doing since the van isn't even visible. As we walk, the mother suddenly collapses on the ground. The husband looks at me in shock-he's still recovering from his climb. I turn her over and watch for her to breathe-nothing. I feel for her neck pulse and yell to him to go call an ambulance and take the kids with him. I don't want them to see what I'm probably going to have to do next. Please be a pulse. I flash back to the wife-beater hung upside down from the tree. He had a raging pulse, but she has nothing. I start to do compressions on her. After a while, I give a couple breaths while holding her nose then back to compressions. I see folks running towards me, thank god. I just keep doing compressions because I don't want to put my mouth on her again. They have me step away, gladly. I see the husband with the kids staying back towards the lodge. He and I lock eyes again. Jake is now running out of the building with some of the other maintenance staff. I hear a machine talking.

"Stand clear, press shock." One man pushes a button. "Resume CPR," the machine says. A woman starts compressions again. She's very good. Standing nearby, I want to go back to my truck and escape the scene, but I'm a little too committed at this point. Soon the machine speaks. "Press analyze, stand clear." She does not look like the same woman who was just crawling across an inclined ladder...then I hear a breaking noise again. I look back to where the van is, and the sinkhole must be shifting more. "Stand clear, press shock, resume CPR," the machine says again. Then she starts to wake up just as I hear the ambulance coming from a ways away. The woman is turned onto her side, and her family runs back towards her. I walk to my truck without anyone noticing. I just want to finish my pizza and hope there are no more sinkholes. Jake can go and get the ladder back.

They take her away, but her husband stays behind. I walk to the back of the lodge to go inside. I can't believe there was a sinkhole. My God, maybe we'll find a mammoth here or something. Is this a known thing in Montana? Where is Jake now? I feel a little tired and sit down in the break room. Nobody is in here. I lay my head down.

"There you are!" Jake bursts in. I think he woke me up. "We've been looking for you, Bill. Come on!" I bet the husband just wants to tell me thanks or something. I thought we communicated enough already and had an understanding. We reach the front doors and people are all over. There are news vans here and cameras. Oh no, I don't want to be on TV. This is not good. I pull my hat down some.

"Jake, why didn't you tell me this was all going on?"

"I knew you wouldn't come if I told you. I can tell you're a private guy, but you saved the day!" He pats me on the back as he leads me right into the commotion. I can't think of how to get out of this. At least, my name has changed, so that will probably help, and this will probably just be a Montana thing. I see the husband now, and he is making his way to me through the crowd. He puts his arm around me, and the cameras look to be rolling. Crap.

"And this is the guy who saved us. He led us out of the sinkhole on a ladder. I thought the earth was going to swallow us all up. It was terrifying." He is hugging me now. "Thank you, thank you for your help." His kids are hugging me, too. Some fancy woman with too much makeup shoves a microphone in my face.

"Sir, what is your name?"

"Um, Bill Cantwell, ma'am"

"We understand that after saving the family from the sinkhole, you then performed CPR on Mrs. Woodward." She seems to be waiting for me to talk.

"Well, she just dropped down, and it all turned out ok. All the chickens made it across the road." Then the woman laughed and took the microphone away, thank you. Jake is standing on the other side of me as I try to get away, but he holds me there.

"If you're just tuning in, we had a sinkhole develop here at Cedar Creek Lodge. Montana has had its share of sinkholes, but mostly they've been south of the Lewis and Clark National Forest along the Belt Meteor Crater. That area is about 200 miles south of here. So, Bill, how long have you been working here at the lodge?"

"Well, a couple weeks now."

"After today, I hope you get a raise." She focuses on the husband now. I slip out of Jake's grasp and back up into the crowd. "I guess you'll be heading to the hospital."

"Yes, I wanted to thank...Bill..." I just go back inside.

7
MIDGET FINSTER

I've been in this prison for over two months now. I been told I might get an early release for overcrowding. Tom has been ridin' my ass every day. At this point, any small miracle will do. I follow all the rules and don't cause trouble. Plenty of people pick on my height, but I'll be out of here long before most of them will. Unfortunately, Tom is a needed commodity. I am hot meat around here-apparently girlish.

Eating lunch in the dining hall always brings on that familiar stench. It doesn't matter what we're eating, the tastes and smells are the same, sausage and rice. I have an oily glaze on my face from the lard oozing out of my pores. I physically feel like pig. A community TV plays the news during lunch. We get to see all that we're missing, which isn't much. Today it's about a sinkhole in Montana that almost swallowed up a family in their minivan. That is crazy.

I hear the news lady talking to the husband. His wife had a heart attack afterwards, and she was rushed to the hospital. Apparently, they can't find the guy who saved them. I hear them talking as I try to cut this sausage brick.

Thank you, thank you for your help. what is your name sir, Bill Cantwell, ma'am. We understand that after saving the family from the sinkhole, you then performed CPR on Mrs. Woodward. Well, she just dropped down and it all turned out ok. All the chickens made it across the road.

I freeze while chewing. What did that guy just say? He talked about the god damn chicken crossing the road. Oh my God, it did sound like the guy from my brother's taped conversation. He's a white guy, too. I stare at him, hiding behind his hat. I see you, buddy-tall, nice looking guy. Where did they say this was? Please speak again, let me hear your voice again. *If you're just tuning in, we had a sinkhole develop here at Cedar Creek Lodge. Montana has had its share of sinkholes, but mostly they've been south of the Lewis and Clark National Forest along the Belt Meteor Crater. That area is about 200 miles south of here. So, Bill, how long have you been working here at the lodge? Well, a couple weeks now. After today, I hope you get a raise.* Cedar Creek Lodge in Montana, very interesting. Bill Cantwell, well, Mr. Bill Cantwell, I think we have a date with destiny. I can't eat any more of this. My stomach wants chicken.

8
LIBBY

Looking out the front window, the scene is beautiful. This house sits up on a hill. The driveway winds down and disappears, and trees surround us. My new favorite trail winds down the hill off to the right. When spring gets here, and the stream at the bottom isn't frozen, I hope to find some fish. I hope to find so many creatures, but I haven't gone far away for fear bigger animals. I often think about water, my old pond, my new stream, my nightmares, and my dead sister. I think about Dad. His murder was so senseless and meaningless. Ivan should have just figured out something else. He was a cold-blooded killer and a physician, sick. Greed, arrogance, and abuse made Ivan a monster. I wish I wasn't thinking about Ivan, but something has happened. I'm not positive yet, but I'm sure something has happened.

I wonder if Mom, Dad, and Cassie are together now. I'm kidding myself because I don't really believe in that. But I do remember the strong feelings I would get down by my pond. I felt a calmness and a stir that happened together. That stupid fish would keep coming by. My dreams of drowning followed by Earl drowning. How does all that all come together without The Powers That Be.

I keep looking out the window, wishing things could be different. Patrick is great and all, but we're hiding in the hills of Montana. Archie got too far away from me a couple days ago, and now he's missing. Patrick hasn't even noticed and I haven't said anything. I just hope he comes back, but I fear Archie was killed. I just can't think about it.

When will I see my aunt and cousins again? I know we weren't that close, but they're all the family I have now. Do they even think about me? They couldn't get a hold of me if they wanted to. Patrick thought they might be tracked or something so we should break all ties for a while. I'm happy about his mom coming to visit; having company would be nice. Tonight it's supposed to start snowing. Spring will be a welcome relief from the isolation. I need to start a new life now that we're away from the dangers.

I've been researching going back to school. There's a school in Kalispell where I could become a nurse aide. Then I could later get a nursing license. Now that the shock of Earl has subsided and the long flight here is done, I've been feeling so much better. Patrick found a job quickly, so it's my turn to start my next chapter.

Patrick has been very patient with me. The other night when we made love, I was ready to be close to him again. He is mine, and I know he wants to take care of me. We'll work out some of the communication problems we have. We're young and in love; we're allowed to not get everything right. Our relationship has had some major hurdles to overcome, to say the least. Everything will work out fine. I see Patrick's truck coming up the driveway. Put on a smile.

He looks very frustrated and doesn't make eye contact when he enters. He hangs his coat and hat on the hook and sits down.

"Well, today was another life changer." I walk over and sit by him.

"What happened?"

"I was outside eating lunch in my truck when a family in a minivan fell into a sinkhole right in front of me. It was crazy. I've never seen such a thing. I used a ladder to get them out. When that was over, the mother had a big ol' heart attack right in the parking lot, so I had to start CPR on her. It was crazy. I think she'll make it; she woke up."

"That's unbelievable," I say with caution. I know he wouldn't want any of this attention on him. Hopefully that is all it was.

"Then later, the place is packed with the news people and I'm suddenly doing an interview with all the cameras. Me!" Oh no, this won't make him happy. This will not be a good time to tell him any more news. Please say we don't have to move again. I don't know what to say. I don't know what consequences this could have. I put my hand on his leg and wait for him to say more. He looks me in the eyes now.

"At least my name is different and I had my hat pulled down some, so I think it'll be okay. I mean, it's probably just be a local thing. The sinkhole itself will be the focus now, I hope."

"Right, thank goodness you did that. I'm sure it will be fine." I hope so. He doesn't look so sure, and he has that look in his eye like when he saw Becka on the floor. He was worried but stayed very calm. I try to distract him. "Maybe we should get ready for the snow coming tonight."

"Right, I'll go out and bring in more wood." He stands.

"I'm making us omelets tonight, first time ever." I get up and walk away to seem busy. He puts his coat and hat back on and goes out. I hate for him to worry about this. He was just getting used to living in peace. We may never have true peace.

The omelets turn out to be more like scrambled eggs with ham and cheese mixed in, but still good. I wash the dishes while Patrick watches the evening news, and there he is. A couple times, I can see his face on the screen, but he's a guy named Bill. Later, I see Jake standing next to him. He does look like a nice guy, and he smiles a lot.

"I wonder if your mom will see this, then we'd know how far they broadcast it," I say. "You could tell her to watch the news tonight to see if you're on it." He just watches without saying anything or acknowledging me. In the zone, like the time he was first planning our escape to Montana. He was shut out from his surroundings. He's a planner. He has planned his way from childhood till now, even though most of his plan was forced on him, but he still had an end in sight. Where will it end now? And when? Now they're taking about the weather and the upcoming snow storm.

I feel almost trapped here. With Patrick worried about his TV appearance, his friend Kull, and who knows what else, I hate to talk about these issues and remind him of them even more. I don't want to be the naggy little woman. He doesn't share many of his thoughts. I feel like I'm that way too. I can't even remember our relationship before the darkness started.

This is where our communication could improve. Sometimes we need to talk about the shit that has happened to us. How is Patrick affected by all he has been forced to do? I don't know. I can't ask him. Does he have nightmares? Does he ever look at his hands and remember what they were used for? I can't think about it. I shove it all into my shell.

We were once kids getting to know each other, so innocent. When was the last time we had fried chicken and potato salad, because I have no idea. I'm starting to second guess my decision again. I had the chance to go away alone and make a start fresh. Instead, I'm holed up in a snowy peak without even a car yet. I could have gone down south. I could be waitressing on the beach, living in a bungalow, and using a bike. All my money could be safely kept and saved. I've lived through enough now that I think I can take care of myself.

But I did come here. I came here to be with this person, but is he permanently damaged inside? A person would have to have some repercussions from being forced to kill, dissect, and bury. I have to put that out of my mind. I do love him. I fell in love almost immediately, and I want to be with him. So why does part of my brain keep telling me a different story? Am I just a stupid girl? Am I meant for something else? Can we get beyond our pasts? Do I need to worry about the dead bodies buried on my land? Just a small detail.

9

Last night there was no cuddling, kissing, or talk, for that matter. Patrick is contemplating, obviously, but he doesn't want to share. "I am right here!" I want to yell, but never do. I think about my house and if I should put it up for sale. I feel like Dad's equipment should be sold off and not sit around, but I also don't want anyone going around the place. I don't want to ask him; I don't want to bring up part of what he used to do. I guess it can wait a while. At least until this recent event passes.

It's morning, and I'm attempting breakfast food again, pancakes this time. Pancakes I can do. Bacon grease in the skillet with some cinnamon and corn meal in the mix. Pure maple syrup tops it off. Patrick is trying to smile this morning. Maybe he realizes he was ignoring me last night. That smile on his handsome face gets me every time. It's Saturday morning, and I have him all weekend. A new thick blanket of snow covers the ground, and it is still snowing steadily. After we eat, we decide to search for a lightly used four wheel drive car for me, or maybe a truck. I have a feeling I'll end up getting some sort of SUV because we'll need the room. I picture the beach again-warmth and sunshine. I could have gone there...

We suddenly hear screaming outside. It sounds like a man, and he's screaming for his life. We look at each other like "what now!" Patrick jumps up and looks out the window, while I'm frozen in place.

"I see someone down among the trees, and a bear is beside him. Now the person is on the ground." He starts putting on his boots.

"Are you going out there? Patrick, you can't go out there. Someone might have found you!"

"I don't really have a choice. I have to find out who it is. Just stay here and keep the doors locked." He pulls some guns out from under the couch. My jaw drops. "Here, here's a smaller one." He quickly shows me how to use it. "Just pull this hammer back and shoot." I peek out the window while he's putting his coat on. I don't see anything but white; the snow is about two feet thick. I grab a chair to stand on to see better. We hear screaming again. Another nightmare to face. Patrick is quickly out the door.

I watch him aim as he's heading towards the trees and down the slope. I hear a shot while he points the gun in the air. Then I can see movement. The bear is running away. I can barely see him standing over something, and he must be talking. He's not aiming the gun or anything. He's bent over now...examining probably. Is someone dead? Who is it? Will there be more? I can't take this. How could anyone possibly find us. We'll never be safe and free. Patrick is lifting someone up under his arms and trying to drag them uphill through the snow. It's too hard for him. I see him look up towards me and wave at me to come down. It must be safe. I feel some relief. I put on my gear and head down the hill. It's hard to walk down without falling, even in his footprints. My anxiety rises again as I'm about to see who it is.

I reach them, and see Jason, the detective. Is he crying from pain or from shock? Our eyes meet, and he seems to show relief. I see some blood on the snow. Then I see blood down by one of his feet and on his shoulder. His coat is ripped and blood is surrounding it. Patrick gives me instructions because I'm speechless.

"Libby, can you lift his feet up so we can get him to the house?" I attempt to lift his feet. He cries out some when I grab the bloody one. I'm not able to keep hold of him and walk up the hill. It's too much weight on the slippery snow. We put him back down. "I'm sorry about this, but it's the only way we can get you to the house." Patrick bends down and hoists Jason over his shoulder and stands up. Jason cries out in pain from the throw over. Patrick stands up slowly and starts walking up the hill. I follow behind watching Jason. He doesn't look up at me. He just tries to keep his arm from moving. "Libby, put a blanket and sheet over the couch." I run ahead of him and open the door. I find a blanket and sheet in the closet and prepare the couch for a bloody mess. Patrick tries to gently place him on the couch while he's breathing hard. "Let's see how bad it is."

Patrick kneels down beside him and takes off his coat. Jason's left shoulder has several claw marks across it. I don't see any bone, but it's bleeding still. "Libby, grab some towels." I gladly walk away while nausea suddenly sets in.

The bloody smell is familiar and revolting. I'm still wondering what he's doing here. Is he here to arrest us? Does he know about the bodies or something about Dad? Why is he alone, or maybe he isn't alone. I grab the towels. "Hold these to his shoulder and press." I comply. Patrick moves to Jason's feet. He takes the boot off the good foot, then carefully does the same with the bad one. Jason grabs the edge of the couch with his right hand and groans while the boot slides off. Patrick rips his pants up his left leg. There are claw marks around his ankle and up on his calf. "You're lucky that was a young bear. The damage isn't bad."

Patrick gets up and goes into the bathroom and comes back with some supplies. "I have supplies ready because I know there are bears. This guy was out there eating a granola bar and watching us, Libby." I am still speechless. I'm waiting for the ball to drop, and I'm surprised Patrick is helping him.

I finally speak. "Should we just take him to the hospital?"

"The storm is still in the area, and it is too far away. I'm sure we can just patch you up right here. Right, Jason?" Patrick talks with sarcasm. Like he has a plan already. He opens up a bottle of something and pours it on the leg wounds. Then he takes tape strips and pulls the skin together as best he can and tapes it up. Then he pours a little more medicine on him. It has a strong antiseptic odor. After wrapping it up in gauze, he places a pillow under Jason's leg.

Next, he moves back to the shoulder. When I take off the towel, the blood has stopped oozing, but nausea takes over again and I run to the bathroom, and vomit, followed by dry heaving. I decide to stay in there, because I don't want to face the consequences that have come along with Jason being at our house. Our hideaway, states away, hidden in the hills and back country. Yet here he is.

Changing my mind, I go back out and face the outcome. They both look at me. Jason's shoulder is bandaged up.

"Jason was just about to tell me what he's doing here." Patrick looks at him. I feel weak in the legs and sit down along a wall, not wanting to get too close to either of them. I'm very confused about how this is happening. "We're waiting, detective." Patrick seems so calm. Here he is fixing him all up, not even knowing why he's here in the first place.

"Well, first, thank you for carrying me up here and bandaging me up." Jason looks back and forth between us, like he's wondering himself what's going on. This makes me all the more confused. How did he find us? "I think we should just call an ambulance to come and get me, and I'll get out of your hair," Jason suggests.

"I don't think so. You'll be just fine. I'd just like to hear why you're here." Patrick says calmly.

"Um, well, I couldn't get hold of Libby anymore, and her house seemed empty. I was worried about her after that last attack from Earl. There's still an investigation going on, and she disappears. I just wanted to make sure she was okay."

I'm stunned. That's why he's here, because he didn't know where I was? He then knows nothing and traveled all this way to check on me.

"Jason, detective, how did you find us here?" Patrick is trying hard to stay calm. I can see he's in the mode that in a split second, everything can change. Patrick has inhuman reflexes and reaction times that blow my mind. He's just waiting to hear how Jason found us. "We're waiting." I look at Jason as he decides how to assess the situation he's in. Perhaps, he can also tell at this moment that Patrick is a sharp tuned reactor. A person you shouldn't mess with, a person who gets the job done. It must have been the spot on the TV.

"When I last saw Libby, she was alone, scared, and vulnerable. I was worried about her and her safety. I put a GPS tracker in her backpack. I just wanted to make sure she was safe." He put a tracker in my backpack? I look at Patrick. He's still looking at Jason.

Patrick asks, "So, you came all this way to see if Libby was okay?" He nods his head. So, it wasn't the TV; it was from me. I left him alone to go to the bathroom, and he went out to his car. That's when he must have planted it. Is that even legal? Isn't that an invasion of my privacy? I have no words to say because I don't know what is going to happen next. Will Jason just leave and everything will be fine? I have a feeling it won't be that simple. Nothing in my life is simple anymore. Just the thought of more stress makes me get up and proceed to the bathroom again. I heave and heave. My stomach can't take any more turmoil. As I lean over the toilet, my breasts are sore. I cry.

10
JASON

I am staring eye to eye with Patrick. I want to thank him again for helping me, but I also feel very vulnerable to this boy or man sitting here. Why are they here? It's like they're in hiding. My wounds hurt terribly, but he did bandage me up skillfully. I saw him use tea tree oil, very archaic. He is definitely not an unskilled boy. I don't know much about Patrick, but he seems to handle situations with authority for such a young person. I can see why Libby loves him. He has a strong, fierce personality, and she needs a father figure to take care of her.

I can hear Libby getting sick again. Patrick seems to be deciding what to do with me. Libby walks back out and slides down the wall again. She looks so pale and frail. Patrick just focuses on me.

"Could I have my phone back now? Thank you for getting it for me." I ask, even though he actually took it out of my pocket when he frisked me on the ground. He checked all my pockets and sides for weapons, I would assume. He didn't find anything. Just my phone. Luckily, I keep my Ruger LCP in the small of my back in a case hooked to my pants. Most people don't want to see a detective with a gun at their side, so I carry mine behind me. I can still feel it there.

"I don't think so. I'm going to keep your phone for now. I found you on my property with no apparent cause, so the phone is mine." Patrick gets up and pulls two more guns out from under the couch and moves them to the bedroom. "You can stay here on the couch where I can see and hear you. When you're feeling better, you can leave, and I never want to see you again. You can see that Libby is fine, so no more worries. Right?"

"Right, I am glad to see that Libby is fine." I look over at her. She clearly doesn't look fine. She looks lost. "Do you have any Tylenol I can take?" Patrick watches me for a short time more and gets up. He takes his dressing supplies with him to the bathroom. Then he goes to the kitchen and comes out with water and two Tylenol. I watch Libby get up and go to her bedroom, I assume, and shut the door. Patrick goes in also and shuts the door. I'm trapped here in their living room. How is this going to work? Do I just act friendly, when they know I'm clearly here for no other reason than to see Libby. My car is close to the end of their driveway. I was just going to walk up close to the house and see that Libby was okay. I cannot believe a bear attacked me, and now I'm wounded and stranded on their couch. I could probably walk, but even with my leg elevated on this pillow, it's throbbing intensely.

I'm thankful for Patrick's help. I don't know how much more damage that bear would have done if Patrick hadn't scared it away. It startled me so much that I hadn't even thought to get my gun out at first. Then I was afraid my little gun would have just wounded it and made it madder, so I didn't want to use it. I threw the granola bar away from me. The bear ate it and came back for more. I've never been more terrified. I'm thankful to be safe and on this couch right now. It's just so awkward. I severely overstepped my detective protocol, but I just had to see her. I decide to slip my gun and holder off my pants and hide it in the couch cushions.

They must be whispering to themselves, no doubt. I look around. I don't see any landlines. There is a TV in front of me. A fireplace is crackling away. I see some dog bowls by the door, but I haven't seen a dog. I do remember Libby having a dog. This house is nice, nothing fancy. How did they ever end up here? I feel tired from the long drive here and the bear attack. I stayed in a hotel last night, but without much sleep. I was flooded with thoughts of how to present myself at their place. This is not how I saw myself ending up. Did I think Libby would see me and run into my arms? I just had to see her.

I'm awoken later on by the noise in the kitchen. I ask Patrick to help me to the bathroom. He stays on my right side so I can put my arm around him as I hop along, then he leaves me alone. Patrick is taller by a few inches and obviously stronger. He has the rugged good looks that most girls probably go for. I keep my left arm down, and it doesn't feel too bad. My leg, on the other hand, feels very swollen. I'm afraid to put any weight on it. It hurts each time I jar it with a hop, but I try not to let it show. He helps be back to the couch.

"Thank you," I say. He just goes into the kitchen. Libby is making something.

"We're having some pancakes and sausage," she says. "Hope you feel like eating."

"I could eat some, thank you again. I hope I won't be too much trouble. I suppose I should apologize for sneaking around, but you understand my concern. I couldn't get a hold of you, and you seem to be a target. I was worried." I look at her, pleading for understanding and not judgement.

"I guess I should have told you I was leaving town. I just wanted a clean break. It seemed like people were looking at me and talking about me. Patrick talked about this place and the park nearby. I just said let's go for it." She smiles. "So he came out and found a place."

"Just like that. You make it sound so easy. Weren't you in Kentucky with your mother?" I look at Patrick and try to be as friendly as I can while asking questions.

"Yes, at first, then I came here. I've been here before and loved the area. I have a friend here and the hunting is amazing."

"Well, that is great. I'm so glad you guys are doing fine. Hopefully in a couple days, I'll be feeling better and out of your hair."

"Yes, that would be great," Patrick says, while looking at me. I would like to just go back to my hotel, but I can see the snow outside coming down. I'm sure my car is buried. I feel so helpless and exposed. I realize my coat is gone.

"Um, where's my coat?"

"I put it in the wash, and I thought we could just duct-tape the scratch marks. That should keep you till you get a new one." Libby is stirring up the batter. The sausage smells wonderful. Patrick gets up, puts on his boots, grabs his coat, and goes outside without saying a word. "Don't mind him, Jason, he isn't much for talking. He's been busy getting this place ready and working. He'll have to go to work tomorrow, and I'll help you get more cleaned up then. We'll find some clothes or something that will fit you and go over that wrapped up leg." I'm relieved Patrick will to be gone tomorrow.

"I really am sorry about this," I say.

"I'm just glad you're okay. That could have been terrible if we weren't here. You come all this way to check on me. I feel bad about that."

"Don't feel bad. I just had a feeling you were in danger, and I had to know if you were all right. You might want to take the tracker out of your bag."

"Patrick already did. He said I can't give you your phone either. He took the card out of it and destroyed it. I'm sorry about that. He still wonders why you're here, a little paranoid." I don't say any more. I just lie here at the mercy of this couple. This mysterious young couple. Patrick comes in with an arm full of wood, even though there's already plenty by the fireplace.

After we eat, he turns on the TV. Patrick sits in a chair beside the couch and watches some YouTube stuff about tractors while Libby sits in front of the fire. She's looking at a book or something. I pretend to watch the tractor show, but I know nothing about tractors. I grew up in the city. Dad didn't know how to fix anything. We kept most things fairly new, and when something broke, we bought a new one. I don't think that's how Patrick grew up. Finding out what his uncle was capable of, it makes me wonder what his dad was like. I did find out that his dad left them several years back. I wonder where he went. Maybe Patrick's dad is in Montana too.

Patrick takes me to the bathroom one more time before they go to bed. I want to ask for a toothbrush, but I don't. The leg is throbbing again. I do ask for more Tylenol. Libby gives me another pillow and blanket.

11

In the morning, I'm greeted with a large stick. Patrick must have gone out and found one that I can use for a cane while he's not here. In other words, use this not Libby. I thanked him, and he was gone. The snow has stopped for now, and the sun is streaming in. I try out my cane to go to the bathroom. The throbbing has subsided a little. My clothes are still ripped and covered with dried blood, and I look horrible. I try to brush my teeth with my finger and wash my face. I run some water over my hair and smooth it down. Stumbling past the kitchen, I cane hop to the window and sit down.

It's so quiet here. It's hard to imagine that just yesterday my life almost ended in this tranquil setting. I'm still in shock over that confrontation with death. I've never been so scared, and I hate that I owe my life to a guy I wish would just disappear. A guy who seems to have everything: the girl, the face, the body, the house, the calm reserve, and the money. How does he afford this place? It wouldn't be my business to come right out and ask, but it is puzzling. I don't even know if he worked back in Alliance. He is working somewhere now, must be a great job. I'm sure a guy like him could do about anything he sets his mind to. Guys like that are maddening. Hope Dad isn't missing me too much yet; he'll be wanting my skills eventually.

Libby opens her bedroom door and smiles as she goes into the kitchen. She looks beautiful with her hair a mess, dark circles under her eyes, sloppy robe, slippers, and a smile that can lighten the entire state. Oh my God, Jason, you need to stop this. She's not yours, and you'll have to leave her. This could be the last time I ever see her, how very sad. I may have to put up with Patrick a few more days just to get a few more days. My ankle hurts really bad...

She retreats back toward her room. She speaks to me before closing the door.

"I'll find you some clothes, and we could change your dressings. We should check how your cuts look." Her bedroom door shuts. She almost acts nervous. I know I feel strangely excited being here alone with her. I did travel across the country to see her. It might be obvious that I have feelings for her, and they would surely know that. So, the fact that Patrick left me here with her is puzzling to me. Do they really think it's just about police work? I stare out the window again. She comes out holding some clothes.

"Here are some of Patrick's sweats that should fit you, and they stretch. I thought you might want to sit in the shower to wash then we can change your dressings."

"That would be great. Do you have a plastic chair?"

"No, but I have a bucket we can turn over." We laugh at that. "Maybe we should put a bag over your foot and around your shoulder."

"Well, I'll just get myself to the bathroom first." I feel the need not to be quite as good at getting around as I could be.

"Oh, let me help you," she insists. She comes right over and helps me in. She finds the bucket and places it down in the shower. "Let me get some bags." When she leaves, I can smell her still, mesmerizing. I shut my eyes and tell myself to stop. She comes back and tells me to tie this trash bag up around my leg. She helps me take my shirt off and tapes a bag around my shoulder and under my armpit. That is a great idea. "That should hold." Libby slowly backs up. "I'll just shut this now." I look down at myself. My body is probably not near as impressive as Patrick's.

I turn on the shower while I pull off my pants. I sit on the floor to put on the bag. I then remember my gun. Surely she won't inspect the couch and find it. Naaaa. I decide I'll just have to stand in the shower. Sitting on that bucket is just asking for a fall. I just prop the leg up on the ledge. There must have been more blood on me than I thought. The water flows pink for quite some time. The hot water feels wonderful. I picture Libby taking a shower in here. No, just finish up without falling. Ignore the erection.

I manage getting out, and I sit back down to towel off and dress. I leave my clothes in a pile. I stand to look in the mirror. I could never get away with the messy hair, rugged outdoors look like Patrick has every day. I find a comb and smooth out my thin hair. I'm not bad looking, just average, I guess. Well, here goes nothing, you ugly stalker. I open the door.

"Do you like oatmeal?"

"Love it, thank you. I smell coffee, heaven." I take a deep cleansing breath. Try not to act weird. I hobble with my stick to the kitchen table. I can see she changed the sheet that was under the blanket. My coat is on the coat rack. The shoulder of it is already taped up. "Love the coat," I laugh.

"I still can't believe that happened, so scary."

"Yea, I was afraid to go to sleep. Thought I might have a nightmare about it."

She looks at me. "Do you ever get nightmares?"

I realize she's asking me this question seriously. "I guess not. Why? Do you?" She brings the oatmeal and coffee over to the table. Sugar and milk are already on the table. I use some of both.

"I have the same nightmare over and over again. For several years, the same one. I wondered if other people do the same thing."

"Do you want to tell me about it?"

"No, I was just curious. Are you in much pain?"

"Not unless I move." I smile. "This tastes good. Thank you again."

"I still can't believe you came all the way here."

"When I couldn't reach you, I was worried something else happened. Then the tracker moved so far from Ohio, I even thought you might have been kidnapped. I went to Earl's funeral, and the people who came obscured the whole incident and wouldn't acknowledge me. Mouths were shut while eyes were wide open. Then you were gone. Nobody talked. I was worried." I look into her eyes to see if she understands and accepts my answer. I don't mention that I couldn't stop thinking about her, and I had to make sure she was okay. I need to change the subject. "Didn't you have a dog?"

"Well, I did till a few days ago. He ran off. I'm afraid something got him."

"I'm so sorry. Did Patrick go and look for him? He seems to be a handy-type person."

"I didn't mention it to him. He has a lot of things going on, and his work has been crazy. A sinkhole opened up at the lodge where he works, and he saved a family that was trapped in the hole." I stare at her. Unbelievable. I hate this guy even more now.

"That's amazing. He works at a lodge."

"Yea, he does maintenance."

So, he does a regular type job, not one that could buy this place. I just have to ask. "Libby, how do you guys afford to live here? Your other houses aren't even sold."

She looks down for a beat. "I got some insurance money when Dad was...you know. We used that for a big down payment here."

I never thought of that. There I go sticking my nose into her business again. She must think I'm judging her life and choices.

"I'm sorry I asked, it's none of my business." Then I think back to the fact that she didn't tell Patrick her dog went missing. Has he not even noticed? That's sad.

"Let's get your dressings changed. We need to check for any infection. Patrick said he would pick up some more supplies on his way home. He texted me that the roads are still bad; the sun is just making ice now."

"I guess your cell phones work good up here."

"They do." She takes the dishes to the sink and rinses them out. I try not to watch her, but I can't help myself. Look at the window. She brings the dressings over. She does my leg first. The ace is unwrapped. Blood soaked through most of the gauze, and it stuck to the skin. She slowly starts to peel it off, then she turns pale. She has to get up and run to the bathroom. I hear her hurl up the oatmeal. Now I feel bad. I continue to peel off the old dressings so she won't have to. The white tape strips are still holding the edges together. I drip some more tea tree oil over the strips and let it dry. I just put the same ace wrap over top without any gauze. Maybe I'm glad she doesn't see how good the cuts look.

As I start to untape my shoulder, she comes out.

"I'm sorry," she apologizes. Crazy girl.

"Please don't, I'm sorry. I didn't know you would get sick with blood."

"I don't, usually."

"What are you, pregnant?" I ask jokingly. She doesn't say anything. She's not laughing or looking at me, but then she does. Her eyes say it all. She is pregnant. "Wow, Libby, you don't look very happy about it. Have you been sick a lot?"

"I haven't verified it, but I suspect I am." I stop messing with my bandage.

"You need one of those tests from the drug store. I'm sure Patrick can get you one."

"No, no, I haven't told him. I don't want to tell him just yet. He has enough going on." I'm a little confused now.

Libby doesn't tell him about her dog, and she doesn't tell him she thinks she's pregnant. Why?

"I'm sure he'll be happy to hear it, don't you think?" She doesn't answer me. I'm confused.

"Let me help you with your shoulder."

"No, no, I can get it. Can you just open a couple packs of that gauze." I finish peeling off the old bloody bandage. The slashes were deeper here, and the cuts are not fully joined together. I drip some oil on and put gauze over top and hope for the best. At this point, I wouldn't want to leave her to go to the hospital. She's still a lost girl. I feel the closeness to her; it's stimulating. The fact that she may be pregnant changes nothing about my true feelings for her. I'm slightly overjoyed that I know something so intimate about her that Patrick doesn't. Is he not the perfect man? Libby was alone after Earl attacked her, and she's still alone here. She keeps all her problems to herself. Patrick has no clue what's going on outside his world. At least, that's what it seems. I put the shirt back on and hop to the couch. After I get my leg elevated, it feels better. I'm still blown away by her news.

"How far along do you think you are?" I ask. Now she looks sick again. "Libby, what is it?" She shakes her head and tears start to fall. She gets up and goes into her bedroom and closes the door. That's when it hits me. Oh my God. Could she be pregnant with Ivan's baby? How long has it been? That was around two to three months ago now. No wonder she doesn't want to tell Patrick.

12

I look around this room again. It looks settled. The dust even looks old. It doesn't look like it was just moved into. Maybe the last owner sold the contents with the house. I decide to try to move my left shoulder around some. It hurts, but it needs to move. I'm so glad it wasn't my dominant arm that was injured. I check that my gun is still in place. I should be good to drive in a couple more days because by then my welcome will be spent. Patrick wants me gone; I'm sure he suspects my true feelings. Again, I think how surprised I am that he leaves me here with her, but then again, he doesn't seem to notice much about her. I just wish that Libby would want to leave with me.

She comes out of her room.

"I don't want to talk about it," she insists.

"Okay, we won't talk about it. I think you're supposed to be on vitamins or something is all I will say."

"I don't have a car or doctor yet. I just got here last week, which you are well aware." She smiles slightly and looks at me with eyes that tell me she appreciates the effort to check on her. She sits down at the table. "I've just been making plans. I'm going to go nursing school. Normally blood doesn't bother me."

"Nursing school sounds great. Is there a school in Kalispell?"

"Yes, I was just checking into it. You showing up threw me off my busy schedule." She smiles again.

"You said that Patrick has a friend in the area?"

"Yea, they met when they were kids. Patrick went to see him, and it sounds like this guy isn't doing so well. He didn't go into much detail." Of course he didn't. Patrick doesn't talk with her about most things.

"Libby, can I ask you something?" She looks at me. "Did you really want to come all the way here?" She looks out the window.

"Do you see it out there? It's beautiful, and I love to be outside with nature. There wasn't anything holding me back." She doesn't include Patrick in that scenario, but maybe I better change the subject before she leaves again.

"You know, if you need to go anywhere, you can take my car. It just might take a while to clean the snow off it."

"I hope you don't feel like a prisoner here. He was just suspicious when you were scoping us out. Now we know you were just concerned. I do want to thank you for caring. I hope you heal up okay."

"Patrick is pretty good at taking care of injuries. How did he learn that?"

"I'm not sure. He's always been aware of being prepared and defending yourself. He has taught me some off the wall stuff."

"Like what?" She hesitates. I can tell she doesn't want to tell me anything else about that subject. "How long have you two been together?"

"It's been about two and a half years now. I feel like it's just meant to be." I was afraid of that. She knows nothing different. Yes, he has saved her, but is he really good for her?

Later on, she makes some lunch. She makes hamburgers out of venison.

"Patrick butchered a deer soon after arriving here and just made most of it into hamburger. I add some spices and lots of cheese."

"So, he has a grinder?"

"He must, probably in the underneath room thing." She motions with her hands under the room. Oh, that is interesting. He does have another room for his stuff. I knew he was a hunter. I never got into that. With my dad being an insurance salesman, hunting was not part of his character. Dad and I enjoy talking about current affairs and politics. This hunting and outdoors life is new to me. I might have known not to eat the granola bar and apple outside if I was a hunter. Or maybe you do eat that stuff if you're a hunter and want to attract animals. I don't know the standard protocol there. I do know I only have a short amount of time left before the hunter comes back home. I need to make the most of the time we have together alone.

She brings the burgers to the table with some oranges. I decide to try to make this meal last a long time so we can sit and look at each other and talk. I'm an expert on how to eat slowly, thanks to my mother's example. She savored everything and could take up to two hours eating a good meal. I smile to myself remembering how she put her silverware down and closed her eyes to bask in the food. I channel her slow methodical chewing while Libby scarfs her food down. I decide to ask her more questions to keep her in her seat while I continue with my slow meal.

"Did you always live in Alliance?"

"Yea."

"Have you talked with your friends? What were their names?"

"Rashin and Hope. No, I haven't talked to them." She looks sad now. Abort, abort.

"You said your cell phones work here, right?"

"Yes, the phones do work up here on this hill. Down towards the creek, it loses signal."

"How many acres do you have here?"

She ponders that question. "I guess I don't really know."

Maybe I better quit asking her so many questions. She looks like she might take flight soon. I'm only halfway through my burger. I can tell it tastes different but still good. I start to peel an orange, but I have trouble.

"Oh, here, let me do that for you." I hand it to her. Her fingers are so small and delicate. She doesn't wear any polish, and I am guessing she isn't wearing any makeup either. Same old ponytail and sweat clothes on. She's so different from the other girls her age. I catch myself staring.

All of a sudden, water bursts out from under the sink. It flows over the floor boards. When she opens the cabinet door, water sprays in all directions. I hop over and reach down to turn off the water valve. Thank goodness Dad taught me that much. We look at each other and all the water and laugh.

"What a mess, now we need a plumber, or something," she says.

I look at the fittings. "I think they just need tightened back up. I can do it with your help." Please let me be good at this. "Do you have any wrenches or tools here?"

"Yea, downstairs. Let me help you go around the house, and you can see what we have."

"Sounds good." We go towards the door, and she pulls a chair out for me. She helps me with my boots and gets my coat on. I wait for her to do the same. I anticipate that we'll be holding on to each other, and I'm super happy her sink broke. A beaten down path winds around the house and down to a door on the back side. Of course it's locked, and she has to go back up to get the key. I stay propped beside the door. Behind the house is just hills of trees. The sight is beautiful, no doubt about it. My ankle is feeling the pain of being down and putting some weight on it. She's back with the keys.

"I don't really know which one it is." She finds the right one on the third try. The door opens, and she finds the light. Before us there is a workbench with plenty of tools to pick from. I see a meat grinder all cleaned up. And there's a big safe. I also notice the cement floor is so clean. It's especially clean on half the floor. Libby is looking at the tools, while I notice some strange marks on the wall. I try not to stare at them. I look up at the tools to find what we need. I point to two things that she can get for me. While she reaches for them off their perfectly positioned spot, I look back down at the wall. It looks like faint, ever so slight, blood stains. Almost like a small trail. The rest of the wall is clean, but right beside the workbench I see it. This is something a detective is trained to look for. My eyes went right to it. I suppose it could be from the deer, along with the clean floor, but it is creepy. The deer would be dead before coming in here; that much I know about hunting. I suppose stuff can happen while cutting. I put the thought out of my head.

"I'll take these up then come back down for you." I nod my head, still a little sickened. After she leaves, I bend down closer to the stains. I can't find any more spots, so I look under the workbench. It's too dark to see. That's when I see some old suitcases, and I mean old. There is no way Patrick brought them here. I stand up, knowing she will return any second. I want to say something about all of this, but I can't right now. I don't want to upset her and spoil this nice time. She helps me back up along the side of the house. It's harder this time going up, and the pain has worsened. Just get the job done.

I get down on my knees this time and tighten the big connector things. It looks good. I turn the water back on slowly. It seems to hold, so I turn it on all the way. All good.

"Yea!" She claps and pats me on the back then helps me get up. "Here, let's get you back on the couch." She fetches some towels and cleans up the floor and cabinet. I notice the cleaners under the sink do not look new either. It makes me wonder what's inside the other cabinets. I wait. Sure enough, she says she's going back down to put the tools away. "Patrick will never even know we had a flash flood." Right, we don't want to upset Patrick, do we?

As soon as she leaves, I heave myself to the kitchen cabinets and look in the ones on the end. I see old glasses and Tupperware stuffed in the back. Stuff that has been kept for quite a while. Not just moved in. I knew it. I hop back to the couch, and I'm almost winded. Calm down. Am I winded from not moving in two days, or winded from the fact that all this stuff was already here?

When she reappears, she returns the keys to the cabinet closest to the refrigerator. She shuts the door and takes the towels to the washing machine. I don't know what to do next. I wait till she settles down.

"I'll try it out." she says as she fills the sink to wash dishes. I elevate my leg on the pillows again and turn my head towards the window. I don't want her to catch me staring, and I have more to think about now.

13
PATRICK

When I come home from work, Libby and Jason are laughing about high school pranks or something. It's nice to see Libby laughing, I have to admit. She does light up a room. I'm sure Jason is having a nice time getting waited on. His wounds should be getting better, and he can be on his way. I think he took his job title a bit too seriously coming clear out to Montana to see if she was okay. It's a relief that that was all he was coming out here for. Good thing I didn't just kill him right off. But the question remains, what is he, in love with her or something? He has hardly been around her. He's also a few years older, sicko. Yet, here he is, laughing it up while I'm gone. I need to just stay cool. Libby would never leave me for this guy, city boy, cosmopolitan type. She's just enjoying some company. If he can help her get over what she has gone through, perhaps I should let him continue. She may need the company. Soon enough, she'll be ready to move on with her life, Jason will be long gone, and we will have a fresh start.

"How was work?" she asks me.

"A bunch of scientists or geologists showed up. They're measuring and studying the sinkhole. It's crowded with people just coming to see it. Too many cars to plow any snow, and I'm playing traffic control more than anything. Get this, that family is coming back next week because they want to thank me...again. The mom is getting out of the hospital soon. I told them, no cameras, and they agreed."

"That is so nice. Maybe I can come and meet them, too. Then I can see the lodge and hang out for the day. I would love that. I could meet Jake."

"It's a date, little lady." I say with a smile and lean in to kiss her. Take that Detective Trespass. I take off my boots and head for the shower. I decide to shave and put on some of my newer clothes. This will make him look like a dork all the more. I can play the game. My hair could use a cut. It's hard to tame down. I need to make an effort at having a polite, friendly conversation with them. Conversations have never been my forte...I'm more of a get the job done and get out kind of guy. Small talk makes my skin crawl. Small talk is like beating a dead horse. Small talk infuriates my logic. I can talk to Libby or Mom or Jake-necessary people, or people I care about, but that's it. Dad probably taught me this. He got right to the point, whether it was yelling or beating, then he was done with you. No small talk there.

When I emerge from my shower and self-pep-talk internally, they're watching TV. Then Libby jumps up and says she's making spaghetti for dinner. Wow, not breakfast food.

"Can I help you?" I ask.

"You can bring in more wood if you want, but you look so nice now."

"That's okay." I slip on my boots without tying them and go outside. That's when I notice the extra footprints going around the house. That's very interesting. I load up my arms with wood, and casually stride back in.

"Libby, were you guys outside today?" I ask nicely while adding to the fire. Jason sure seems quiet.

"Oh yea, the sink here broke. The pipe fittings were loose so we went around and found some tools so Jason could fix it. It was a mess."

"That's crazy. I'm surprised you didn't mention it."

"Well, I just didn't want to bother you about it. All fixed." I look over at him on the couch.

"Luckily, it was just a couple loose connections," Jason adds. Why does he look a little different to me. He almost looks more uncomfortable now than he did yesterday. Why would that be? I realize he was in the cellar, but that shouldn't be a problem. Did he do or say something to Libby? She seems the same.

"Yes, that is lucky. Are you feeling better and getting around better now?"

"I suppose, and I haven't developed a fever, which is good. I want to thank you again for bandaging me up. How did you learn to do that?"

I don't even know how to answer that. I had to bandage my mother and myself up many times growing up. It was second nature to take care of bleeding wounds. I could show him my backside.

"Hunting accidents, I guess. Read a lot of survival books."

"Libby said you like to be prepared." The small talk is clawing at my back like more wounds. I stand up and walk back towards the kitchen. Jason and I lock eyes.

"Smells good in here already." I say. "I'm working tomorrow, but the day after that we can do whatever you want."

"Let me think about it. I'm sure I can come up with something we can do around here. I think it's done snowing for a while, so that means hiking will be on the list. I can't wait to see some of the trails towards the park." I look over at Jason, letting him know that by then he should be gone. I'm sure he can tell exactly what I'm saying with my stare. I don't need a lot of words. Turning away, he then looks at the TV.

Libby and I eat at the table while Jason decides to stay on the couch. He says his leg is sore from being up on it today fixing the pipe. We play some country music and eat. Not much conversation taking place now, fine with me. Libby looks around the room while we eat. We don't make much eye contact. We used to not be able to take our eyes off each other. This makes me wonder about her now. I don't want to be the paranoid, possessive guy here, but I feel a presence. I feel like I'm hunting again, the peace mixed with the tense. Occasionally, I would bury myself partly in the ground. I could stay there for hours with the deer urine spread about. I could sense the heartbeat of the bucks when they passed by. I felt the tension in their movements, urgency. I feel some of that now. Just be cool. He'll be gone soon. She needs to see that you're confident and hospitable. Keep your switch turned on to nice guy.

I wash the dishes while Libby is doing some laundry. I see that Jason helped himself to the books. There's a small bookshelf with old western books and natural remedy books. He's reading a Zane Grey.

"These look like old books, Patrick. Did you bring them here with you?"

"No, a lot of this stuff came with the house. Someone must have died." Now I know what he's thinking. He can tell this house is not a recent move in but lived in.

"You didn't mention that. Did they die in here?" Libby asks.

"I don't know, best not to know. I haven't seen any ghosts. Do you want me to call the realtor?"

"No, you're right, best not to know."

"Guess whoever it was didn't have any family." Jason mentions.

"Guess not," I answer. I need to end this conversation. I look at Libby. "I'm going to look for a car for you, sound good?"

"Okay, babe." I go into the bedroom and shut the door. I don't want to answer any more of his questions. I hope he doesn't pursue this line of questioning anymore. I may have to kill him yet. The small talk is definitely over. It wouldn't be hard for him to find out the owner of this place has the same last name as Ivan. Jason might need to stay until I feel he's not a threat. I need to work tomorrow to look like I have nothing to hide. Glad he has no way to use the internet, unless he asks Libby to use her phone. I hope Libby won't miss him too much after he leaves. I just realized I haven't seen her dog, Archie, for a while.

Libby pops in to see me later. "Did you find anything?"

"I can't find much used. We may have to buy a new car." I say with a smile. No problem. Especially since this place has not cost me anything. Libby wouldn't even have to work, but I know she'll need her own thing. I wouldn't really have to work either, but I need to keep up appearances. I do like my job with Jake. When all this sinkhole drama is done, all the better. "I'll look a little more then come back out. Hey, Libby, where is your dog?

She hesitates. "He ran away. He just got too far away from me." I see the sudden sadness in her eyes.

"Why didn't you tell me?"

"Patrick, I know you have a lot going on with work, and you can't do anything about it."

"Come here." I say holding out my hand. She comes over and lies across me, and I hold her tight. Have I seemed too busy for her to talk to me? She hasn't shared much of her day-to-day life with me. "Libby, I'm sorry. Please tell me if you need anything. I don't always know the right way to act. I love you and want you to be happy."

"I'm fine. I'm afraid to get another dog. It might run away, too."

"I could put up a long line a dog could run on but can't run away."

"Okay, then let's go look for a dog after our hike. That's what we can do. I like having someone here with me."

"Great, but I'm not just talking about a dog. Are you okay with Jason being here? Is he asking too many questions?" Does she actually like having him here?

"No, I think he still feels embarrassed. I bet he'll leave tomorrow. He's moving his ankle more now, so I think he can drive. Then we can get back to us." That's all I needed to hear. She gets up to leave. How long can I stall in here before acting like a recluse? I'd like to know if he wants to ask me more questions in his innocent little way. I'll just have to ask him questions first. I power up to go out. I grab a soda from the fridge and ask if anyone else wants one. No takers. I sit on the chair beside the couch while Libby sits at the table. A Modern Family episode is playing. I like the little blonde.

14

The next morning, I get up for work. Last night, they talked a lot about high school. I didn't have much to add to the conversation. Jason and Libby had lots to say. I wasn't into any clubs or sports. School wasn't high on my to do list. I was too busy following Ivan's orders. Honestly, I don't remember much of a childhood at all. Most of it needed to be blocked out of my memory. Sometimes I want to be mad at Mom for keeping us in that house, but I think there was a time she did love him.

I remember that time when Uncle Jay visited us. It might have been when Grandpa died. Mom had everyone over to the house to eat. I must have been around eight. The real beatings hadn't started yet just the yelling. I never liked Jay, and neither did Dad. I can remember most of my cousins had left. My cousin, Poodle, was my favorite. Jay was still there. I remember Dad pulling him out of their bedroom, and Mom was crying. I saw Dad hit him outside a couple of times, and then he left. I never saw him again till Dad and I took that trip out here to Montana. Before we went home, we stopped here at this house, and Dad asked him for money.

Dad told me Grandpa gave all his money to his favorite son, Jay. He decided to see if his rich brother would spare any. Jay wouldn't even let us in the house. Jay told us that their Dad knew which son would amount to something. He looked at me and called me a scrawny little bastard. After that day, Dad became quite a bit meaner. I blame my uncle for part of my miserable life. I knew that someday I would see him again. His wife died young of cancer, and I never met her. They didn't have any kids.

I doubt we'll stay in this house for too many years. Someone might catch on to his disappearance. I pick up his mail at the post office. I'll tell them he had a stroke, if anyone ever asks. He didn't have a phone line or cell phone that I could find. I decided living in his house would be easier than finding one. It was also free of charge. I torched his safe open, but there wasn't much in it. That's okay. I don't need his stinking money. I pay his bills with his checks and his signature I easily found on documents.

I killed him quickly. He didn't even know who I was or saw it coming. A fire took care of most of him. The residual went down by the creek. I suppose I'm not quite as innocent as I was. This kill was not forced, but it sure was just as easy. I know Libby wouldn't like hearing this story. I know I don't deserve her. It is a troubled life I lead.

I see Jason sleeping on the couch, but he's probably faking. I would be. I hope he plans on leaving and there are no more surprises today. On the way to work, I picture Uncle Jay standing inside his door saying he doesn't want any help plowing his driveway. He told me to go find some other old person to bother. I acted like I fell on his sidewalk to get him out of his house, and I popped him right between the eyes. I wanted to quickly hide him, so I drug his fat ass around to the back of the house and that's when I found the back door. I pulled him inside and went to work. For once, I didn't want organs just revenge.

The traffic has already started with people coming to see the sinkhole. Police are here today to control the crowds. I flash my badge and get to pull into the designated area for employees. Being an employee is a new experience for me. I like it. I find working a legitimate job amusing. It's like going to an amusement park or something, which I have never done before. But I wonder how long I'll be on this ride. I have ended lives, taken over a house, changed my name, and now work an ordinary job. Can I carry on being William Noble Cantwell? How long can this charade last till another hurdle surfaces?

Jason found us, a sinkhole put me on the news, and the owner of the house I now live in has vanished with no explanation. Can I pull this off? What am I forgetting? Do I have reason to think Jason will cause a problem? Does he suspect more than he lets on? I'm sure he does. Will he investigate the previous owner? Maybe the owner died in the woods somewhere? He's just gone. My last name was Sipos before Mom changed us to Kessler after Dad's unfortunate exit. If Jason is gone when I get home, I'll feel much better, but if he is still there, tensions will surge. Maybe if he does like Libby, he wouldn't do anything to disrupt her life. Or would he do anything to get her away from me? If I ever had to leave her, I would hate it, but I would do it. I know she deserves better.

Jake is having coffee and joking with one of the lobby girls. When he sees me, a big smile crosses his face.

"There he is. Hey, Bill, the lodge is full, and we have to help out with the indoor maintenance today. Apparently, the kitchen ventilation went out, and until the repairs can be made, we have to get some fans set up." He starts walking towards the exercise room. "We're going to take these fans to the kitchen and close the fitness center." Yep, this job is hilarious. "I'm glad to be indoors for once. The police can handle the traffic today. When are you going to see 'your family' again?" He likes to joke about my heroism.

"Next week, sometime."

"I still can't believe that. It was really me who saved the day because I had you bring that ladder out."

"I don't remember anyone talking about you at all," I say with a smile. Jake is so corny. I've never met another man like him, corny and giggly, like a girl. My life would have been so different with him in it growing up. The evil in people, how does it even start? It passes through the veins in the blood. Am I evil? It runs through me, pumping me with known elements. Known evils. I suddenly fear for Libby. She should be free from me. What will I be forced to do next? I'll have to uproot us in a few years. What will I tell her? Well, Libby, the thing is, I killed the owner and took over his life and house. It's now time to go. He was another relative of mine, so no big deal.

It's no big deal to me, but I fear the rest of the world might think differently about my past actions. I should have just killed him and left, but the house is so perfect. Perfect size, setting, and the basement room is great for projects.

Just focus on the day. Set up the stupid fans and whatever other mundane job we take care of.

At lunch, I'm tempted to call home and see what's going on. What do they do all day? No, no, just wait and see. I don't want to know he's still there and be pissed off the rest of the day. If he needs taken care of, I'll take care of it. Libby still seems to be recovering from Earl. She stares off, seems quiet, reserved, and vulnerable. I guess Jason being concerned about her safety and keeping her company and them laughing can't be bad for her. He just needs to keep it professional. If he thinks the bear was scary, he hasn't seen me mad yet.

On my way home, I get a text from Libby saying Jason is still there. She says he plans on leaving tomorrow and that his ankle is still very sore. She knows I want him to leave and is giving me a heads up. I'm surprised he wants to be in my company another night. How can I stomach small talk with the lounge boy again? He doesn't know what pain is. I ask her if she wants me to bring anything home for dinner. She says no, she's making pancakes. Again...

When I get home, Jason is on the couch and Libby is nowhere.

"Where's Libby?" I ask.

"She went for a little hike, and took that little gun with her for protection." He looks me in the eye. "I know you're ready for me to be gone, but I have quite a long drive back. There's still a lot of swelling, and my temperature has increased. I'm getting the sweats. If it's higher tomorrow, I'm going to take myself to the hospital. I don't want to be on the road getting septic."

"Right, good idea," I agree. I walk back outside and look around. Is he stalling or really getting a fever? He didn't look bad. I noticed he had on different clothes, more of mine. I walk towards the little trail which leads to the creek. I don't see her anywhere. Do I want to take a walk or go back inside? I decide to head down. She must be sick of him, too. The snow on the trees has not melted off. It's beautiful. I'm sure Libby is ready to explore. I reach the creek, and I see her far off sitting on a log. She looks towards me and smiles. She stands and walks toward me.

"This doesn't count for my hike tomorrow." She grins.

"I don't know. I walked a whole 600 feet to get here." She hugs me and holds me tight. I feel relief and apprehension both. "You okay?"

"Yea, I'm ready for him to go, too." Fantastic news. "I feel bad about him coming all this way, but who asked him." I chuckle to myself. She is carrying a long stick. She hits the creek with it and easily breaks the icy layer on top. The creek underneath flows slowly. We listen to the quiet trickling and hear some birds chirping. This is the peace we both need. I see her looking at the trees and the landscape. Her life is not as simple as it once was. I'm sure she couldn't handle much more tragedy. It would probably put her in a state of complete darkness. I know I should make her leave to get away from me, but I'm selfish. My family was all selfish. Hopefully, the little part of Mom in me can be enough for her.

We walk back up to the house. Jason needs to be on his best behavior tonight. I don't want questions; he just needs to go. I look at the house. Maybe we'll never have to leave this place. Maybe this is where we're supposed to be. Bears or no bears, the woods here are not boring. The area is not overpopulated, and everything we like is in our back-yard. Where else would we go? I'll have to get the deed to the house changed, and that will be the tricky part. There might be a will somewhere, but I never found it. I did find a number for a lawyer. That's probably who has it. Small complication.

15

I mention all of us going to the little diner down the road tonight for dinner. I'd like to see how well Jason is getting around on his leg. He doesn't move much when I'm around. They agree. I jump in the shower to wash off the small layer of dust from the fans. Such an insignificant thing to consider a shower for, but I'll act the part, observing normal hygienic standards.

I watch Jason use his cane to get to the truck, not bad. Libby sits in the middle. He has a sock over the bandage, likely because he can't get his foot into his boot. It doesn't look swollen, but I suppose it is some. He definitely doesn't have a fever. I can tell just from his smell.

We pass his car on the way out. I can't even tell what he's driving. The quick ride to town is quiet. Libby points out another house high on a hill. That driveway must be three times the length of ours. I make a mental note that I haven't gotten security beams that cross the driveway yet. I then think of Kull-the way he's being treated and how his life has turned out. I want to help him. Maybe I can get him a little shack and insulate it to make him a small home and put it somewhere on the property. It can have a little wood furnace and whatever else he wants. We'll first get rid of this unwelcome guest, and then I'll talk to Libby about it. I know she won't mind.

We arrive and make our way to a booth. Jason sits across from Libby while I sit next to her. I sit facing the door out of habit. We all order something different. The people around us look our way, probably because they don't know who we are. It's like no one in the whole place is even talking. Then I notice the conversations start up. I decide we need to talk before it gets more uncomfortable.

"Where're you headed tomorrow, Jason? Going back to Ohio?" I'm not being subtle. No small talk.

"Well, I thought I might see some more sights while I'm out here."

"Like what?" Libby asks. Participate in the small talk, you can do it.

"Well, Mount Rushmore is on the way home and I've always wanted to see that. I'll need a phone to scope out destinations." He looks at me after that remark. Libby shifts. The silence falls again. It seems like there's been a shift between them. The laughter is gone. Do I even want to know? I'll ask Libby later on tonight, and hopefully he can leave freely. She comments about the old wallpaper and the pie display case. The register is a huge bronze hulk, and they seem to still use it. The city of Kalispell is large, modern, and ritzy, but our little corner of the city is far from it. I like it. Hope I can manage to stay.

Jason is eating his country fried steak and mashed potatoes like he's starving. I chuckle to myself. I eat a meatloaf sandwich and fries. Libby has her pancakes.

"Do you need to swing by a store for anything on the way back?" I ask. "It might start snowing again tomorrow, and the back roads are cleared off now. The earlier the better to get out of the mountains." I want to make his exit as swift as possible.

"Sure, I wouldn't mind grabbing a few things." I know the stores are a few miles away. We could get some supplies, too. Shopping with Jason would be better than one more evening at home with him. He even offers to pay for dinner for all of our hospitality. Isn't that nice.

Yep, I think he's walking on that leg perfectly fine. The evening is going so well, and we stop for ice cream before going home. It's a celebration in my head; the not so big bad wolf will be leaving.

The next morning, I emerge from the bedroom anxious to see Jason up and around. He's still sleeping on the couch. I never did offer him the spare bedroom. I thought he would leave quicker this way, wrong. It's like he's still trying to find something to arrest me for, or that could just be my paranoid imagination. I make a lot of noise in the bathroom to make sure he wakes up. Libby is up when I come out, and they are talking about cell phones. Libby apologizes for me killing his phone. I say nothing.

Our front door suddenly bursts open and Bert leaps in wielding a gun. Ernie is right behind him without a gun. My stomach drops to the floor. How can they possibly be here? How did my handlers find us? This is it.

"Nobody move! Stay calm, I don't want to have to shoot all of you!" Bert yells. Libby is close to me now while Jason remains on the couch. Our hands instinctively go up to show compliance. This cannot be happening. I'm enraged inside. I fear for Libby more than I ever have before. Even when I saw Ivan standing over her, this feels much worse. "Well, what do we have going on here? I thought I would find this guy dead with his car still covered in snow at the end of your driveway," Bert says as he notices Jason's bandaged leg. "What happened to you? Did Patrick hobble you so you couldn't get away?" Now he laughs. We all stay silent as Bert aims the gun at us. "So, Patrick, did you decide to take a little trip? You didn't tell us about it. Shame on you." I'm still speechless, trying to figure out how they found us. Jason looks puzzled. "This sure is a cozy arrangement. Hey, Mr. Detective, are you having fun here with her?" I look at Jason again.

"Who are you? What are you talking about?" Jason asks, obviously terrified.

"Your little girlfriend, Libby. We know how much you love her."

"What are you talking about?" Jason's eyes go wild.

"We put a virus on your computer through an email we sent when you first came to Alliance to investigate the disappearances. We can see and hear everything you do in your office. We had to keep tabs on your lack of progress. We could hear you talk to yourself about her. It was hilarious. 'Libby is so beautiful and so alone. I want to be there with her.' I'm sure Patrick would like to know that."

So, he is here because he's in love with her. However, that is the least of my problems right now. Ernie stands behind Bert, noticeably uncomfortable. Ernie needs to get a different job because he has never shown an ounce of balls. Stay calm and watch for an opportunity.

"I'm going to have to take you back with me." Bert is looking at me.

"Not interested," I say calmly and keep my hands up to keep his gun from going off.

"I don't think you understand. You *are* coming back with us, and you are going to continue your job."

"Can't you just get other worker bees? Why are you clear out here to get me?"

"Apparently, your organs have the best survival rate. Most of the other guys are sloppy and don't slice and pack as well." At that comment, Jason looks at me with an appearance of acknowledgement and shock. "You mean he still doesn't know?" Bert laughs. "You don't know that Libby's perfect boyfriend has been killing all those wasted young men for us? Well now you do?"

"How did you find us here?" I ask calmly.

"We saw the detective enter this address into his computer while he was mumbling about 'Why has Libby gone so far away?' He led us right to this address after he put a tracker on her. We've been watching the place for a while. Finally saw you all leave together last night. We couldn't quite figure out what was going on here, but I don't really care." Bert looks over at Jason. "I guess this guy will have to die now, and then you two can come along with us. If that won't work, I can just take care of Libby too." Bert looks at me to let me know he's serious. I'll be going with him back to Ohio, and if I cause any problems, he'll kill Libby. But first he's going to kill Jason. Ernie is still behind, and he looks ill.

"Wait, hold on, I don't know anything. I don't want to know anything," Jason pleads while Libby sinks to the floor right beside me. I lean over to help her.

"Just leave her there!" Bert yells to me. I thought she was passing out, but she just sits, staring out the window. Very pale. Jason pleads again. Bert was pointing the gun at Libby, but now he points back at Jason. How do I control this? Do I care that he kills Jason? Will he really shoot him right here?

"Wait, wait!" Jason pleads as Bert is looking right at him. Jason is holding up his hands in front of himself, waving them. I react. Before anyone can respond, the knife that is always on my side is sticking into Bert's chest. He reacts with a shot that goes above Jason's head. Jason leaps to the floor. Bert is stepping sideways looking down at his chest. I'm on him immediately and force the gunned arm away from everyone. I hold him down until his eyes go dead. Ernie just stands there without a weapon or comeback, no surprise there. Some blood is coming out of Bert's mouth. I take the gun out of his hand and hand it to Libby. She takes it. I grab a hand towel from the kitchen and stuff it in his mouth so more blood doesn't leak out. Then I go over to Ernie and pat him down, nothing.

"Ernie, have a seat," I say. Ernie knows I'm in charge now, and he sits. "Now, you aren't going to give us any trouble, right?" He shakes his head no. He looks terrified. I pick up Bert's feet and drag him right out of the house and towards the basement. I'm sure someone will shut the door.

16
JASON

This man and I look at each other. I'm blown away by what I just witnessed. These two men bust in here, and I find out Patrick is the Ohio killer. Does Libby know this? I look over at her, and she's still sitting on the floor with the gun in her hand. She's looking at me with tears in her eyes. Then I see blood underneath her. She realizes it too and stands up. She hands me the gun and walks to the bathroom and shuts the door. I open the gun to see there are still four bullets in it. I'm not sure what to even do at this point. There is blood where Libby was sitting and more where it ran out of that man's mouth. What is Patrick doing now? I'm completely confused. I remember that my gun is still in the cushions, but I don't feel threatened anymore. I stand up and decide not to bother with my cane-stick; nothing can hurt anymore.

Ignoring the other man, who seems like no threat anymore, I walk towards the kitchen and get a drink of water. Nearly being killed makes life seem like I am just floating along and it isn't real. The man makes no move to leave or talk. The house is eerily quiet after the shocking event that just transpired. I'm still trying to wrap my head around what's happening. Patrick's organs are better? This is incredible. How did I not know this all along? How can Libby be involved in this? Was her father? Earl was right. I bend over the sink feeling like I need to vomit all thoughts out, but I just stare at the sink bottom. The drain. What is Patrick doing now, and should I be afraid for my life again?

I turn around and walk towards the bathroom. I think I know what happened to Libby.

"Are you okay?"

"Yea," she says but nothing more. I don't know what to do, so I go back to the couch and sit. The fact that I'm a police officer/detective has no value at this time. I've been plunged into another man's twisted world, and my own is stranger still. I stare at the frightened soul beside me, and the two of us are silent for another 15 minutes. Then the front door opens. Patrick is standing there with just a T-shirt on and some stains on his pants. A cooler sits at his feet.

"Here, take this to your boss and tell him I'm done. I'm not coming back, ever! You're lucky to be leaving alive, you know that. A very lucky chicken about to cross the road safely. These won't be any good." He points to the cooler. "So don't bother getting there fast." The silent man gets quickly to his feet, and he picks up the cooler to leave. Patrick and I watch him frantically stumble down the driveway.

Patrick pays no attention to me as he walks into the house. He immediately sees the second blood stain on the floor. He looks up at me. "What's this? Where's Libby?" It's then that he notices the gun in my hand, which I am defiantly not pointing towards anything.

"She's in the bathroom." He runs over to the door.

"Libby?" He tries the door, and it opens. She's standing there. "Are you hurt?"

"No, I'm okay." She still looks pale from across the room. I look away to give her privacy. The door remains open.

"What is the blood from?" She is going to have to tell him.

"I was pregnant, and I think I just lost it."

"Pregnant? You were pregnant?"

I walk outside to get some air. Do I still leave? How can I leave her with that person? I still might be killed at this point, but Patrick did just save my life, again. I'm sure that man was about to shoot me right there on the couch, and Patrick stopped him. I think about that man about to shoot me. Where is he?

Did Patrick take him down to the basement and cut his organs out? This cannot be happening. Patrick is sick; he is beyond sick. Why is Libby here?

Patrick opens the door and walks right towards me. Oh my God, he looks like a different person- his face. He walks right to me, takes the gun out of my hand, like I wasn't even there, and goes back around the outside of the house.

I retreat back inside in time to see Libby emerge from the bathroom. She has a robe on and goes into her bedroom and closes the door. I don't even know what to think or do. They ran away to Montana to get away from those people, that's one fact. The other fact is that I've been staying with a killer. This doesn't make any sense. Why am I still alive at this point? I need some answers. Patrick is the last person I want to confront. Libby is going to have to tell me.

I walk to her bedroom and open her door. She is lying on the bed on her side facing the other way.

"Libby, I'm sorry about the baby, but I need to know what's going on here. You have to tell me the truth now!" I wait for a response. She is crying quietly. "Did Patrick kill those people in Ohio?"

"It's not what you think," she answers.

"Then tell me. I feel like I need to arrest both of you. Please tell me how this is not what I think?" She turns over and sits up. She wipes her face off with her sleeve. Her eyes look into mine. We were sitting right here just yesterday when I kissed her. I knew it was going to happen. We were having a serious conversation about how life leads you to crazy places. She seemed a little lost, and I wanted to embrace her and tell her it will be okay. I leaned in and our lips met. She didn't turn away. I held onto her like she might fall off a cliff and kissed her deeply. She kissed me back, then she broke away and ran outside. She stayed outside till Patrick came home from work. Now, I'm looking at her again, but this time it's completely different. She is not the vulnerable girl, but a girl hiding a criminal secret so horrid, I want to tell her she is not alone. "Libby, you have to tell me."

"Well, you know that Ivan was Patrick's uncle. Ivan was blackmailing Patrick and making him kill those people. We tried to escape that world by coming here. Patrick didn't want to do it. Ivan knew he could hunt and butcher, and

Ivan was a monster. You know, then he attacked me." I agree with that part. But I'm still puzzled.

"How was Patrick being forced?"

Reluctantly, she answers, "Patrick killed his father when he was 13 and buried him in his yard. His father was beating him and his mother. If you don't believe me, you can see the scars all over Patrick's back side. Ivan figured it out. Ivan told Patrick that if he didn't do the jobs, he would tell the police, and he and his mother would be put in jail." I'm starting to understand but still blown away.

"Do you know who killed your dad?"

"Ivan did. Dad was noticing stuff going on in our yard. That's where all the missing people are buried, so Ivan got rid of him." With this additional information I have to stand up and walk away from her. What am I supposed to do now? I walk outside to get some more air. So, Ivan made Patrick kill people for profit, buried them on Libby's land, killed her father, and attacked her. Then they ran away to get away from the organ-ization. I led these people to this place because they have been spying on me all this time, because I was the detective on the missing person's. It's hard to comprehend what Patrick has been through. I knew he was off somehow. I walk back into the room.

"Libby, how long have you known this?"

"I found out after my Dad was killed?

"You still wanted to be with him after knowing all of this?" I try to understand.

"I didn't at first, but when I considered everything, it wasn't Patrick's fault. He was just trying to protect his mother."

"Libby, you have to know that even being forced to kill will still change a person. He's broken. I'm also wondering who lived in this house. I saw blood splatter on the wall in the basement room. The floor is very clean in half of the room. Did you not notice that?" She looks at me with questioning eyes. "I have to wonder if you already knew about that?" She shakes her head slowly while she is contemplates what I'm saying.

"No," she says as tears run down her face. I sit down beside her, still trying to piece everything together. "I can't believe he has killed anyone else here." She does not sound convinced.

"Libby, I think Patrick keeps a lot of things from you. He may not be bad, but he is definitely broken. You are an accessory to all this, now that you know. What am I supposed to do with this information?" I let my head fall into my hands. I suddenly remember another piece of the puzzle.

"What about Becka, your dad's girlfriend?" She looks away. She looks scared.

"She's buried out there, too." Libby states so matter of factly. I'm sick. She has a son still looking for her.

"Did Patrick kill her?" She doesn't answer. Oh my God, she doesn't answer this question. "I don't want to know. I don't want to know." I look over to a small scratch on the wall. I focus on it. A small insignificant scratch that doesn't mean anything. Breathing becomes hard to do. What is Patrick even doing right now? How do I feel about Libby right now? She's a victim in all this, too. There's no going back from knowing this. I still want to rescue her in some way, but how is it even possible? How can I even look at Patrick? He could have easily killed me when he found me snooping on his property, and he could have let that man kill me. He seems to know right from wrong, but he's still a killer and his reflexes are nearly inhuman. There must be a reason he's in this house.

"Why did you guys pick Montana?"

"He picked it. He had been in this area one time before and liked it." I ask to use her phone and look up the Montana public residential records. I plug in this address and the owner of the property's name is Jay Alan Sipos. Same as Ivan's last name. I know that Patrick's mom changed their last name back to her maiden name at some point. That was apparently after the father's execution. It looks like a family member lived here, and Patrick took him out.

"Do you know Jay Alan Sipos?" She hears the last name, too. She shakes her head as she starts to cry again. Libby curls up into a ball again and faces the other way. Why did Patrick get rid of this Jay person? Is he dead or just gone? What happened in the basement? Maybe I didn't see what I know I saw. I look back at the scratch. "Libby, I'm not going anywhere right now. I'm half afraid to stay, but I cannot leave. I don't even know what to do with all this information. I care deeply about you; I think you know that. I don't think you should be with this man. He is mixed up with too much crime." I hate acting like I'm a completely innocent person. She shouldn't be with me either, but I still want her.

"Please just leave me," she says. "He's trying to get away from it." I stand up, leave, and shut the door behind me. I have to remember that she just lost a baby, too. Under the circumstances, it might be a blessing. The circumstances she is dealing with or not dealing with are beyond her reason. She has to know they can't just live on like nothing has happened, especially now. When will those people be back again? They'll have to move. She cannot be with him. He is flawed. Damaged like a dog, damaged beyond repair. His past will always linger underneath. I know this is my chance to just limp down the driveway, get the snow off my car with my good arm, and just leave. But I can still taste that kiss. I felt the urgency she had in her. She needs someone who can love her properly not someone who is caught up in his own sadistic life. Does she even know him at all? How does he juggle his various roles? Patrick is broken and scary. I look towards the path that leads to the basement door. I am not as bad as him...I'm not.

17
MIDGET FINSTER

I remember the name of the lodge and the state, Montana. I was recently released from my living hell. Tommy was sad to see me leave. I decided to leave on good terms with him; I believe in karma. My ass will never be the same. I'll never look at a public restroom the same, and I'll always fear what might be right behind me. Thank God Grandma didn't spend all the money she was holding for me. I gave her some and split with the rest. My Range Rover had a lot of spilled pop in it. She'll have to go back to using her piece of shit car. Her handicap sticker is hanging from the rear view mirror. Sorry, Grandma, I'll mail it to you.

It takes me three days, but I drive to Cedar Creek Lodge in Columbia Falls. I can still see his handsome face on TV talking about his chickens crossing the road. I hope he still works here. I try to rent a room for a couple nights, but the place is booked up. I can sleep in my car; anything is better than where I just came from. I won't hear the crying, snoring and jerking off. I watch the people coming and going from the handicap parking space. If anyone questions my handicap sticker, I'll just get out of the car and walk slanted. Short little man with a slant, and for good measure, I usually throw in a stroke look to my face. It got me out of a few jams.

I'm furious Collin was taken. Guess I loved my brother more than I even knew. I'm going to find this guy, and kill him myself. It's my third day here scoping the place out. Maybe I could act like a reporter and ask for the guy who "saved the day." I wouldn't mind walking over to see that sinkhole, but I stay focused. Just then, I finally see him. Tall, handsome, and obviously strong. He's carrying a large fan. Another guy is pulling a fan on a dolly. I can't believe it. How did this guy end up here? If I could hear him talk, I might be totally sure it's him. I follow them as they go towards the kitchen. I wait by the coffee machine, empty. I find some water in a pitcher, same pitcher as the prison. My ass tightens up.

He and the old guy walk out together.

"I didn't want to make two trips. Now we can clean out the traps."

"Slow down, Bill, let's savor this time we have inside." That's it! Bill Cantwell. It is really him. I head back out to the Range Rover after I urinate in the restroom- the clean danger-free restroom. I'll wait for him to leave, and I'll just follow him home. I practically run to the car, I don't need to stroke walk now, suckers...

18
JASON

I have no desire to see what Patrick is doing right now, and Libby wants to be left alone. Do I play policeman at this point or run far, far away? Why is the owner of this house and possible relative gone too? I don't think I'll ever find out the answers to all my questions.

I try to picture Libby during those few precious days we had together while Patrick was at work. She made me feel welcome and made sure I wasn't hungry. She took care of me. Libby is not broken or damaged yet. She's just an accessory to Patrick's life. I still want to save her and take her away, but is it too late? Is she willing to leave this man she followed clear across the country? Do they talk about high school or future jobs or funny jokes? I don't picture that happening. I know she would be better off with someone who doesn't have to run and hide, and she's already good at keeping secrets.

I go back to the outside of her bedroom door. It's quiet, no crying. She's probably all cried out. I speak through the door. "Libby, I'm going to stay another day, but I'm going to go into the guest room and shut the door. I would love for you to come with me tomorrow, but that has to be your choice. I'm not going to report any of this, because I don't want you to have to deal with the outcomes. Please just think about it. I doubt you'll have much of a life staying in this situation. I pray Patrick lets me or both of us go in peace. You can tell him where I stand, because facing him actually terrifies me. I would leave now, but I want you to think about my offer while you lie there next to him tonight." I turn to go, thankful he isn't behind me now. My ankle hurts, and my arm hurts, but I don't really feel it. My mind full of thoughts is much worse, and I retreat to the spare room, shut the door, and lock it. Not that locks would really help.

I hear him come in later on. He takes a shower. I must have slept part of the day and night, but my body stayed frozen in place the entire time. Can I look into his eyes this morning? Can I actually drive a car and never think about these two people again? I know she will still pick him. He's a victim to her, and he's her first love. Unfortunate and sickening. I know that the clothes I have on are all I have along with my coat and boots by the door. I purchased a bigger pair of boots so my swollen foot would fit into something.

I open the door to find an empty room. Thankful, I go to the bathroom. When I emerge, they both are sitting at the table. She doesn't look at me, and her face is a red mass of turmoil. Patrick and I lock eyes. Nothing is said. He has that way about him, where nothing needs to be said. I only have one thing to say.

"Patrick, would you please scrape the snow and ice off my car and around it so I can leave?" He nods yes. He gets up to put on his boots and coat and walks out just that fast. Is he giving me a chance to say good bye to Libby, or does he even realize that's what I wanted?

"I can see you're staying here." I say.

"I can't leave him. I will miss you and our talks, but I just can't." Tears are forming in her eyes, but I don't know for which reason. I could assume she does want to go with me and that's why she is crying, but she might be crying because she loves this broken man. I'll have to let her go. The kiss was powerful but not enough. It doesn't take him long to clean off my car. I look out the window while I think of anything else I can say to change her mind. Libby sits in silence. Patrick is walking back down the driveway towards the house, and then he starts walking over towards the trail that goes down to the stream. Doesn't want any goodbyes from me. Then I see a figure moving in the trees behind him. I see it again. A small figure crouching along. I think I see him holding up something. It looks like a shooting stance towards Patrick. I lunge to the couch cushions and find my gun. As I look back towards the figure, I hear a shot and then the figure starts moving faster. I open the door, and as he sees me, he stops and aims a gun at me. I open fire on him. He goes down. I don't see Patrick standing anymore as I dart out with no shoes on and my ankle screaming. I know I'm out of ammo, so I pocket the gun in my pants. The figure stays down. I glance towards where Patrick was, and he's starting to get up. We both now slowly walk towards this new presence, a figure that implicates me now.

The wind chills me to the bone, but I keep going. We reach the figure at the same time. He's not moving or breathing. He looks very small, almost childlike. Patrick finds a wallet in his back pocket and opens it.

"Martin Stevens from Ohio." Patrick doesn't seem to know who he is, but he also looks defeated. It's like he doesn't even know I'm standing here. He looks up to the sky as he turns away from me. I see the blood now. Patrick has blood forming on the back of his pants.

"You were shot. Let's get you inside." He turns to me.

"I'll be fine. Don't tell Libby. I need you to take her with you. I don't know who this is, and I don't know who else could be coming. She needs to get away from my world. Thank you for saving me this time." He starts to walk away from me towards the house. I look back down at the little man. My body is numb, and I realize my teeth are chattering. I look in the direction the man was coming from, hoping I don't see anyone else. I stumble towards the house now. Patrick has already disappeared inside.

When I reach the porch, I walk inside. Patrick is standing against the wall, and Libby is moving about the bedroom. Then he walks right past me to the basement. I put on my boots and coat without a word. I wait. Libby walks out of her room with a small old suitcase, and she looks at me with fresh tears in her eyes.

"I'm coming with you..."

"I'm glad." My heart is overflowing.

"Patrick is getting some of my things out of the safe." She looks ready to leave. She doesn't even look around. There isn't much in this house she wants. Patrick returns with a duffel bag and hands it to her. As they embrace, I walk outside, wondering if he is bleeding to death right now. He isn't going to tell her about the shot. I won; I get the girl in the end. Libby won't have to get involved in what I do, and nobody will come chasing us.

Dad and I have a great partnership. We started our side business years ago. The abused women that came into the hospital would have nowhere to turn. I met several of them working with my mom. Dad informed me of a plan that would benefit the three of us: him, me, and the women. He would set them up with a life insurance plan on their husband. But the women had to be patient. They were told to deal with their abusive husbands another two years or so then they will reap the rewards. The kills couldn't happen too close to obtaining the policy. I would then perform the drive by shooting, usually at a gas station. Some of them I even robbed for effect. Dad and I would get a nice cut from the grieving widow. We moved around a lot, and Mom always ran into more abused women in the ER. She had lots of phone numbers for Dad to call. The two year mark was very exciting for the women. Some of the bigger policies Dad had them use another insurance company. Didn't want to bleed ours out, and we still got a nice payout. The women are all so appreciative.

Libby and I walk down the lane. Neither of us look back. She's not even crying. What a strong girl. I knew she would be perfect for me.

ABOUT THE AUTHOR

Kristi lives in Ohio with her husband where she has been a nurse for over thirty years. *Out of the Wormhole* was her first novel and *Veins of Evil* her second. Besides nursing and writing, she's a bookkeeper, drives a dump truck occasionally, and manages a private dog park. She loves the outdoors and visiting national parks.

NOTE FROM KRISTI DOWNARD

Word-of-mouth is crucial for any author to succeed. If you enjoyed *Veins of Evil*, please leave a review online—anywhere you are able. Even if it's just a sentence or two. It would make all the difference and would be very much appreciated.

Thanks!
Kristi Downard

We hope you enjoyed reading this title from:

www.blackrosewriting.com

Subscribe to our mailing list – *The Rosevine* – and receive
FREE books, daily deals, and stay current with news about
upcoming releases and our hottest authors.
Scan the QR code below to sign up.

Already a subscriber? Please accept a sincere thank you for
being a fan of Black Rose Writing authors.

View other Black Rose Writing titles at
www.blackrosewriting.com/books and use promo
code
PRINT to receive a **20% discount** when purchasing.